MED EMERGENCY!

The survivors of the blast were drifting through space in the personnel module, injured but safe . . . for the not-quite-eight hours their air would last.

And the computers' cold equations were clear: the only ships that could bring them to Tom Noels' orbiting hospital could not reach them in under thirteen hours.

Medically, it was not important that one of the survivors was the only woman who had been close to him in a long, long time.

But, whatever the reason and whatever the risk, Tom Noels knew that he was about to make the longest-distance house call in the annals of medicine!

SPACE DOCTOR

Lee Correy

A Del Rey Book

BALLANTINE BOOKS • NEW YORK

A Del Rey Book
Published by Ballantine Books

Library of Congress Catalog Card Number: 81-65101

ISBN 0-345-29263-4

Manufactured in the United States of America

First Edition: June 1981

Cover art by Rick Sternbach

TO:
Dr. John Paul Stapp

Chapter One

"Doctor, the senator wants to talk to you on the phone!"

Thomas K. Noels, M.D., didn't look up from where he was working on the young Chicano lad with the dirty, infected gash along his left arm. "I'll call him back, Dolores," he replied absently to his office nurse. "Now, son, this will sting a little bit, but don't be afraid."

"Doctor, he does not speak English," the plump woman who was his mother said in halting words. She lapsed into a rapid stream of Spanish to the young man, who bit his lip, tried to look brave, and obviously steeled himself.

"But, Doctor, it's the *senator*!" Dolores persisted.

Noels looked up briefly and told her firmly, "I'm busy with a patient, Nurse. I'll call him back." Carefully, being as gentle as possible, he began to swab the festering wound with a mixture concocted from the roots of several Chihuahuan desert plants added to ordinary sulfadiazine. If the AMA had known—to say nothing of the New Mexico Board of Medical Examiners—Dr. Tom Noels would be in trouble. But since his clinic in Socorro, New Mexico, was almost a hundred miles from anywhere else, he didn't worry. He had studied enough folk medicine to know what he was doing with the young migrant farmboy who had let the gaping wound become infected.

Dolores Sandoval wouldn't give up. She had been raised in New Mexico, and she knew of the senator and his power. You didn't call him back; you answered

1

when he called. Besides, his H-Bar-S Ranch was one of Dr. Tom Noels' best clients; it sent all its sick and injured ranch hands to Noels' Socorro clinic or had Noels fly up to the ranch itself. Since Dolores also handled Noels' bookkeeping, she knew how important the H-Bar-S Ranch was to the financial status of Dr. Thomas K. Noels.

"Doctor, it isn't just the H-Bar-S Ranch calling. It's Senator Hocksmith himself—and he's waiting on the line for you!"

Noels ignored her this time. He had given her an order and he expected her to follow it as a nurse should: stat and with no questions. But he told her lightly, "Tell him to take three ounces of Cutty and call me in the morning."

Obviously vexed, Dolores closed the examining-room door.

"Did that hurt?" Tom asked as he finished cleansing the wound.

The young Chicano obviously understood more English than his mother realized. He shook his head, but Tom could see tears in the corner of the youth's eyes that told him otherwise.

"How did it happen?" Tom asked for the fourth time; he hadn't yet received a satisfactory answer.

"An accident . . . in the fields, down by the river," the mother finally replied.

Dr. Tom Noels knew it might have occurred in one of the irrigated lettuce fields, but he also was certain it hadn't been an ordinary agricultural accident. The gash was a knife wound, and there was no way the young migrant farm worker could hide the other superficial cuts of the same vintage as the deep wound on his arm. Noels had seen too much of this and too much hygienic neglect that led to such festering infections.

Knowing what he was about to say to mother and son would be wasted, he warned them anyway. "This is badly infected, and it could get worse if the wound isn't kept clean. I want to see you both here in three days."

"We do not have the money," was the excuse.

"There's no charge here for those who can't pay." From the look in the mother's eyes, she didn't believe him.

Dolores opened the door and stepped in. "Doctor, the senator says he'll hold the line until you have a moment to speak to him."

Noels smiled. "Thanks, Dolores. I figured he would."

He dismissed patient and mother, knowing full well he probably wouldn't see either of them again unless the wound didn't heal or there was another fight in the migrant labor camp. The situation bothered him. He was doing his best to provide good medical care for those in the Socorro area who wanted it, whether or not they could pay. And his special interest was the isolated people of the American West who didn't have medical care readily available.

Yet they didn't seem to want it.

They had spent decades—centuries—without good medical care. They had never been taught to seek it out. And they wouldn't unless the problem was serious, such as the badly infected knife wound in the young Chicano's arm . . .

Dolores' voice suddenly interrupted his reverie. "Doctor, the *senator* is still waiting on the telephone!"

"Nurse, Owen Hocksmith's no *alcalde*. And if he wants to wait, it's his nickel."

Dolores obviously couldn't fathom her boss's attitude, which was understandable since Dr. Tom Noels never took telephone calls from Senator Owen Hocksmith in public. Finally, in the privacy of his small, Spartan office, Noels shut the door and sat down at the old oak desk, battered by decades of use first by the Army at White Sands and since by countless New Mexicans. He picked up the telephone handset. "Howdy, Smitty."

The voice that came back was gruff and hoarse, but without a trace of the soft New Mexican drawl. "Hello, T.K. What's wrong? Don't you have video on your set yet?"

"Smitty, I know you gave me that check to buy a videophone, but it was more important to get the automated blood-fraction analyzer instead. I was having to send all my blood samples to Albuquerque and wait four days for data."

"Well, never mind. I got something I want to talk to you about," the voice grated over the handset receiver. "Can you fly up for dinner tonight?"

"Smitty, the weather's turning sour. Can't we talk about it on the phone?"

"No. The front won't move through until about midnight, so figure on spending the night."

"Smitty, are you all right? Something you don't want to talk over the phone about?"

Hocksmith's laugh was hearty and deep. "Me? Sick? T.K., I'm as healthy and fit as a bull Charlerois servicing a herd of cows. No, I'm fit. Leave your black bag at home, because nobody up here's sick or hurt this time."

"I've got a hospital staff meeting tonight, Smitty."

"You and the other two doctors there? They can get by without you. T.K., this is important."

"How important?"

"I've got a license to save the world. That's all I can say right now. I'll expect you at eighteen hundred hours. Bounce your ass up here, T.K.! This is the sort of stuff we used to talk about on the Hill."

Noels hesitated, then replied, "I'll be there, Smitty."

The line went dead.

Tom Noels sighed and hung up. Senator Owen Hocksmith's words took him back more than fifteen years. If not for that, Tom would have delayed the flight up to the H-Bar-S until the weather front passed through on the following day. But the remark referred to an old, old agreement between the two men, who had only been boys when they had made it. There was no question in his mind; he had to go to the H-Bar-S Ranch high in the western mountains of New Mexico that night.

"Dolores! Cancel my appointments for tomorrow morning. Emergency up at the H-Bar-S Ranch. Then call Dr. Jarvis and tell him I won't be able to make the meeting tonight. How many patients left for me to see this afternoon?"

"Was the senator angry?"

"At me? Don't be silly."

This response completely befuddled Dolores. She was a good nurse, especially for a private medical practice in the Southwest. Born and raised in Truth or Consequences, seventy miles south, she spoke English and Spanish and she knew the people better than Tom Noels himself. But she didn't understand the doctor's cavalier attitude toward one of the most important men in New Mexico. "Doctor, how long has the senator been a patient of yours? I've worked for you since you first set up your practice here, so it has to be longer than that." She was searching for some bond that might exist between the two men.

Tom Noels smiled slightly. "It's been a long time."

When he reached Socorro Airport at 4:30 P.M., the feeling of snow was in the air. A brisk, dry, cold wind was blowing out of the northwest, so the normal thirty-minute flight to the H-Bar-S Ranch in the Gallinas Mountains would take longer. The Flight Service Station in Albuquerque confirmed that the cold front, with snow, was expected through about midnight, with rapid clearing following. Freezing level was on the ground at Socorro, and as much as six inches of snow would accumulate in Albuquerque by morning.

"Climate is what we want in the Southwest, weather is what we get," Tom observed. "Ready to copy my flight plan?"

"Uh, we don't advise flying into the Gallinas Mountains area tonight, sir."

"I'm a doctor. I'm going," he told them. "Ready to copy my flight plan?"

"Uh . . . roger, sir, but if something happens, Air Rescue won't be able to get to you tonight."

"If something happens, the people at the H-Bar-S Ranch will find me long before you ever get the word."

Tom wasn't worried. He had a mountain airplane, a Maule M-20 with STOL modification that had a full house of navigation equipment and could carry a stretcher and a nurse or paramedic. The plane wasn't his but had been designed to his specifications. He leased it for one dollar per year from Eden Investments Corporation, one of Owen Hocksmith's companies. Hocksmith wanted him to have the necessary transportation to get to the H-Bar-S Ranch and elsewhere in western New Mexico in a hurry if there was an emergency—and often there was.

He knew the route, even though it was already plotted in the course-line computer of the Maule as a backup. By the time Tom was airborne off Runway 34 into an increasing wind, the sun had set behind bands of clouds over the mountains to the west.

It was a rough flight, and he didn't have much time to think about why he was flying to the H-Bar-S Ranch in the teeth of a winter gale that roared over the mountains and through the passes, shedding turbulence that bounced the little Maule around like a cork in the surf. It took him fifteen minutes longer than the normal half hour before he keyed the mike and called, "H-Bar-S Unicom, Maule Lifeguard Four Three Niner. Twenty miles southeast, coming through the pass. Please turn on your lights and the nav equipment."

"Maule Four Three Niner, H-Bar-S. Roger. 'Evening, Doctor. Kind of rough up there tonight?"

"Roger that. Expecting snow from the northwest?"

"That's what we're looking for. Okay, you've got lights and nav gear."

The airfield at the H-Bar-S wasn't just a rough dirt strip dragged through the yucca and cactus, but a 7000-foot paved runway equipped with edge lights and flashing-strobe approach lights, and capable of handling Hocksmith's LearJet Longhorn-XI or any other modern jet. It also featured a full instrument-landing system plus its own omnirange station, one of the few private units in the United States. That didn't puzzle Tom Noels—how else would a rancher, entrepreneur, financier, and political figure manage to maintain a ranch as headquarters of an industrial and financial empire? The private airport was as much a tool to Owen Hocksmith as a stethoscope was to Tom Noels.

Tom made a mid-field landing next to a turnoff to the low metal hangar, and a jeep with a lighted *Follow Me* sign led him to the hangar, where he shut down. But even before he could unstrap, the hangar doors slid apart, and two men pushed the Maule inside, nestling it beside Hocksmith's LearJet and a Gulfstream-III that Tom didn't recognize.

"The colonel's waiting for you at the ranch house, Doctor." The speaker was a lanky man wearing boots and Levi's but bundled into an old Navy fleece-lined flight jacket.

"Thanks, Jim. This bird won't know what to do, being hangared all night. But it'll keep me from having to de-ice it in the morning." Tom grabbed his coat, his black bag, and his overnight case from the cabin.

"We'll preheat it for you anyway. And the runway'll be plowed whenever you're ready to take off in the morning. I'll close your flight plan with Albuquerque."

Another jeep took him up a winding road to a sprawling house settled naturally among the ponderosa and fir, looking as if it were actually a part of the mountain. The house was a combination of the old and the new—the old was above ground, a sturdy wood-and-stone structure built piece by piece over the years as the ranch had grown. The newest part, built since Owen Hocksmith had taken over, was mostly underground, typical of the new energy-efficient buildings. Debouching from the jeep, Tom walked down the covered ramp to the front door. The wind baffles on the sides of the ramp were so effective that the biting northwest wind on the surface had been quieted to a cold, dead calm at the door, which he had to open himself.

The home of Senator Owen George Hocksmith wasn't a sterile, impersonal place; it had atmosphere, the most obvious part of which was the smell. There was the faint tinge of burning mesquite and pine, just a hint of the smoke from one or more fireplaces, and a piney mustiness emanated from the rough wood paneling. The Spanish-American furnishings were massive.

The big Navaho rugs on the floor were worth a fortune and would have provided a prime exhibit in Phoenix's Heard Museum or the Palace of the Governors in Santa Fe. They alone spoke of the incredible wealth and power of Owen Hocksmith. His was a Western American home, albeit large and considerably more comfortable than a simple summer cabin among the pines.

Mrs. Cameron, Hocksmith's white-haired Scots housekeeper, met him. As long as Tom could remember, Mrs. Cameron had been a fixture at the H-Bar-S Ranch—when Tom had visited Hocksmith during school breaks from Roswell those long years ago, before Wayne Hocksmith had passed away, even before Owen Hocksmith's wedding to Frances Valencia in what was the state's biggest social affair that year. H-Bar-S *was* Mrs. Jeanne Cameron, and she ruled the ranch house in no uncertain terms.

"Hello, Tom. You're looking well. I'll have your bags and coat put in your usual overnight room," she told him, taking his heavy coat. Her words rolled out in Aberdeen brogue, her "r's" fluttering off her tongue. "Smitty's in the study, working as usual. You're his doctor; tell him to relax a spell now and then. He's working too hard."

"He does what he pleases, Mrs. Cameron. He's always worked too hard," Tom said. "That's why he's gotten where he is."

The ancient housekeeper nodded. "Smitty's waiting for you. Dinner in a bit. Still like your steak raw?"

"Barely dead," he told her, and headed toward Hocksmith's study.

It was a ritual. Tom Noels knew that Mrs. Cameron had alerted Owen Hocksmith to his arrival. So Tom rapped smartly three times on the heavy carved door of the study. From within came the sharp command, "Bounce and brace!"

Tom opened the door quietly and stepped in, shutting it just as quietly behind him. He followed up with his part of the ritual. "To hell with you! You recognized me twenty years ago."

Owen G. Hocksmith grinned from where he was seated in a chair with an arm writing-desk. "Wait one, T.K.," he said, then turned his attention back to the video communicator and continued the conversation Tom's arrival had interrupted. "Sorry, Pete. Tom Noels just walked in."

The image on the color screen was that of New Mexico's senior senator, the Honorable Peter Archuleta Otero, and it was obvious that Otero was in the study of his Chevy Chase home because the background was that of a Colonial American house. "I hope you can get that problem straightened out with him. In the meantime, whatever possessed you to propose locating the ground rectenna on the Hassayampa Plains over in Arizona, for God's sake? Haven't we got enough open land in New Mexico for that thing? Why'd you give it away?"

"I didn't, Pete," Hocksmith explained. "Look, we've got the launch site pegged for the Jornada del Muerto; that's where the action's going to be. The rectenna's only the first of many, but the launch site stays the same throughout the whole program for the next thirty years. Hassayampa's a site where it never snows, a technical factor that figures into the initial evaluation of the system. We'll want to find out what snow cover on a rectenna does to the reception of the beam, but not at first. And Hassayampa allows us to tie into a major node of the western power grid at the Palo Verde nuclear plant."

"Spare me the technical justification, Owen. That may sell the committee, but what's behind it?" Otero's image asked.

"Always looking behind the facade, aren't you, Pete?" Hocksmith said with a sigh. "Well, without benefit of a scrambler, all I can say is Jerry Cleator wanted a piece of the action for Arizona . . . and you know his trust fund's stake in the corporation."

"That's what I thought. I'll collect on that account down the line when I need the senior senator from Arizona."

"Pete, play whatever political games you have to back there in Washington," Owen Hocksmith announced bluntly in his gravelly voice. "But keep me free of them so I can get this job done! It's going to take everything I've got to pull it off, and everybody's a winner if I do. If I don't, maybe we can buy one from Japan in ten years or so—if we're prepared to meet their price."

"They'd make OPEC look like merchants in the Casbah, wouldn't they? Have a good evening, Owen. Please stay in touch."

Hocksmith cut the connection, rose from his chair, and limped over to Tom Noels. He was a huge man, big all over, with a craggy face and squinty eyes that told the world he was from the American West. He wore a heavy plaid woolen shirt clasped at the throat by a silver-clipped bola tie, and his Levi's and boots were worn and spattered with just a trace of the winter mud of the high New Mexico mountains. His classic cowboy appearance belied the fact that he was perhaps the sharpest businessman and most astute politician in the Sun Belt. He extended a massive hand. "Glad you could make it, T.K."

"You feeling okay?"

"Sure, why not? Tired of all this crap I have to put up with from Washington, but that's part of the game. Siddown." Hocksmith indicated a leather-covered easy chair near his desk-arm chair.

The office of Owen G. Hocksmith never failed to amaze Tom Noels because the room was totally unlike any other business office the doctor had ever seen—no desk, no filing cabinets, no book-laden shelves, just an impressive array of computers, peripherals, communications equipment, and a large paper shredder. Otherwise, the room was simply a very comfortable living area with easy chairs scattered about, a small coffee table, a bar cleverly blended into the decor, Hocksmith's desk-arm chair, and a fireplace in which a real fire fueled with ponderosa logs sputtered and popped, radiating warmth. A large window displayed a sunny scene of the ponderosa grove outside the house.

"That bother you?" Hocksmith asked, indicating the scene in the window.

Tom nodded. "Yes, it's dark outside now."

"Got a favorite scene?" Hocksmith asked.

"No, suit yourself, Smitty. I've seen enough of this world to know there are a lot of beautiful places in it. I prefer the real thing to something on a videotape loop."

"Still the iconoclast, eh?" A pass of his finger darkened the window and replaced the scene with one showing the Gallinas Mountains in the moonlight.

"Still bothers me, Smitty," Tom told him quietly. "It's one hell of a night out there, regardless of what your magic window shows. It'll be snowing hard in a few hours, and the wind's cold enough to freeze the balls off a billiard table. I don't want to seem gross, but I canceled appointments and a meeting—and I flew up here through a headwind that bounced me all over the sky. I wouldn't have done so except for what you told me on the phone. So let's get to it. What's this about a license to save the world?"

"Pleasure before business," Hocksmith remarked, sensing that his friend needed a spot of relaxation. "What are you drinking?"

"Nothing. I'll be flying back tomorrow. 'Eight hours, bottle to throttle.'" Tom never broke the strict rule against flying within eight hours of having a drink.

"Don't be so sure. Besides, you'll have a night's sleep between the bottle and the throttle. Scotch and branch water?"

Tom shook his head. "No, make it bourbon neat."

"When'd you take to drinking rotgut?"

"When I was ship's doctor on the good old S.S. *Patrick Miller*. Once I finished off all my Scotch, the only stuff left to drink was the captain's bourbon or my medicinal alky. Tramp steamers don't go very fast, there isn't much to do, and it's a long time between ports," Tom replied, recalling with some bitterness his three years of beating around the world after Julie Lea had gone.

"Bourbon it is," Hocksmith said.

"Now, again, what's this about a license to save the world?"

"I thought that'd get you."

"It did."

"I'm glad you remembered."

Remember? How could he ever forget—even after all these years and all that had happened since the days on the Hill—New Mexico Military Institute in Roswell? Of all the upperclassmen, Owen Hocksmith had hazed New Cadet Tom Noels the worst . . . and then had "recognized" him as an equal months before Tom's first year as a "rat" was over. This had come about because of an innocuous conversation between them: "Mister Christmas, what are you going to do when and if you grow up?" he'd asked for the millionth time, using the nickname that Tom hated but couldn't object to. Previously, New Cadet Noels had always replied with the stock answer, but then one day he added, "Sir, when I grow up, I'll lay all the whores in Juarez, tell the Commandant of Cadets to mount the flagpole in front of Headquarters, and do what I damn well please— which is to help save the world, sir."

They roomed together for the two years until Hocksmith graduated. The tough cowboy from the H-Bar-S Ranch revealed only to the spare, thoughtful, tough farmer's son from Carlsbad that there was a philosophical side to him. It had come from lonely nights in the New Mexico mountains, from lonely days when one could see thousands of square miles with only the sky above, and from what experts would call an "existential experience" but which Owen Hocksmith told Tom Noels was his personal discovery of God. Tom had experienced the same thing, but in an intellectual way while reading, studying, and experimenting in the primitive biology lab of a Carlsbad junior high school, trying to discover what the books didn't tell him about why he was here and what he was supposed to do with his mind and his hands.

The two young men, so unlike each other in appearance, background, and personality, became extremely close friends because they found they could talk to one another without rancor or ridicule, and in perfect understanding . . . not usually at first, but always after a bull session that might last, with interruptions, for days.

"So you're gonna save the world, Puck?"

"Yeah, Chrissy, just like you are."

"How, Puck?"

"I don't know yet, Chrissy. But I'll find a way."

"Yeah, there's gotta be a way as long as it's apparent there's room for improvement."

"When you find it, let me know, huh?"

"Sure, and you do the same."

Times had changed. Years had passed, the school nicknames had faded, and the two had gone their separate ways. Their friendship was a bond that couldn't be broken by time or distance—and there had been plenty of both. But nothing more was said on the subject until Hocksmith's telephone call that winter day.

Owen Hocksmith set a tumbler of bourbon on the coffee table in front of Tom Noels, then settled his big frame into the desk-arm chair that was his working place. "T.K., I wasn't kidding. I didn't expect to get it at all, but I *do* have a license to save the world."

"Smitty, you never kid me about important things, or I wouldn't have come tonight. But I'm confused. If you got a license to save the world, why did you call me? To ask my advice based on my somewhat dubious expertise on saving my own life's work, regardless of my ability to save lives of others?"

Hocksmith raised his glass. "None of the above. But I once promised you I'd let you know about it. Here's to saving the world!"

Tom raised his glass, too. "The world . . . if it's worth saving." He took a swallow and set the glass on the table. "Okay, I appreciate the fact you remembered. But was it important enough to get me up here on a night like this?"

Hocksmith nodded.

"Well, I don't know exactly how you plan to do it, but I know you've got one hell of an empire carved out for yourself: ranching, investments, high-tech industry, banking, politics," the doctor admitted. "You've covered all the bases, Smitty. Eden Corporation's something to be proud of, and you own it. It's a real force in the Southwest. And you run the Democratic Party here in New Mexico. But regardless of how much you're worth or how much political power you hold, I'd be interested to learn how one man from a very isolated region can put it all together to save the whole show."

"Easy," Hocksmith said, but not with diffidence. He looked at his glass, then at the doctor. "I learned what the key was—and then they dropped the key in my lap. So I've got to defecate or abdicate. T.K., what makes the world go?"

"People like you talking to people like Senator Otero."

"Nope." Hocksmith shook his head. "He's just a tool to make things happen. What *really* makes everything happen? I'll tell you: *energy.* Natural energy. We take it from the world around us and use it to make things better for us. Take energy away, and what happens?"

"We freeze in the dark."

"Not for long, because things would get pretty damned hot pretty damned fast," Hocksmith explained. He reached around, picked up a small, transparent plastic box, and handed it to Tom.

The doctor didn't need to open it to see the small piece of bubbly greenish glass inside. "Trinitite. Some of the stuff we picked up from Trinity Site before the Army bulldozed it under to keep souvenir hunters off the White Sands Missile Range."

"What's kept the whole world from being covered by

trinitite? After all, there's a bunch of big, playful boys out there with enough plutonium and uranium and lithium hydride to do the job five times over. Answer: energy that we've turned into systems to keep most people from killing other people most of the time." Hocksmith took another swallow of Scotch, then continued. "We're going to run out of natural energy here on Earth someday, T.K., and it may be sooner than we'd like. Even before it comes to that, we won't have the energy to maintain those systems that keep people from killing one another. We won't freeze in the dark for very long; thermonuclear bombs will light up the place and provide a little too much heat for our liking."

"So?"

"So I'm going to save the world, T.K., but not as I thought I would. Politics won't save it. Business won't save it. Money won't save it. Only more energy'll save it. And the only place to get more energy is where there's lots of it all the time: *space*." He stood up, went over to the bar, and refilled his glass with Scotch and water.

Turning to his perplexed guest, Hocksmith explained, "T.K., they dropped in my lap a license to build the prototype Solar Power Satellite—followed by the rest of the system if the prototype's successful. And it will be. So I called you up here not only because I need your help but because you can save the world with me."

Chapter Two

"What's a Solar Power Satellite, Smitty?"

"It's just the biggest engineering project of the Twentieth Century, T.K.," Owen Hocksmith replied, and flipped a switch, whereupon a wall screen lit up. He punched a keypad, and an illustration by Stonebeck flashed on the screen. "The Sun's our ultimate source of energy, and it always shines in space. So a big photovoltaic collector in geosynchronous orbit would collect solar energy constantly. By big, I mean six miles long and three miles wide. It'll generate five gigawatts of electricity—that's five billion watts, or one percent of our national electrical capacity."

"Big numbers impress only small people, Smitty. After you generate this electricity from sunlight in space, how do you get it to the ground? In buckets?"

"Microwave beam to a ground rectifying antenna—or rectenna."

"A five-billion-watt microwave beam's likely to fry people and animals, isn't it?"

Hocksmith shook his head. "Not by several orders of magnitude, T.K. The rectenna measures ten by fifteen *miles*. The energy density's only twenty-three milliwatts per square centimeter at the center of the beam. Out at the rectenna edge, it's a tenth of a milliwatt per square centimeter, one one-hundredth of the United States' standard limit of safety. It's not even in the same league as a microwave oven by several orders of magnitude. Forget frying airplanes or birds flying through the beam; Department of Energy's spent nearly a decade studying the environmental effects." He punched the keypad, and another illustration of the rectenna appeared. "The rectenna's a simple unit—really just a bunch of aluminum structures like sheds. But the output's switched onto the existing electric-power grid. That's why I told Otero the pilot rectenna's going to be sited in Arizona."

"Neat. But what kind of a sky hook are you going to use to put that big mother in space?"

"The biggest damned space transportation system ever built!" Hocksmith keyed the display again to show a map of New Mexico. "Launch site's over on the Jornada, just west of the White Sands Missile Range. Got the Santa Fe railroad there, plus a pipeline, plus a good electric-transmission line. For the pilot powersat, everything's lifted up from Earth." A series of drawings showing very large rocket vehicles flashed by on the screen. "Materials go up in StarLifters, big rockets that carry a million pounds into low-Earth orbit on each flight. People go up in StarPackets, which are winged shuttle vehicles. The StarLifters and the StarPackets are reusable. They land at the Jornada launch site when they return."

"I've heard rumors of something going on east of T-or-C and Elephant Butte," Tom admitted. "I knew you owned the land, but I didn't know what you were doing there."

"Building a spaceport, T.K."

"Seems the expensive way to go, Smitty. What's wrong with Cape Kennedy or White Sands? Some of the facilities are already there."

"White Sands doesn't have the transportation facilities; and besides, it's tied up with weapons research," Hocksmith explained. "And there isn't enough room at the Cape for this operation."

"And you didn't own the land there," Tom pointed out without rancor. He knew how his friend operated.

Hocksmith shook his head. "No, that isn't it. It's cheaper and easier on the Jornada because H-Bar-S Land and Cattle Company already owns the land, so I don't have to look for it, dicker for it, and buy it."

"Smitty, I don't understand all the ins and outs of your proposed project, much less what you're already doing, but as a word of advice from a friend, I hope you'll cover yourself pretty well. Sounds like just the sort of thing they're hanging entrepreneurs for these days."

"You really don't grasp the magnitude of this operation yet. Look, just for the pilot plant SPS operation, I've got to launch ten flights per week. In payload terms alone, that's ten million pounds to orbit every week. Got to have that railroad to bring in the cargo and the Four Corners Area coal. It takes a lot of propellant to boost that much payload, so I've got to build a propellant plant on the Jornada to convert coal and San Juan Basin natural gas into methane, liquid hydrogen, and liquid oxygen.

"All this Earth-based activity's just straightforward engineering and management, using well-known techniques, but it becomes a different story in orbit." A diagram flashed on the screen. "The subassemblies are put together at a Low-Earth Orbit Staging Center called the LEO Base, then transferred out to the Geosynchronous Orbital Construction Center—GEO Base—where the powersat assembly modules are put together." Hocksmith paused. "We're going to have about three hundred people at LEO Base, and eight hundred people at GEO Base. Does that tell you anything, Doctor?"

"Yes. What's the largest number of people in orbit together at once to date? Seven in the Space Shuttle?"

"Twenty in the Soviet Cosmograd cluster, and twelve in NASA's space station made out of used-up Shuttle External Tanks," Hocksmith corrected him. "Things have happened since you took off around the world on that tramp steamer, T.K."

"You're right. I never paid too much attention to the rest of the world after I went aboard the *Patrick Miller*. But, Smitty, what you're telling me just leaves me cold so far."

"Tom, I'm surprised at you! Here you are, a doctor who's wanted to specialize in frontier medicine."

"I don't see what your project has to do with that. I'm a doctor, not an engineer."

"Okay, T.K., look at it this way. Those three hundred people in LEO Base can get back to Earth in less than an hour if necessary; we'll have lifeboats, so to speak, in case of an emergency. But out there at GEO Base, it's a long way home. Takes eight hours or more just to get back to LEO, where you have to transfer from the deep-space passenger ship to a StarPacket that can enter the atmosphere and land. It takes maybe as long as a day to get back to Earth from GEO Base— and there's a lot of stress involved in the trip."

Hocksmith paused, and seeing no response from the doctor, added gently, "We can get by with a simple first-aid dispensary at LEO Base, T.K., but not at GEO Base. I'm required by my license from the Department of Energy as well as by the regulations of the Industrial Safety and Health Administration, ISHA, to set up a hospital at GEO Base."

He finished off his drink and set the glass down. "If building this powersat and the system of powersats that follow is the biggest engineering job of this century, T.K., then the GEO Base hospital's going to be the biggest medical challenge of our time. It'll be in weightlessness; it'll have to handle construction accidents of an entirely new type; it'll have to handle emergencies resulting from a totally alien environment; it'll require the development of a totally new area of medicine— true space medicine. The job requires a doctor who's worked with people in isolated places—like the Southwest or aboard a tramp steamer. It's the sort of medicine you've specialized in. In short, T.K., you're the only man I know who could do the job . . . and I need you." This was the closest Owen Hocksmith had ever come to voicing a plea to his friend.

Tom Noels remained silent. Hocksmith's project gave him a visceral excitement because he understood what his friend was trying to do, even though he didn't understand the technology and finance behind it. It was a big and dynamic plan. It was new. But, he told himself, he didn't know anything about space or space medicine. He was just an Earth-bound doctor with a small clinic in an out-of-the-way New Mexico town.

Sure, he had had great dreams and plans once. He'd always been fascinated by the frontier on which he had grown up. His interest in people and their well-being on this Southwestern frontier had first led him to medical school. It was one of the things he had talked out with Hocksmith back in their days as roommates at the Institute in Roswell. Even then he had known exactly where he was going with his life. He would graduate from medical school; he did. He would marry his childhood sweetheart from Carlsbad, Julie Lea; he did so when he graduated from med school. Julie Lea would become an R.N., and together they would set up a clinic in Albuquerque devoted to bringing modern medical technology to the isolated people of the Southwest. With Owen Hocksmith's backing, he and Julie Lea had accomplished it all. And there had been one wonderful year followed by unspeakable horror.

Tom Noels really didn't like to think about the snowy night in Albuquerque when his life had come apart. He had stayed late at the clinic to finish up a consultation via satellite TV link with a rancher near Luna, New Mexico, one of whose cowboys was suffering from frostbite. Working with the two-way TV link, Tom could tell the ranch cook exactly what to do and could watch while his instructions were carried out.

Julie Lea Noels had died seven minutes after leaving the clinic. A trailer truck had jackknifed on the snow-slick pavement of Interstate 40, and she had been killed instantly when her car skidded under the trailer.

Tom still believed he might have saved his eight-month-old unborn son. But the paramedics hadn't thought to notify Tom immediately, and the internist in the trauma center at Bernalillo County Hospital had pronounced her DOA and never thought to try for the baby by Caesarean. Although Julie Lea never had a chance, their unborn child might have been saved except that the police and the hospital had followed standard procedures.

As a medical student and doctor, Tom Noels had seen many gruesome sights and was perfectly capable of switching off his emotions to permit himself to work with the professional detachment of a medical doctor. But the sight of the mutilated body of his wife, the love of his life for as long as he could remember, had been too much for him. Medically, he knew, he had gone into profound shock. But he simply had not been able to do anything to prevent himself from coming apart. The horror of his loss was one thing, but it was added to the horror of his realizing exactly what was happening to him and being unable to stop it. He had needed three years and twice around the world to reassemble his life into even a mere shadow of what it had once been.

"Smitty, you may need a doctor out there in space. But frankly, I'm not sure I'm the one."

"Tom," Hocksmith said intensely as he stood up and put his hands on his hips, "I'm in a bind. You don't know yet just what kind of a problem I bought on this. I could hire any number of doctors, but my work isn't technical or button-counting; it's working with judgment calls about people. It's the same here on the ranch, or in any of my business dealings, or even in the New Mexico Democratic Party. Now, I could turn this whole medical thing over to my personnel department. But I know you, I trust you, I want you, and I need you to do the job."

"I'm flattered," Tom admitted frankly, fully aware of the fact that Owen Hocksmith was devoting a considerable portion of his very valuable time to the doctor when it was possible for him to hand the whole thing to a lackey. "But, Smitty, I'm not sure that I need you."

"I think you do, just as we've needed each other since those days on the Hill."

A piece of electronic equipment chirped. Hocksmith waved his hand in front of it. "Yes, Mrs. Cameron?"

"Dinner's ready, Owen."

"We'll be right there." He waved his hand again, then turned to his friend. "Let's chow-down. Man can't think straight on an empty belly."

Mrs. Cameron sat at the table as usual, but Tom was surprised when they were joined by a small, bespectacled man in a neat business suit, white shirt, and tightly knotted tie. He was introduced as Robert Eddy of Eddy, Torrance and Curry, a law firm in Santa Fe that handled Hocksmith's complex legal affairs. Tom knew of Robert Hagerman Eddy not only through his long association with Hocksmith but also from the machinations of New Mexico politics.

Hocksmith may have taken time to talk with Tom, but he didn't waste much time otherwise, even over dinner. The table talk was brought around to Hocksmith's affairs early on by the rancher-entrepreneur himself. "Bob," he said to the attorney, "how's that government pass-through corporation coming along?"

The lawyer primly wiped his lips with the napkin, adjusted his glasses, then explained, "The SPS Investment Corporation was formally incorporated in the District of Columbia last Thursday."

"How soon before we have to deal with that matching-funds appropriation mess?"

"That's something that S.5439, the SPS Implementation Act, fails to spell out," the attorney replied, then reached to take a sip of water. He spoke very precisely, choosing his words carefully. "We'll have to work it out with the Department of Energy, because the Act doesn't specify what must come first."

"I'm on a tight rope if we have to raise risk capital first and then wait for Congress to match my equity activities with an appropriation," Hocksmith admitted.

"Don't let them know it," Eddy advised.

"They probably already know." Hocksmith's reply contained more than a bit of distaste. "The only thing I don't like about this SPS project is having to deal with the government as a partner in fact if not in name. I've had to open a lot of my affairs to their scrutiny."

"Well, if it bothers you too much, you can get out," Eddy noted. "I'll have to look at the license again to determine what the cancellation would involve."

"I don't want out. I took this on, and I'll carry it through," Hocksmith stated flatly.

"Owen, please don't make statements like that," his attorney objected. "Don't burn any bridges behind you, particularly when you face the whirling knives of politics. I want to keep an escape route open. I'd rather have you get out with your hide intact than take you through an involuntary bankruptcy."

Hocksmith sighed. "You're right, Bob. Okay, look into the options available and work with my comptroller, John Curry. He'll want to know what it'll cost me at any point to bail out if I'm forced to do so." In spite of his rough rancher appearance, Hocksmith knew how to talk the language of the money men and could blend with them if necessary. A Harvard M.B.A. had taught him that. "If I can outsmart the idiots in Washington and keep my colleagues in finance happy, I'm not going to quit, even if we hit some rough spots about the time we're ready to put the pilot satellite on line."

"Excuse me," Tom put in, "and I don't want to pry into your affairs, Smitty, but I thought you had this whole powersat thing sewed up."

"I do and I don't," Hocksmith replied. "I started out wanting only a part of it because of Eden Corporation's subsidiaries. But there was no way I could bid subcontracts for Solar Photovoltaics, Argonarc, or NoArc. So I asked for the whole DOE license, hoping I'd get the subcontracts. My political intelligence sources told me Department of Energy issued the offer to license because it had to under federal law, but that DOE was going to reject the bids and act as prime contractor itself because it'd be cheaper."

"I told you it wouldn't work that way, Owen," Eddy said, "especially when the federal government can't own the SPS system when it's finished."

"I still don't know whether I should've listened to you or not, Bob," Hocksmith replied. "Ask me in ten years or so. Anyway, Tom, I bid the whole package—and I was sole bidder for the license."

"The *only* bidder in the whole United States?" Tom asked incredulously.

"Nobody else was willing to risk building the SPS pilot system, even though it'd put them on the ground floor to build the rest of the sixty powersats the program calls for in the next thirty years."

"It wasn't the risk, Owen," Eddy reminded him. "It was the SEC regulations and the Sherman Anti-Trust Act that kept everyone else away. Rockwell, Westinghouse, Alcoa, and three other Fortune-500 companies tried to form a consortium, but the Department of Justice told them they'd be hit with an antitrust action if they did."

"I don't get the logic of that, Bob," Tom remarked. "I thought consortiums were formed all the time."

"The Europeans do a great job of it, but they don't have to contend with the Sherman Anti-Trust Act," Eddy explained. "A consortium would need some agreement among its participants concerning the division of costs, and therefore the division of income and profits would have to be based on that division of costs. To the Attorney General, under the Sherman Anti-Trust Act, an agreement on division of costs means an agreement on price. Q.E.D.: Justice would have to file antitrust actions against the consortium and its participants. The law is clear on that point."

"Sometimes," Tom observed, "you lawyers make the game too complicated."

Eddy shook his head. "Only as complicated as the rest of the human race forces us to make it. We're experts in the prevention or resolution of human conflict. If two people can possibly disagree, history shows they'll figure out a way to do it. See Genesis 4:8."

"So you're like the dog chasing the car, Owen, and you managed to clamp your teeth around the rear bumper," Noels remarked. "Now that you've got it, what are you going to do with it?"

Hocksmith nodded. "No, T.K., I was glad to get the

whole project. It meant I could do the job the way it should be done: *my way*. Or so I thought." He looked briefly at Tom, who he knew would understand without further elaboration. "The basic problem was financing. Even the 'legendary senator' couldn't hack it," he went on, deliberately using the nickname given to him by friend and foe alike. Hocksmith the Politician knew where he stood. "But I managed."

"Took an act of Congress."

"That it did, Bob."

"Explain," Tom requested. "I can't follow the twisty affairs of our federal government."

"Even I didn't have the financial clout to do the job, and I couldn't raise the risk capital."

"Why did the Department of Energy award the license to you, then?"

Hocksmith tried to explain. "Otero and Cleator convinced DOE that my single-contractor systems approach was better than DOE trying to juggle five thousand subcontractors. Since Eden Corporation has fewer than twenty-five stockholders, it's not subject to SEC restrictions and isn't an antitrust consortium. And I was the only game in town. Otero and Cleator wanted me to have it because of what the program would do for New Mexico and Arizona. They rammed through the SPS Implementation Act and passed it over the President's veto. It allows the government to share the risk by providing something they call Matching Funds Appropriation. Congress will match any equity capital Eden Corporation raises, and they'll appropriate these matching funds in the form of a low-interest, long-term loan with an interest rate pegged to that on government bonds. My investors are protected because the matching-funds appropriation goes into an escrow trust fund drawing compound interest and insured by the FDIC. If something goes to worms in the finance area, the government's SPS Investment Corporation can tap the escrow fund, but then I've got to pay the government back unless *I* go belly-up."

"You won't," Eddy said. "They won't let you declare

bankruptcy, Owen. DOE will move in and take over to protect the government's position, you'll be serving time at Anthony or Safford, and I'll be working for some government corporation."

"Don't remind me!" Hocksmith snarled. "I'm not going to fail, Bob. The Hocksmiths haven't worked their butts off here in the Southwest for a hundred years so the government could come in and take over everything. And I didn't get involved in this to go broke. My great-grandpappy made it when nobody thought the land was worth anything. Tom, do you know what they were saying about this region?"

"A lot of people still don't think this state's worth anything."

"Well, see if you think it's changed. The Honorable Daniel Webster stood up in the United States Senate in 1848 and made a statement my father never let me forget: *I have never heard of anything, and I cannot conceive of anything, more ridiculous, more absurd, and more affrontive to all sober judgment than the cry that we are profiting by the acquisition of New Mexico and California. I hold that they are not worth a dollar!* Well, Hiram Hochschmidt came into the Gallinas Mountains with two Colt revolvers and a mule—and with debtors chasing him from Mount Carmel, Pennsylvania." Hocksmith paused a moment, then continued. "He paid them all back in full within ten years—and owned half the New Mexico Territory within twenty-five years. And not by shady tricks, but with the same sort of hard work and brains that enabled the Pennsylvania Dutch to transform the wilderness of Pennsylvania. I wasn't handed the Hocksmith affairs as a keeper. It's my job to keep them growing. I can't do that in the Southwest or even on Earth any longer. The only way I can grow is upward and outward." He stopped as if he suddenly realized he had said too much in front of his attorney.

But Robert Eddy seemed to understand, because he added in a low voice, "Excelsior!"

Hocksmith looked at him. "Robert, set up the Excelsior Corporation as quickly as you can. I want to own that name."

Eddy took a small, leather-covered pad out of his coat pocket and made neat and careful notes as he nodded.

"We'll register the name in Delaware, too," Eddy remarked, putting the notebook away. "By the way, I should have those contracts ready to discuss with you by tomorrow morning, unless you want to work on them with me after dinner."

"No, Tom and I have some jawing to do," Hocksmith said, tossing his napkin on the table.

Once they had returned to the seculsion of Owen Hocksmith's study, Tom Noels told the entrepreneur, "Look, Smitty, you talk as if I'd already agreed to work as your doctor in space. Well, interesting as the prospect sounds from a medical point of view, I've got news for you: I'm not going to work for you."

"I'm not asking you to." Hocksmith keyed the video window to display the scene outside the ranch house. Heavy snow made up of small, swiftly blowing flakes had begun to fall. Almost an inch already covered the ground, but none had yet stuck to the branches and needles of the ponderosas.

Tom continued as if he hadn't heard what Hocksmith said. "I'm a doctor, not a wage slave. A company doctor on the payroll amounts to the corporate version of socialized medicine, and I won't have a thing to do with it!"

"T.K., I wouldn't trust my life to any doctor who was a kept medic. Now listen to me: I'm not asking you to come to work for me."

"Then what sort of a proposition did you toss at me before dinner?"

"I didn't. I told you I needed a medical facility at GEO Base and you were the best man to handle it. For ten years, you've practiced frontier medicine. But you're working on an old frontier in the Southwest that's about *gone* now because of communications and aircraft. What I've got is a new frontier, and you'll have to develop a whole new field of medicine for it. Do you want to do it, T.K.?"

Tom Noels hesitated. "I don't know, Smitty. I'm not so sure now that I want to save the world anymore or even to practice frontier medicine. Most people don't care; they'd sooner go to a witch doctor whose magic satisfies them because they don't understand it. Thanks to communications these days, everybody thinks he knows more medicine than a doctor." He paused for a moment, then continued. "Anyway, I've still got to figure out where I go from here alone."

"My God, T.K.! I didn't think Julie Lea's death had gouged you that deeply!"

"Keep Julie Lea out of this!"

"I can't because you can't . . . or won't," Hocksmith told his friend gently. "T.K., when Julie Lea was killed, you came apart. That period was as rough on your friends as it was on you . . . and you *do* have friends. In some cases you really strained their friendship. You threw away our clinic in Albuquerque and ran off around the world. By rights, I shouldn't offer you the GEO Base deal at all, because how do I know you won't run into something out there that makes you throw up your hands and quit because you can't handle it? Shut up, I'm talking!" Hocksmith was standing over his friend now and quashed the doctor's attempted interruption.

"I don't think it's going to happen again. I know what Julie Lea meant to you. I knew it back on the Hill when you'd go Absent Post and I'd cover for you."

Tom Noels sighed deeply. "Smitty, you shared the dream Julie Lea and I had, you helped us start our clinic. That dream disappeared with Julie Lea."

"How do you know? What would Julie Lea say if she were here? How do you know this isn't part of what you were trying to do, but a bigger part than you thought existed?"

"I'll have to think about it."

"Okay, you deserve that chance. And while you're at it, there's something else to keep in mind: You won't be working for me."

Tom looked up suddenly at the big man. "What do you mean?"

"Dr. Thomas Kenneth Noels, P.C., will be a subcontractor to Eden Corporation." Hocksmith reached over, punched the computer keypad, and waited while the printer zipped out several pages of hard copy. "Here's the contract Bob Eddy drafted this afternoon. If you want to come aboard, fill in the blanks with costs, advances, and so forth. I won't haggle with you."

Tom looked at the printed contract in disbelief. "You had me pegged to sign this even before I came up here?"

"No, but I hoped you would once you found out what was involved . . . and if you could unscramble yourself enough to realize this is part of your dream after all. I know you, T.K., and I know you wouldn't even be here tonight if you didn't still remember." Hocksmith paused, then added, "I've told you about the project. I've told you you're the one to handle the medical side of things. I'm not going to give you the hard sell, because I can't. It'd be a mistake to have a doctor at GEO Base who didn't believe that what he was doing was the greatest thing since Hippocrates. Think about it, Tom. I'll see you at breakfast. You'll have to excuse me now, as I've *got* to handle some other matters—or Cheops' Law will have me by the short hairs."

The guest bedroom in the old part of the ranch house was the one Tom used whenever he visited the H-Bar-S. The room was more familiar to him than his apartment in Socorro because it had been part of his life for a very long time. It held many memories, some pleasant, some disturbing. He knew he had been a wanderer. Every place he had called home was now gone, including the farmhouse near Carlsbad. The H-Bar-S Ranch was the one thread that ran through his life.

The proposed contract was straightforward. Tom admired Robert Eddy's style, the nonlegalistic terminology that was understandable and yet legal. But he couldn't read it in detail. The words soon became meaningless. He was tired. He was confused.

"Physician, heal thyself," he muttered and did something he rarely did. He took a flurazepam capsule and went to bed, knowing that by suppressing his arousal threshold the sleeping pill would insure him of a sound night's sleep without the usual nightmares. He could not handle one of Julie Lea's frightening visits that night.

In spite of the sleeping pill, he found himself awake at first light, so he dressed and went for a walk. The snow had stopped after the front's passing, and the sky was crystal clear. The new snow squeaked under his boots as he walked through the pines. The pungent smell of pine logs burning in ranch fireplaces filled the clear air. It was completely silent in the groves as he wandered, trying to put his thoughts in order.

Was it right for him to abandon what he and his wife had started? He was practicing in Socorro because he couldn't bear to return to Albuquerque, or even to Santa Fe. Those places held too many memories.

But was his work in Socorro meaningful? Suddenly, he found himself asking if, in a modern world of vanishing frontiers, there would really be anything to pioneer in the long run. Had the dream been valid at the beginning? Was he now wasting his life, his knowledge of medicine, and his expertise?

Tom stepped out of a pine grove on the uphill side of an east-facing clearing. In the wan predawn light, he noticed a white-tailed deer pawing the light snow cover, foraging for breakfast. He had been walking so silently that the deer, upwind, hadn't sensed his approach. He stopped and remained absolutely motionless, watching.

His father had loved to hunt, and when the old man was alive, such a discovery would have meant venison on the table. But it had been years since Tom had taken out the old scope-mounted Remington .270. The doctor was not a hunter or a fisherman. He merely liked to watch.

The deer finally sensed his presence, raised its head, and suddenly leaped into the cover of the pines, putting prudence ahead of curiosity in a bolt to escape an unknown new factor in its immediate environment.

But it was an animal, Tom suddenly realized. To survive, it had to run from the unknown. Human beings were different. They faced the unknown as their insurance of survival. Someday, as the Earth and the Sun changed—as they had and always would—the deer's progeny would probably become extinct. Human beings might not, because they had already sought survival and genetic immortality not only by the conquest of distance and climate but also by the conquest of pain and disease. Thomas Kenneth Noels was a human being; he knew he could no longer run from the unknown of a life whose plans had gone awry. Somehow, he had to stand his ground, then manage to forge a new life plan.

The Sun was about to rise over the hills. In the sky of late-dawn twilight, a bright star moving slowly in the southeast caught Tom's eye. The Soviet Cosmograd? The NASA SkyPark? He didn't know, but the point of light was so bright and was moving in such a path that it had to be a large, low-orbit satellite. People were out there already. They were people just like himself. They would have medical problems like anyone on Earth—perhaps some that were different.

What was he doing here on the ground?

Hocksmith was right: *There* was the frontier.

Chapter Three

"Smitty, I can't sign this contract after all."

It was lunchtime at the H-Bar-S Ranch, and Tom had had the chance to do a great deal of thinking and planning during the morning.

Hocksmith looked surprised. "What the hell's wrong, T.K.?"

"The blank spaces," the doctor admitted, then went on to explain. "I could easily set up a budget for establishing a clinic for eight hundred construction workers—on Earth. Or for a ship's sick bay—also on Earth. Very straightforward stuff. But the GEO Base clinic has me stumped."

"Why?"

Tom ticked some points off on his fingers. "One, I don't know how much room I'm going to have available up there."

"No problem. I'll get you together with Dan Hills so you can go over the space available at GEO Base."

"Two, I don't know how much it's going to cost me to get equipment and supplies lifted up there. I understand rocket transportation's pretty expensive. Somewhere I heard that current NASA costs are running about five hundred dollars a pound."

Hocksmith shook his head. "That's NASA. I've got to lift payload for ten bucks a pound. But don't worry about it. Bob"—he turned to his attorney—"can you modify Tom's contract to stipulate that transportation costs will be borne by SpaceLift, Inc.?"

"I don't see why not," Eddy replied carefully. "But it might be better to have the doctor go over the whole contract, decide what changes he wants made, and then make them all at once. Otherwise, the basic logical integrity of the agreement could be compromised by paradoxes."

Hocksmith waved his big hand. "Fine. Do it that way, T.K. Work with Bob on the details you want changed."

"You're being unusually agreeable today," Eddy pointed out.

"Big load off my mind. Got the best man available for the medical side. Once all these preliminary details are hammered out, I'm going to let Tom run his show and forget about it," Hocksmith explained. "I've got other big problems to worry about until I get good people riding herd on them."

"Smitty, maybe I didn't make myself clear," Tom said. "I can't sign this contract in total ignorance of what's going to be required of me. It's not fair to either of us."

"Look, you're a doctor. Within reason, I don't care what it's going to cost for the GEO Base clinic. It's a DOE and ISHA requirement—but I require it, too."

"But I can't tell you what it's going to cost, Smitty! And I won't sign a blank contract." Tom could see that Hocksmith was becoming irked because he couldn't understand the matter from a doctor's point of view. "There are clinics, and there are clinics, Smitty. One to handle the sort of emergencies that result from making semiconductor control systems at Precision Digital will be different from the one at PlastiComp, where toxic chemicals are involved. I've got to anticipate the sort of accidents and other medical problems involved with constructing a solar power satellite in the space environment. I've got to talk with some of your people planning this project."

Hocksmith grinned and nodded. "Okay, no problem. Bob, draw up a consulting contract for Tom—fee plus expenses, whatever he feels he needs to study the medical problem at GEO Base and come up with recommendations on how to proceed."

"Hold on, Smitty," Tom objected. "I don't expect to be paid a professional fee for not working."

"What do you mean, not working? You'll work your ass off! Since when are studying and planning not work? Don't tell me med school and residency weren't work, T.K."

"Well—"

"And stop arguing with me. I'm going to provide whatever you need to do the job. I won't haggle about details."

"Smitty, that GEO Base medical facility could be *very* expensive."

"To you, the GEO Base clinic may seem like a complex and very expensive undertaking. But to me, it's only part of a much bigger and much more expensive job. I've got to have that medical facility." Owen Hocksmith tossed his napkin on the table and stood up. "T.K., we've never really worked together before, and you've got to understand I'm not going to hold your hand. You're a professional and one of my subcontractors. Tell me what it's going to take to do the job, then do it. If you run up against problems with my people or problems that my people can't solve, then come to me. Otherwise, I'm going to consider that the med facility will be open for business at GEO Base on schedule. Confer with Bob on the contractual details. I'll put you in touch with John Curry, my comptroller in Albuquerque, and Dan Hills, my chief engineer. That should get you started." He laid a hand on the doctor's shoulder. "I'm not fobbing you off on subordinates, T.K. I expect to hear from you because I'm interested in what you've got to do. Now, let's go do it. We've got a schedule to keep, and the world won't wait."

"How much room will you need, Doctor?" Dan Hills was a tall, skinny engineer with thinning red hair. He wore rimless half-moon glasses because, like most older engineers, his eyes had started to go. He was attired in the uniform of his profession: dark suit, white shirt, neatly knotted tie, and a breast pocket full of pencils.

Tom shrugged. "I haven't the foggiest notion, Mr. Hills. I don't even know what GEO Base is going to look like."

"Well, if those idiots don't screw up in fabrication and assembly, I'll show you what we *think* it's going to look like." He set his glasses on the desk and punched the keypad on his computer terminal. A drawing appeared on the twenty-four-inch color-TV screen above the keypad. "You read engineering drawings, Doc?"

"Looks like a jumble of lines to me," Tom admitted. "No, I don't guess I do. Not the way you do them now on computers, Mr. Hills."

"Call me Dan. Okay, try this." He punched keys, causing the drawing to metamorphose into an apparently solid object which then rotated into perspective view. The GEO Base resembled an array of beams and columns in an open latticework pattern. "This is a big mother, and I have trouble getting the idea of its size across to people. Each of the subassembly bays that comes up from LEO Base is about half a mile on a side. Takes two hundred fifty-six of them to make up the SPS photovoltaic collector. GEO Base consists of as many of these little hexagonal cans as needed. Each of these little-bitty hex modules you see here is twenty feet in diameter and a hundred feet long."

Breath whistled out of Tom Noels' lips in a quiet gasp.

"So much for the gee-whiz stuff. This whole project's full of gee-whiz stuff," Dan Hills admitted. "Great for the newspapers and TV people. But hell, engineers build things as big or as powerful as necessary to do the job. Same deal here. What's cute about the design is that a hex module's made of flat wall sections that can be stacked disassembled for transportation. They're assembled in orbit by bolting them together. Then hex modules can be stacked end to end or nested in a honeycomb cluster if necessary. If the guts of a hex module are complex, we can assemble it on the ground at the Jornada launch site. An assembled hex module fits right into the payload bay of a Shuttle, a StarLifter, or a StarPacket—any one of them. Then we can transfer the assembled hex modules from LEO to GEO in a couple of hours using a Cot-Vee."

"What's a Cot-Vee?" Tom wanted to know.

"Acronym for Cargo Orbital Transfer Vehicle, or C-O-T-V. Damned project's lousy with acronyms. Sometimes it sounds like alphabet soup. It's a nasty little legacy from the DOE studies—and any time you get a government agency involved, you're going to get screwy acronyms. They love 'em." It seemed that Dan Hills was a raconteur, because he went on to explain to Tom how he had come up with what he called an X-rated acronym for one of the assemblies. "It sailed right past the DOE people; they didn't notice it at all. The Hawk caught the reference during a planning meeting, and I damned near got fired over it."

"The Hawk?"

"Owen Hocksmith. Well-deserved title. In spite of the fact that he runs the whole show, he knows every detail of what I'm doing, understands it, and watches it like a hawk. Caught my acronym on the first pass, but didn't know where he could find another chief engineer with my sweet and lovable disposition." The engineer smiled, then began calling up illustrations on the color monitor screen. "Here's a Pot-Vee, a Personnel Orbital Transfer Vehicle that's a sewer pipe with a rocket engine on its tail end. And here's one of the pressurized hex modules. It's twelve feet wall-to-wall and fifty feet long. That's almost eighty-five hundred cubic feet. Will that be enough for you?"

Tom shook his head. "I really don't know, Dan. I'm not used to thinking in terms of cubic feet," he admitted.

"Up there you have to. Unless it becomes absolutely necessary to spin your medical facility, you'll be in weightlessness, or zero-g," the engineer explained. "I hope you can do things in weightlessness. If I have to spin your sick bay to provide you with pseudogravity, it's going to screw up the whole GEO Base because of the torque, moments, gyro precessional effects, and so forth."

"Could you spin the sick bay if I had to have gravity?"

"Yes, but only if you let me know *now*. I'll have to redesign GEO Base for it. Everything there will be in weightlessness to save time and money. You have no idea how it runs up the mass and the cost when we have to spin-up part of a facility to provide even a tenth of a gee. And you run into problems with a transition hatch and a large rotary joint, plus having to stress the structure to take the centrifugal forces and the precessional forces. If we spin your sick bay, you'll have to handle a gravity gradient plus Coriolis forces. If you can get by in weightlessness, it would certainly help. Is there any medical reason why people need gravity? We've been told by NASA that there are no irreversible physical effects on people subjected to weightlessness for up to six months. Since we'll be rotating our crews every ninety days or so . . ."

Like Dan Hills, Tom was an Earth-born person who had lived his whole life in a gravity field. Neither man was thinking yet in terms of zero-g. "I'll go with weightlessness. But, Dan, do we have a storm cellar?"

"Storm cellar?"

"I've talked with the NASA people at Johnson Space Center, too," Tom explained. "GEO Base is beyond the Van Allen Belts. If the Sun coughs up a pretty good flare, we'll have a severe radiation problem and only minutes to get behind shielding. We'll need a storm cellar."

Dan Hills thought about this for a moment. "Why the hell didn't those idiots at NASA tell me that when we started the design of GEO Base?" he erupted, slamming his hand down on his desk.

"Did you ask them?"

"Hell, no! I didn't know what to ask them. Those space engineers down there live in a different world, and none of us at Eden has ever designed a manned space facility before." The engineer stopped for a moment, then asked, "What kind of radiation do we have to worry about?"

"Mostly solar protons and X-rays, I'm told."

"What level?"

Tom shook his head. "I'll find out."

"Can I use shadow shielding?"

"I think so. Just get enough mass between people and the Sun."

"Okay. If you'll get me the data, I can design your storm cellar. And thanks, Doc."

"No sweat. It's my job to look out for the well-being of the people out there." Tom decided he liked the lanky engineer's no-nonsense approach and his affable way with words. He glanced at the drawing of the hex module on Hills' screen. "I think one hex module will handle the sick bay. And, Dan, I think it should have a completely separate life-support system—just in case."

"All the modules have independent life-support systems—just in case. Cute little redundant design philosophy. In ten years we'll know enough about long-term life-support systems in space to get rid of some of the redundancy, but I'm not buying any system without a backup. Not on this job, even though my budget includes the usual estimate of fatalities."

Tom looked up sharply. "You people always figure that into your costs? How many people did you budget to lose on this project?"

"One hundred and fifty."

"Dan, I'm going to reduce your estimate."

"Miss Gordon, under what sort of conditions did you take your residency in nursing?" Tom Noels asked the attractive young woman seated with him in the executive lounge of Eden Corporation's headquarters in Albuquerque. He had to have a nurse at GEO Base, and he had already interviewed several applicants for the job.

However, Tom was more than a bit wary of this woman. Not only was she disturbingly beautiful, but Angela Mae Gordon was being interviewed because word had reached Tom Noels that Senator Otero would appreciate courtesies on Miss Gordon's behalf. So the doctor planned to be a bit more thorough in his interview and evaluation.

"I worked for three years as a general R.N. at the hospital of the University of Pennsylvania in Philadelphia," she told him, repeating basically what was on her professional résumé, which he held. "Following that, I've been two years at Georgetown University Hospital, where I spent fourteen months as a scrub nurse in OR."

That was probably where she met Senator Otero, Tom told himself. He didn't know what the relationship between the beautiful young nurse and the senator might be or might have been in the past. But the senator's aide in Santa Fe had been insistent that Tom interview her. "That's not what I meant, Nurse Gordon. I don't question your professional background or qualifications. I was interested in the conditions under which you worked."

"I'm afraid I don't understand your question, Doctor." She crossed her very attractive legs. No question about it: She was an unquestionable Nine—or maybe even a Nine-Point-Five. Her face fit her name: angelic.

"We'll be working in relative isolation," he explained. "I don't know what we may face in the way of medical emergencies, because nobody's done this before. I must have a medical team that can handle *any-thing* that comes along. For example, if we run out of Number Six Silk suture, we've got to be able to improvise with what we've got on hand. Frankly, I was hoping for someone with nursing experience in the Navy, on a cruise ship, or in an out-of-the-way part of the world."

Angela Gordon tossed her blond curls back from her shoulders. "Doctor, basic medical technology doesn't depend upon where one is. It's there to use as it can be adapted to the circumstances. Three months of my surgical nursing at Georgetown was in the trauma center. Often, we didn't have time to obtain the correct equipment. Sometimes we couldn't even get the proper drugs. But we had to act fast, using what we knew and trying to be as versatile as possible."

He changed the subject. "Are you afraid of heights?"

"I don't think so, Doctor."

"Have you climbed mountains?"

"There have never been any mountains around for me to climb. I was born and raised in Indianapolis."

"Afraid to be in tall buildings, then?"

"No, Doctor."

"Are you afraid of falling?"

"No, Doctor. Why do you ask?"

Tom sighed. "Because at GEO Base, you'll be falling all the time. You'll be experiencing weightlessness."

Angela Mae Gordon did have a certain magnetism about her, an aura of pleasant professionalism as well as being attractive. Tom was capable of maintaining professionalism in relationships with other medical personnel, including both female doctors and nurses. This iron discipline had been drummed into him thoroughly during med school at Colorado General in Denver. He knew that doctors and nurses off-duty were quite likely to be as human as anyone else. However, his social life had been somewhat different because of Julie Lea—the long childhood and adolescent courtship, the waiting with anticipation of completing med school, the satisfaction of their all-too-brief marriage, and the impotency that had gripped him since that winter night in Albuquerque.

Tom spent more than two hours interviewing Angela Mae Gordon. In spite of the fact she had been pressed upon him, he couldn't fault her attitude or background. But she did lack one qualification that Tom Noels felt was necessary for the job ahead: isolated medical experience away from the big city hospitals.

Nonetheless, she seemed professionally competent and apparently was unafraid of the position at GEO Base as Tom described it. She exuded excitement for the work and a willingness to endure what were likely to be very primitive living conditions, at least for the first few years at GEO Base.

"Nurse Gordon," he admitted to her, "I had strong doubts about you at first. However, I consider that to be a consequence of my ideas about the part of the country where you trained and worked. I must say I'm reasonably pleased with your background and attitude. Though it'll be several weeks yet before I make a decision, I hope you won't accept a position in the meantime that would prevent any further consideration of this one."

"Is there anything I might do to help you expedite your decision?"

Tom looked her straight in the eye. "No."

"Dr. Noels," she told him with a radiant smile that accentuated her disturbing beauty, "I'll be at Georgetown University Hospital—and I'll be waiting for your call."

John Curry, comptroller of Eden Corporation, looked disturbed as he scanned the sheet of budget figures Tom had submitted to him several days before. "Doctor, I didn't realize you'd have to set up a *complete* hospital at GEO Base."

"We'll need a complete trauma center, as well as an intensive care unit," Tom explained. "I'll also have to be prepared to handle something more than runny noses; I'll need a pathology lab and a blood lab. I'll need radiology equipment because I can't send an employee back to the Jornada with broken bones I don't know about; the accelerations of return and atmospheric entry could kill a person if we didn't know where the break was and take steps to protect him against acceleration. If we could let him come back to Earth at all. We might have to let him heal up there."

Curry drummed his fingers on his desk top while he studied the budget sheet once again. "But a ten-bed hospital? Isn't that rather large for a construction-site operation, Doctor?"

"That's fewer beds per thousand people than the state of New Mexico has right now—and you know this state's desperately short of hospital beds," Tom told him bluntly. "I'm going to be twenty-two thousand miles away with no possibility of getting help in an emergency and no way to get an injured or sick person back to the ground in less than a day. And those time estimates are under the *best* conditions with Pot-Vees and StarPackets on hand and ready to move."

Curry sighed. Questioning expenditures of Eden Corporation was his job, but it was a thankless task, and a comptroller needed the hide of a rhinoceros. Putting that medical facility at GEO Base, a requirement of the government license, was going to cost several million dollars more than he had estimated when he submitted the project budget to Hocksmith. And the president and major stockholder of Eden Corporation didn't like to have the comptroller come back for budget supplementals without exceptionally good justification. He was between a rock and a hard place here, however.

"Doctor, I realize you're a subcontractor on the SPS project and that the basic contract between you and Eden Corporation has yet to be finalized pending agreement on costs. I'm not questioning your professional qualifications or judgment in this matter, because we *must* have that medical facility at GEO Base, regardless of what our license agreement says. Eden Corporation cannot unreasonably risk the lives and health of its employees or the employees of any of its subcontractors—here or in space." He didn't mention the liability situation because of additional clauses the doctor had insisted be inserted into the still-unsigned contract. "The cost of the equipment doesn't bother me," Curry went on. "We'll work that out so it's a capital expense properly written off in a way that'll keep the IRS happy and the government auditors pleased. What's difficult is the cost of *getting* the equipment there."

"I know," Tom admitted. "That's why I've tried to choose equipment that weighs as little as possible. In some cases I've specified new equipment that has yet to be tried and proved. I've got to take certain risks, however, because I understand the costs of getting the equipment to GEO Base as well as the costs in terms of electrical and cooling energy to operate it once it's there." He was glad that Dan Hills had been so helpful in going over the engineering aspects of his GEO Base clinic. Things he took for granted on Earth became serious problems at GEO Base. For example, he had to consider thermal efficiency of equipment, since the heat load of GEO Base *had* to remain in balance. Calories coming in had to balance calories going out; otherwise, equipment heat losses would literally burn the place up. The drawings of the GEO Base hospital already showed the hex module festooned with heat radiators.

"I wish there were some way to beat some of these lift costs," Curry remarked, shaking his head. "When we get rolling on the two-per-year production phase, that won't be so important. But the start-up costs of this pilot-plant phase are all out of proportion."

Tom thought about how he might have to handle things at the H-Bar-S Ranch if there were a number of injured or sick people and no way to get equipment in or patients out. It was a problem he had faced before. "Uh, John, maybe I can skimp a few things to start with *if* I have outstanding communications links."

Curry began to nod slowly. "I think I see what you mean, Doctor. GEO Base will have a communications capability with a large number of broad-band, high bit-rate channels. Uh, would a high bit-rate computer link and an interactive video system help?"

"That's what I was thinking about," Tom acknowledged.

"What could you eliminate if you had good communications capabilities?"

"Some of the analysis equipment. If I have rapid access to one of the medical computer networks, I could squirt raw data to lab facilities here on Earth. I could also eliminate most of that microfilm medical data I specified, because then I could tie in with any computerized medical library here . . . or I could go interactive on a video channel with one or more specialists if I ran into something where I needed consultation."

Curry reached down into his desk, pulled his terminal to desk-top level, keyed it, and looked at the display. "We can set you up with any number of nets. How about GALEN—General Analytical and Library Electronic Network?"

"Never heard of it."

"One of the best medical nets going, it says here."

Tom stood up. "Let me look into it, John. Then I'll go over my equipment list and budget again. I can probably take some weight out of it."

Curry smiled. "Doctor, that would be a load off my mind."

Over the phone, the detail man from the large multinational pharmaceutical company was very persistent. "Doctor, let me repeat my offer. You are familiar with our line. You've used it for years. You know my company's already involved in pharmaceutical production in space. We want to stock your GEO Base clinic on an exclusive basis. We'll stock you and keep you stocked at a *sizable* discount. I'd really appreciate it if you could find time to see me for a few minutes so I could go into the exact details with you in person. I don't want to discuss actual numbers over the telephone. When would you be available?"

"Not until your company improves its quality control." Tom hadn't even switched on the video. He had known pharmaceutical detail men for years; some of them were very good and he could trust them. But he couldn't trust this man, nor the company he worked for. "I won't have your junk in GEO Base clinic," he continued testily. "I made the mistake once of buying some of it when I was aboard the S.S. *Patrick Miller*. Damned near killed the first officer. The whole lot of that vaccine was bad. Worse than that, it was toxic! Good thing I was on the high seas at the time, or I would've turned the matter over to the FDA. Now, quit wasting my time!"

* * *

"There's a schedule to worry about," Dan Hills told him. "Your hex module's scheduled, so don't worry about that. It'll be at GEO Base in time, and so will your equipment. But I can't afford to slip another hex module out of the schedule so you can do a ground mock-up, Doc. Sorry about that!"

"Okay, Dan, if I can't get the real thing, I'll try for a wood mock-up—if I've got enough contingency budgeted into my contract. What do you think? How much would you estimate a full-size plywood mock-up would cost me?"

"Built from the existing drawings, or built from drawings made expressly for a wooden mock-up?"

"Probably from special drawings. No sense duplicating all that structural stuff when I'm only interested in how my equipment's going to fit."

"No soap, Doc. We haven't got the engineers and draftsmen available to do the drawings. My guess is that you couldn't afford the man-hours anyway, not at the rates I'd have to charge with overhead and all. And you'd probably have a quarter of a million sunk into a plywood mock-up made from working drawings of a hex module."

Tom stared in astonishment at the engineer. "That's beyond reason!"

"That's exactly what I think of my family's doctor bills these days."

"Dan, can you help me at all? I can lay out a whole hospital on a sheet of paper if it's on Earth, but this GEO Base clinic in weightlessness is a nightmare because it's in three dimensions. If I try to plan it in two dimensions, there isn't enough room to fit everything in. So I have to lay the thing out in three dimensions, taking advantage of volume. Is there any way I can build a model? Can I get some computer time? Would you help me figure out how to use a computer to solve my problem?"

"Well, I happen to have a cute little computer over here that we use for design work. I can't get any time on it until about eight o'clock tonight. So buy me dinner, and we'll come back and plug in your layout problem. Bring along the dimensions of the gear you've got to stuff into the clinic— Hey, did you hear the definition of a metallurgist?"

Tom knew Dan Hills was a great storyteller, so he replied with some relief in his voice because of Dan's response to the call for help. "No, Mister Bones, what's the definition of a metallurgist?"

"Why, he's a guy who can look at a platinum blonde and tell at first glance whether she's virgin metal or just a common ore! Yuk, yuk, yuk!"

"Pretty bad, lad. Now I know why a chief engineer is a person totally devoid of engineering knowledge who married the boss's daughter," Tom returned.

"On second thought, forget dinner. I just became nauseated."

"Dan, I've got just the medicine for you. I'll bring it with me!"

Owen Hocksmith leaned back in his desk-arm chair and put his hands behind his head. "Tell me how it's going, T.K."

"A little bit here and a little bit there, Smitty. Piece by piece." Tom sipped at his bourbon and put his feet up on the coffee table. "I never thought it'd be this difficult when I took the job. Smitty, I just hope I haven't made some big mistake or forgotten some absolutely critical item."

"Some mistakes can be forgiven, T.K. Remember, nobody's done this before."

The doctor shook his head. "No, there isn't a single mistake that I could make that would be forgiven, Smitty, not when I'll be working with the medical problems of people. As old Gossmeyer used to ask us in Materia Medica, 'What price the human life?' I'm going batty trying to cover all the bases. Thank God you've got good people in Eden Corporation."

"That's the secret of success. Hiram Hochschmidt learned that on the Goodnight-Loving Trail, bringing cattle over from Texas. Get the best trail riders available. Put the right man on point, the right men on outriders, and even the right man on drag. That's just exactly what I'm doing, T.K." Hocksmith took a hearty swallow of Scotch, then set his glass down on the desk-arm somewhat heavily. "It'd be working, too, if it weren't for the damned federal government! Be glad you're making progress on schedule, T.K. It's good to know that somebody working with Eden is."

Tom was certain Owen Hocksmith hadn't asked him to spend the weekend at the ranch without a reason. The excuse had been to rest and enjoy the quiet and solitude of the Gallinas Mountains. The latter was impossible; with the communications available to Hocksmith at the ranch, business was conducted at all hours of any day. But if Owen Hocksmith wanted a sympathetic and friendly ear, or even a shoulder to lean on, Tom Noels figured he owed the man that much, if not more.

"Politics, Smitty?"

"You might say that, but I've lived with it for fifteen years, T.K. My biggest pain in the ass is the Washington bureaucracy. I *never* should've gotten mixed up with them! Officious busybodies poking their noses into every nook and cranny of my affairs! Reports and forms to fill out. I've had to create a whole new company just to handle the reports and forms required by DOE, ISHA, OTA, OMB, EPA, and the rest of the alphabet soup back there! Fortunately, I've been able to stay out of the clutches of the SEC, even raising as much equity capital as I have. It's been a matter of outsmarting them at every turn, and God help me if I ever stumble." The entrepreneur finished off his glass of Scotch and went to get some more. "And don't you start telling me I've been drinking too much, T.K.!"

"Did I say a word, Smitty?"

"Sorry. I've been dealing with too many people who've been trying to tell me how to live my life as well as how to do the job I set out to do." He turned to the doctor, squinted, and pointed at him. "To hell with them, T.K.! I'll get this job done—*my way!*"

"Smitty, suppose there's another way?"

"There isn't! Not if we're still going to save the world."

Chapter Four

"Doctor, I'm sorry, but there's no way I can fit you into our lift schedule." The young woman seemed distressed as she indicated the computer display in front of her.

"I'm the medical subcontractor for GEO Base," Tom Noels said quietly. "My contract permits me to request priority transport status at any time."

Obviously, scheduling cargo and personnel payloads for so immense a project wasn't an easy job, even with computer assistance. The girl was harried and distraught, and exhibited the highly defensive attitude typical of a person under mental stress great enough to push her to her limits. Tom didn't try to argue. "Doctor, you're not on the priority list."

"May I use your telephone, please?" he pushed on. "I don't intend to pull rank on you, but this is a snag in the system that I've got to straighten out or I'll have trouble later."

The girl's distress changed to anger at Tom's intention to go over her head. She picked up her telephone and slammed it down on the desk in front of him. "Go right ahead, sir!"

Tom got through to the chief engineer in another part of the rambling Eden Corporation complex on Albuquerque's West Mesa. "Dan, Tom Noels. I've got a problem."

"You and a million others!" Dan's voice cracked back. Clearly he was under pressure, too. The last few months during the buildup of the Jornada launch site, the test flights of the StarPackets and StarLifters, and the first payload launches to establish LEO Base had been difficult. "What's wrong, Doc?"

"Somebody goofed," Tom told him. "Get your terminal on line. Call up the lift priority list. I'm not on it."

There was a pause. "You're right. So?"

"My contract says I should be."

"Your contract text in the memory bank?"

"Yes, but you'll need a special access code to call it up."

"Never mind, I'll cover myself later. If you say you are, I trust you, Doc. But tell me," the engineer asked, "why do you require priority status?"

"I'm a doctor," Tom replied simply.

"I know that. But why were you bugging the people at Flight Scheduling?"

"I must get to LEO Base as soon as there's a slot open in the lift schedule."

"Oh?"

"I've never been in space before, Dan," Tom told him. "I've never had to contend with weightlessness. According to your schedule, in two months I'll be practicing medicine in weightlessness at GEO Base. I've already discussed with you my need for a prior visit to LEO Base. I've got to get a handle on the conditions I'll be forced to deal with at GEO Base."

"Yeah, that's right, we did talk about it, and it sounded like a reasonable approach," Dan said. "Dammit, what idiot screwed up? I thought I'd put your name on the priority transportation list."

"It's not there."

"It will be. Let me talk to the scheduler there; I'll get you on the first available StarPacket."

"Uh, won't you want me to go through ground school first?"

"Why should we?"

"Well, NASA always requires a six-week training course in simulators at Houston before anybody can fly as a passenger on a Shuttle mission," Tom pointed out.

"That's NASA, not Eden Corporation. We can't afford the time or the facilities. An airline passenger doesn't train before making a flight!"

"What if a person can't adapt to weightlessness or doesn't know how to seal an air-lock door?"

"Tom, we've never had anybody incapable of adapting to weightlessness," Dan replied. "And a lot of the people we're hiring were caisson workers, high-iron men, offshore oil riggers, that sort of person. If they can't cut the mustard after a day or so at LEO Base, back they come on the next StarPacket. As for operating the equipment, do you know how much we've spent on designing stupid-proof equipment? And on putting easy-to-read instruction decals on sensitive gear?"

"Some people don't read instructions," Tom reminded him.

"And they're going to die."

"But they may take several other people with them."

"We can't protect our facilities against stupid people except by trying to be very careful that we don't hire stupid people in the first place. Any other design philosophy would've been too damned expensive and would've taken too long. We've become experts here at finessing those idiots at ISHA. Incidentally, have the ISHA people descended on you yet?"

"No."

"They will, Doc. And good luck when they do! Let me talk to the scheduling gal, please. Have a good trip!"

Tom had to agree with Owen Hocksmith. This might well be the biggest engineering project of the century, but its reality didn't dawn on the doctor until the day before he was scheduled to lift for the new LEO Base on the StarPacket SP-05 *Salkeld.*

The Jornada del Muerto in New Mexico was an ideal location for the major launch site of the pilot SPS project. That the Spanish name meant "journey of death" had nothing to do with the project. Its derivation was historical, from the fact that the trail from Chihuahua to Sante Fe had had to leave the Rio Grande

River valley at Las Cruces and proceed northward over a flat plateau east of the river because of ravines that cut into the valley between Las Cruces and Socorro. Thus, the route had created an overland journey of more than a hundred miles without water for the wagon trains of two centuries earlier. Many of them hadn't made it, falling prey to accidents, to poor planning, or to Indian raids. The flat desert plateau of the Jornada del Muerto was littered with the skeletons of wagons, horses, and people, and with some of the early rockets from White Sands. But the Jornada would be the beginning of a journey to the planets and the stars unless finance, management, and politics failed.

The Jornada Space Port, JSP, stretched forty miles north and south along the plain. A pall of dust hung over it from the extensive construction activity engaged in completing the eight StarLifter launch sites and the two StarPacket pads. Three landing fields, each with an asphalt runway 15,000 feet long, were going in. One had already been completed and was in use. The Santa Fe railroad had been double-tracked north to Belen and south to El Paso, and all tracks were in use. Huge pipelines had been installed to carry water into JSP from Elephant Butte and Caballo reservoirs on the Rio Grande, and additional wells had been drilled to tap the flow of the underground Rio Grande that passed beneath the Jornada. Propellant manufacturing complexes were under construction to produce millions of gallons of liquid methane, liquid oxygen, and liquid hydrogen using coal and natural gas brought in by train and pipeline.

The road in from Rincon to the StarPacket site was raw with newness. For as far as Tom could see along the Jornada, huge prefab steel buildings dotted the vastness.

At that point in its development, JSP really wasn't a spaceport; it was a construction site covering a thousand square miles of high desert, an area almost as large as the state of Rhode Island. There were few better sites in the continental United States because it was removed from people and traveled air routes while still enjoying the benefits of the nation's transportation network between two transcontinental railroads and the clear, dry weather of the Sun Belt. For the next quarter of a century, it would be one of the major spaceports, eventually swallowing the White Sands Missile Range on its eastern border to become the prime spaceport in the Western World, surpassed only by the huge Soviet Tyuratam Tsiolkovski Gorodok in Central Asia.

But Tom would always recall what it was like in the beginning with the dust, the shimmering heat, the isolation, and the desolation enhanced by the construction activity. Except for the cloudless blue sky, the topography reminded him of photographs taken on the Moon.

The courier car left him in front of a low prefab building with a sign over its door, *LEO Base Passenger Check-In Terminal.* As he hoisted his fireproof flight kit over his shoulder, Tom's attention was grabbed by a rippling, rolling, tearing thunder of sound. He looked up, trying to pinpoint it, and saw the most incredible sight of his life.

A StarLifter heavy-lift launch vehicle was climbing slowly into the blue sky; it was as if the Sun had furnished it with a mile-long, eye-searing flare that lashed and whipped like a tail. The liftoff took place at least twenty miles away, but the StarLifter was plainly visible because of its size and the clean air. The sound of its departure shook the ground under Tom's feet and drummed in his chest and belly. Five hundred tons of payload was on its way to low-Earth orbit.

Every day, a StarLifter thundered aloft from JSP. Tom shook his head; it was difficult to believe. He remembered well when his father had taken him to see the launch of Apollo 15 at Cape Canaveral; in those long-ago days, a major space launch every three months had been considered incredible. Now he was beginning to appreciate the problems Owen Hocksmith was having with finance and risk capital. Even at $10 per pound, a million pounds to orbit costs a bundle . . . and it would be years before the sale of electricity from the SPS system would begin to repay that investment.

Tom felt somewhat guilty. *His* flight to LEO Base would cost Hocksmith almost $5000 because the price for an orbital flight in a StarPacket was still $25 per pound. It would be several years yet before the technology of scheduled space transportation could achieve Hocksmith's goal. But Tom knew he had to be ready for the people who would be traveling to space even before that.

Inside the building, he presented his ID card to the receptionist, who slid it into a slot on her computer terminal. The display that flashed on the screen was apparently to her liking, for she turned to him, handed back his card, and said, "Welcome to Jornada Space Port, Doctor. You'll be staying in Room Thirty-five B on the first floor tonight." The computer spit a stream of paper from a slot. The receptionist tore it off, glanced at it, then handed it to Tom. "This is your boarding document, Doctor. You're in plenty of time to beat the rush this afternoon. Please begin your processing by checking through Pre-Flight. It's the blue door there."

The door opened for him, and he stepped into another world.

"Good afternoon," he was greeted by a recorded voice as the blue door closed behind him, leaving him in a barren hallway with doors on both sides. "Your flight actually begins now. To eliminate the possibility of terrorism or sabotage as well as the transportation of hazardous items into space, you're requested to make yourself and your flight possessions available for examination. You may refuse if you wish, but refusal may result in delay of your journey. Please enter any of the rooms displaying a sign that it's unoccupied."

Tom knew he would have to go through preflight inspection. He had helped set up the procedures himself. It wasn't a government requirement, but a method established by Eden Corporation on the basis of a thorough systems study of the vulnerability of the SPS system to military and quasi-military activities as well as of the corporation's liability for personal injury to the people it transported to space.

He stepped into the first room along the hallway. It was furnished like one of his own examining rooms, with the exception of a low bench in addition to the chair and examining table. No equipment was visible. Tom knew that anything needed by the examining doctor would be located behind the doors of the cabinet in the wall.

Another recorded voice greeted him. "Please unpack your flight kit and display its contents on the low bench so that they may be inspected. Also, please undress, then put on the clothing waiting for you behind the cabinet door marked *Number One*. Your clothing sizes have been determined from data you have previously given our computer. Place the clothing you are now wearing in Cabinet Number One. Your new clothing is fire-resistant and will produce no toxic chemicals in the space environment. Your regular clothing will be stored here and available upon your return."

Government regulations make people expensive to a private corporation, because personnel can't be expensed, capitalized, depreciated, and used for investment-tax-credit purposes as can equipment. Consequently, the corporations's preflight procedures had been automated to the fullest extent. Tom knew that his flight kit—which he had put together in accordance with instructions to bring only specialized items, no clothing, and approved toilet articles—would be scanned by visual spectrum TV as well as infrared, X-ray burst, and chemical sensors.

As he was pulling on the velcro-zipped nomex flight coveralls, the door opened and a white-coated man walked in. "Howdy, Tom. Going to make the big jump, eh?" The label on his lab coat read "Dr. Vanderhoff."

"Hello, Van. Yup, going up to LEO Base to find out what I let myself in for."

"Sit down over there and let me look you over." Vanderhoff indicated the examining table. "You'll have to let me know what it's like when you get back.

Frankly, you've got more guts than I do. That GEO Base clinic of yours sounds like trouble."

"That's why I took the job, Van," Tom admitted. "I couldn't give routine exams. I hired you because you like 'em."

"I get to see a lot of flesh this way," Vanderhoff explained. "The data's going into my long-term project concerning the basic characteristics of humans in good health. We doctors rarely see people when they're healthy, only when they get sick. We need base-line data on what people are like when they *don't* come to see us. That should make it easier for us to help them get back into good health. Say, I didn't know you had this benign melanoma on your neck, Tom."

"Long story, Van. Been there for thirty years."

"Well, we won't mess with it. Sorry, but I've got to ask you the standard questions we worked up for this exam—you're just another space passenger now, you know. Ever have bad dreams about falling?"

"No."

"Ever have any spells of dizziness, vertigo, nausea, motion sickness, air sickness, seasickness, or other illness caused by motion or affecting your sense of balance?"

"No."

The examination went on for fifteen minutes, at the end of which Vanderhoff looked at the computer readout of Tom's vital signs from the sensors in the table and scribbled on the sheet. "One-twenty over eighty, and pulse rate ninety-two. Excited, huh?"

"Yeah."

"I'd be excited, too, if I were about to ride on top of a couple million pounds of explosive rocket fuel. Good luck, Tom. Drop by on your way back." Vanderhoff shook hands with Tom, then left.

Tom had just started to dress when the door opened and a Pinkerton guard walked in. "Good afternoon, sir. Sorry for the intrusion, but the sensors picked up some unusual equipment in your baggage. Do you mind if I have a look?"

"Uh, not at all. What's the problem?"

"Well, *all* our sensors picked up things we'd like to check," the guard replied. He was very polite. "They noted electronic gear, drugs, and a few other things. Care to tell me what you've got and why?"

Tom sighed, partly in relief and partly in exasperation. "I'm Dr. Tom Noels, director of the GEO Base clinic. What you've picked up are the contents of my little black bag, so to speak." He stepped over to where his belongings were arrayed on the low bench. "Here's an electronic stethoscope, electronic sphygmomanometer, subminiaturized ECG, high-pressure pneumatic injector, drugs—everything from aspirin to morphine—just the tools of a general practitioner's trade."

"Hmmm. May I call in a doctor to look at these?" the guard asked, obviously not familiar with the equipment.

"Please do. Bring Dr. Vanderhoff back, and then bring in your security supervisor. We'll give you a little seminar concerning this stuff, who might be carrying it, who shouldn't be carrying it, and what to do when you find somebody trying to smuggle some of this up or down from LEO Base. Okay?"

Tom chided himself for not having thought to forewarn the security people. Accompanied by Vanderhoff, he started to rectify the situation. Afterward, he spent some time with the JSP doctor going over procedures Vanderhoff should establish for security personnel training. Tom himself had not spent a great deal of time worrying about that aspect of things; his mind was already in space at GEO Base, trying to anticipate what would be required of him.

Van turned down Tom's invitation to have dinner. "You've got to eat here," Vanderhoff said, "and, quite frankly, I don't like the bland, low-residue diet we worked out for people taking their first jump into space. Sorry, but it tastes lousy. I'm going to make you jealous as hell, Tom, by telling you that I think I'll have dinner at La Posta in Old Mesilla tonight—just out of spite!" He grinned.

"Well, Van, one of these days you'll come see me at GEO Base, and I'll serve you a space gourmet meal," Tom told him.

The food at the Pre-Flight Terminal wasn't very good after all, Tom decided when he had to eat it. He made a mental note to do something about it. There had to be a better meal that would do the job. Low-residue, high-protein, bland, and easily digested meals were furnished because the trip to LEO was so brief that StarPackets weren't equipped with even simple lavatories. Furthermore, Tom and the doctors he had worked with on the preflight menu wanted food that would be easily digested, passed into the intestines quickly, and therefore not present in the stomach during lift; they couldn't forecast individual reactions to weightlessness. Even though there were sick sacks at each StarPacket seat, it would be better if nobody whooped his cookies during the flight to LEO Base. The life-support system might not be able to handle the odor, which, alone, would tend to make other passengers sick. And nobody would be aboard who could take time to clean things up.

This was a consequence of routine, everyday, regularly scheduled space transportation. It wasn't like prior space flights where up to ten highly trained passengers were involved. StarPackets would be lifting and landing thousands of people, fifty at a time. "Orbital cattle cars," Dan Hills called them.

The cafeteria was crowded, and Tom could find only a single chair at a table for four. He stepped up and said, "Looks like this is about the only place left. I hope you don't mind if I join you."

"Not at all," a man with a lean face and a very bushy mustache replied, indicating the empty chair. "Eat, drink, and be merry, for tomorrow we boost!"

"I'm Dr. Tom Noels. I'll be running the GEO Base clinic once GEO Base gets built."

"Oh, so you're the sawbones!" exclaimed a large, dark-haired, craggy-faced man. "Well, we're going to have to deal with each other. I'm Herb Pratt, chief engineering manager and your boss at GEO Base. Glad to meet you, Doc!"

"Glad to meet you, Herb, but you aren't my boss— I'm the doctor who's running the sick bay under contract. My boss is Owen Hocksmith."

"Oh? Well, we'll see! There can be only one boss out there, and I've got the responsibility from Eden Corporation to run GEO Base," Pratt replied without rancor. "Plenty of time to knock heads about it later, Doc."

"I'm Nat Wallace," the young man with the bushy mustache introduced himself and offered his hand. "Former naval aviator. I'll be command pilot on one of the Pot-Vees—that's a Personnel Orbital Transfer Vehicle, Doc."

"Hi, Nat. How are the Pot-Vees coming along?"

"The usual grungy little problems you have with any machine that's new and different. We had some bugs, so Ross and I came down to work on some redesign and bring back revised hardware. Meet our Ancient Astronaut here, Ross Jackson."

Ross Jackson was obviously an older man than Wallace, but he had the trim body of a person who took care of himself. The only factors that gave away his age were the crow's-feet around his eyes and a hard face that had obviously seen a lot of airspace. "Howdy, Doc. Glad to meet you. And, Nat, knock off that Ancient Astronaut bit, or we'll have a little go at it out behind the building—and then we'll see who's ancient!"

"Aw, Ross, I was just kidding! No offense. We've gotta work together."

"Just remember that."

"Okay, Ross," Tom interrupted, "tell me why Nat calls you the Ancient Astronaut."

"Just because I've been in this game for twenty-five years, these young jocks think a pilot's reaction time has gone to hell at age forty-seven," Ross Jackson explained. "I was flying hot airplanes long before this youngster was out of diapers. And, Nat, old buddy, don't forget I've got nine NASA shuttle missions under my belt. How many space flights have you logged?"

"How many carrier landings have you made?" Nat Wallace fired back.

"The Air Force didn't screw around making controlled crashes on boats," Jackson noted. He turned to Tom and continued. "Doc, hot airplanes and hot spacecraft have been my life, and I intend to keep right on driving them until you medics won't let me do it anymore."

"No reason a man can't fly just because he gets old," Tom pointed out, "provided his health remains good. Old Max Conrad was twenty years older than you are when he set a bunch of aviation world records that still stand."

"Doc, you're my kind of man," Jackson remarked.

"You've been out there, Ross. How much trouble are we going to have with people unable to adapt to zero-g?"

"I'm glad you asked that question, Tom, because it's a very important question that deserves an answer," the older man replied. Then he shrugged. "Damdifino. Never had any problem when we were running NASA shuttle missions. Of course, mission and payload specialists had a lot of training before lift. But even the scientists we took along who didn't have much training seemed to do pretty well. As I recall, the only problem we had was with that famous TV newscaster. You know, the one who used to anchor the evening news. What was his name? Anyway, the only thing that pulled him through that flight was Marezine. Just have plenty of motion-sickness remedies, Doc. Some people can't stand falling constantly, and even Dramamine doesn't help. Those unfortunate souls have to be knocked out."

"So, in short, you can't give me a pat answer."

"Nope. Look, there was even a Gemini astronaut who got on a mission, went EVA, and discovered when he was out at the end of the umbilical tether that he suffered from acrophobia and total spatial disorientation," Ross admitted. "Top-notch military pilot, too. He flew after that, but never went outside the capsule. He was okay as long as he was in an environment where he knew which way was up."

"So I guess we're just going to have to see," Tom remarked. This was, he told himself, only one of the unknown medical factors he would have to contend with. True space medicine was still a very primitive science. Tom again realized he was going to be the one who laid the real foundation for orbital medicine. That thought rather excited him.

He had trouble getting to sleep in his little, Spartan room that night. Two things kept popping up in his mind. He worried about what he was getting into. Had he thought the whole thing through carefully enough? Had he analyzed everything that could possibly happen? Had he really taken into account the strange new environment of space?

He doubted it. That was one reason he had bulled his way into this exploratory trip to LEO Base for a short stay. He had to get out there, experience orbital living for himself, and reevaluate everything he had done to date. Precious little time remained in which to make changes based on the new experiences. His equipment was on order; it had been integrated into the lift schedule, and it would be difficult to make changes.

Tom had worked out eight basic medical areas he would have to be prepared for. First, there were the usual job-related injuries that were physical: cuts, bruises, burns, abrasions, and even severed limbs. Then there were the pathological aspects, basically public health measures to block entry of infectious bacteria and viruses into space facilities as well as to counteract them when they did sneak in, as they always managed to do.

He also had to be prepared for what he termed the congenital afflictions—appendicitis, tonsilitis, cholecystitis, toothaches, etc. There would also be stress-related illnesses manifesting themselves in hypertension, cardiac problems, and psychosomatic conditions—plus psychological problems caused by isolation and phobias such as the one Ross Jackson had mentioned with the Gemini astronaut.

He had to keep watch for biochemical problems that might be exacerbated or brought on by dietary deficiencies, glandular imbalances, and so forth, plus the medical problems created by social interaction, because there were certain to be fights and alcoholism, and even some drug abuse, strict as the preflight inspection might be. Tom knew enough about human nature to realize somebody would either manage to sneak the stuff up or cobble together a vacuum still.

But the biggest problems were still environmental, the medical aspects of the space environment itself. At GEO Base, he knew he couldn't take a lot of things for granted, earthly things like food, water, temperature, atmosphere, and radiation. These were items that really had him worried.

He fretted. He couldn't sleep. He knew he would have more answers in the next few days. But he couldn't shake his anxiety about them. And he recognized that his unease was due partially to the other problem that had nagged at him for months, in spite of that beautiful cold morning in the Gallinas Mountains when he had made his decision to take on this new thing.

He kept dozing off . . . and dreaming of Julie Lea as he entered into twilight sleep. She seemed to be there, and then she would fade away . . . and there was nothing Tom could do to stop her from going. She never spoke to Tom in his dreams; she had never spoken to him in dreams since that night of horror. He would reach for the one he had loved, but in his dreams he could never touch her. She would fade and disappear—and he would wake up shaking.

That restless night in the Pre-Flight Terminal at Jornada Space Port, Julie Lea appeared. Somehow, without speaking, she conveyed to him that she knew he had given up their joint dream, that he was in pursuit of a new one. She didn't admonish him. She didn't express disappointment. She just disappeared, smiling.

And she didn't return.

About midnight, Tom woke for what seemed the hundredth time, exhausted physically and drained emotionally. He brought himself fully awake, realizing he would be replaying the same dream over and over again . . . except that Julie Lea now no longer appeared in it.

"Doctor," he told himself aloud, "you'd better shape up here, or you're going to be worse off than anybody else come lift-time. Dammit, you took on this job knowing it meant giving up the old one. You've got nobody to blame but yourself. And you can blow the whole thing and maybe even kill yourself in the bargain. Better shape up." He took a flurazepam capsule. Twenty minutes later, he was getting the sort of deep, restful, dreamless sleep he needed.

The StarPacket SP-05 *Salkeld* looked like a big black and gray bat squatting on the ground, its broad delta wings drooping slightly. Dan Hills had described the StarPacket as a "single-stage-to-orbit ship, vertical takeoff and horizontal landing." The StarPacket-II on the drawing boards would use horizontal takeoff and landing like an airliner, but even the StarPacket-I design represented a major step forward in space technology. The resemblance of the StarPacket to the old NASA Space Shuttle Orbiter was only superficial: Both designs had delta wings. Beyond that, the StarPacket was strictly a passenger-carrying vehicle.

"Scared, Doc?" Ross Jackson asked as they waited their turn to climb the boarding stairs.

"No, not really. Excited, maybe. I've been strapping into flying machines of various kinds all my life. This is just another new one."

When Tom finally ducked through the fuselage hatch into the passenger cabin, he discovered that the Star-Packet cabin was far removed from the plush interior of a modern jet airliner. It was more like the interior of a cargo aircraft modified to carry people. However, Tom knew from his discussions with Hills that the StarPacket had been designed from scratch as a people hauler. Even so, not a pound of material had been wasted.

The StarPacket designers had limited the boost acceleration to three gravities. But Tom noted that everything in the cabin that was intended to carry a load during boost was beefy and probably overstressed to handle six to ten gees, while auxiliary equipment such as ladders seemed to be somewhat flimsy, designed to carry a load only under Earth gravity or to support only themselves under flight acceleration. As a pilot, Tom had grown used to such design philosophies in light, general aviation aircraft. He made a mental note to mention to Hocksmith that if Eden Corporation ever set up the orbital tourist business as a spinoff of the SPS space transportation system, the tourist StarPackets should be redesigned to provide somewhat more psychological reassurance to the passengers.

He found his seat in the cabin between Ross Jackson and Nat Wallace. "Well, I see I'll have good company during lift."

Nat grinned. "And we've got a medic standing by. The Ancient Astronaut may need you."

"Knock it off, Wallace, or I'll stuff you out the hatch at max-Q!" Ross snarled.

Eden Corporation had subcontracted the design and construction of the StarPackets to a consortium of aerospace companies. The operation of the passenger transportation system had been farmed out to another consortium, made up of several transportation companies and headed by the former president of a major airline. The influence of these old-line transportation companies was evident because a steward and a stewardess checked that each of the fifty passengers was properly strapped in.

The seat harness was almost identical to those Tom had worn during aerobatic training in a Citabria. The seat itself was not cushioned; it was formed of fireproof fabric net stretched over a frame.

Pounds of dead weight meant pounds of propellant, which meant dollars wasted on nonrevenue payload.

Tom expected to hear the usual speech about cabin pressurization and oxygen masks, but it didn't come. He asked Ross why.

"Doc, if this cabin loses pressure during powered flight, the pilots'll get us back down fast. If it blows a leak in space, assume the crash position by unfastening your shoulder harness and putting your head down between your legs," the older astronaut told him.

"Oh? Why? What good will that do?" Tom asked, playing the straight man.

"That's so it'll be easy to kiss your ass good-bye. There ain't a damned thing they can do if this cabin gets vented to vacuum. But that isn't likely to happen, so don't sweat it," Ross assured him quietly.

There were no cabin windows, but Tom knew what was happening because Hills had explained it to him and because he had seen film clips of the first StarPacket launches. The StarPacket was backed in over its launcher and flame pit by a tug. A hydraulic strongarm rose from the concrete pad and slowly lifted the craft to a vertical position, placing it carefully on the jack pads. The noise of the launch crews driving the shear pins into the pads barely made its way to the cabin. But when more than a million pounds of liquid oxygen and liquid hydrogen began to gush into the tanks in the wet wing and the fuselage behind the cabin, the StarPacket trembled and creaked and groaned as the supercold liquids hit the precooled tanks.

Less than thirty minutes passed from the time Tom had boarded, and the cabin hatch had closed before the cabin loudspeakers announced, "All hands, this is the captain." It was the same old professional pilot's drawl—cool, calm, and competent. "Stand by for lift."

There was no countdown.

Tom suddenly heard a muffled rumble behind him, and he knew that ignition had taken place. This was followed almost immediately by a slight jerk as the en-

Chapter Five

"Up ship!"

There had been no broadcast countdown. No apparent reading of checklists. No rapid exchange of information between the StarPacket *Salkeld* and Mission Control was overheard.

But there had been a countdown, conducted silently by computerized equipment and monitored by the two pilots. There had also been a checklist, just as there always is for even the simplest airplane flight, but it was quietly read in the cockpit. And Mission Control, in this case called "ETO Operations," was just a building full of computers with only a few people overseeing what amounted to traffic control because the conduct of the flight was in the hands of the pilots.

All the external trappings of early space exploration had vanished with the coming of true space transportation. Time-wasting manual procedures and bureaucratic overmanning became totally impractical once flights to LEO Base were being made daily—or even more often on occasions.

So far as Tom Noels was concerned, however, it was a noisy, stressful ride with strange sensations assaulting his vestibular apparatus. The rumbling thunder of the rocket motors, full of subaudible frequencies, slowly diminished as the StarPacket rose through the atmosphere, passing Mach-One and maximum dynamic pressure. The acceleration rose to three gees and stayed there because the rocket engines were throttled back to maintain this acceleration while the StarPacket was growing lighter as propellants burned off.

"All hands, stand by, free fall," came the captain's voice over the speakers. Then, suddenly, the now-quiet vibration of the rocket engines stopped, and the force of three gravities holding Tom back in the webbed mesh of his seat disappeared. He began to fall. The whole ship began to fall.

Tom knew what it was, and he had been waiting for it anxiously because, except for brief moments when he had deliberately created weightlessness in his Maule M-20, this was the one factor in space he was most concerned about.

The sensation made him a bit queasy at first, until he convinced himself that free fall was natural and that he wasn't really falling. The web straps holding him to the net seat helped alleviate the feeling of complete weightlessness. The passenger cabin remained right side up. Everything else was as it had been before engine cutoff. But he found he had trouble orienting himself if he turned his head quickly. Whenever he did so, he became momentarily disoriented, unable to tell the floor from the ceiling.

"You okay, Doc?"

"Sure, Ross. So this is weightlessness?"

"Yup! Great stuff! Love it! Glad to be back again." The former NASA astronaut was obviously enjoying himself. He looked across Tom to where Nat Wallace was strapped into his seat. "Hey, Nat, you don't look so good."

Wallace had very little color in his face, and what little remained was tinged with green. "I'm okay," he replied through clenched teeth. "Just takes me a few minutes to get used to it every time."

"You'd better get used to it, youngster," Jackson told him, "or we'll just have to ship you home."

"I'll be all right!" Wallace insisted. He took several deep breaths, and color began to return to his cheeks. "It's a little like seasickness. I'm okay now."

"Yeah, you look better."

"Mind over matter," Wallace quipped.

Tom leaned over and felt for Nat's pulse. He

checked the young pilot's breathing as well as the feel of his hands. The doctor considered the possibility that Wallace could go into shock, and he was checking for symptoms just in case he had to act fast. But he didn't. Wallace obviously regained control of himself.

"I thought Ross said you'd worked on the Pot-Vees before," Tom remarked. "Do you have this trouble every time you go into free fall, Nat?"

The young space pilot didn't nod. "Just at first . . . then I'm all right."

"All hands, please stay strapped in your seats," the captain's voice requested. "We're less than thirty minutes from rendezvous with LEO Base. There'll be some small lateral and longitudinal accelerations as we trim orbit and change attitude. I don't want to bang anybody up against the bulkhead when I do that, so please stay strapped in place. You'll have lots of time for zero-g games later."

The two stews were floating up and down the aisles, checking the passengers and moving from handhold to handhold. The sight didn't bother Tom at all. In fact, it didn't seem to bother any of the passengers. Thanks to films and TV, a human being floating freely in weightlessness was no longer a strange sight.

"Ho-hum," Ross Jackson said with a yawn, "another successful lift."

LEO Base smelled of people living in close quarters and of machinery, but a strange new machinery smell: no oil smell, but a newness odor that was unlike anything Tom had experienced before. He realized this was because everything lifted to LEO Base was painted or otherwise treated to reduce outgassing of potentially toxic chemicals under low atmospheric pressures. The smell was sterile, but quite different from that of a hospital O.R.

Tom quickly discovered that privacy did not exist at LEO Base. It wasn't a space station; it was a work camp. A young steward showed him to his living quarters, which turned out to be a one-third segment of a hex module about six feet long that he shared with twelve other transients. But there wasn't room for twelve people in the module segment, and there were no bunks, in spite of the fact that the steward explained that the system operated on the "hot bunk" arrangement—*i.e.,* there were places to affix four sleeping sacks to the walls of the segment. With three working shifts, this meant that the compartment always had four people in it during the sleep period of their three-part day.

"You're Shift Two," the steward told Tom, giving him a velcro-backed badge to affix to the front of his jump suit. "You're authorized to sleep in the compartment during Phase Three. During Phase One, you can use the common-room modules, but you can't enter the work areas except during Phase Two."

Tom sighed. Obviously, the schedule was set up for construction crews, not for visitors and certainly not for such people as him and his staff, who would be expected to be available constantly. "Can you take me to the base boss?" he asked the steward, knowing full well that the latter didn't have the authority to approve any change in scheduling.

The boss turned out to be a balding, bespectacled, stout man named Charlie Day, who looked up at Tom Noels from the consoles that comprised his place of work. "Okay, Doc, what's your problem?"

"Your three-shift work schedule's set up for the SPS and GEO Base construction workers, and I can fully understand that," Tom told him, "but I'm up here to learn what I can about living and working in space. I've got to run the med clinic in GEO Base in a few months."

"So? What's your problem?"

Tom tapped the cloth badge on his jump-suit pocket. "I must be able to go where I need to go when I need to go there."

Charlie Day looked pained. "Look, Doc, I've got three hundred people in LEO Base right now—no, the exact count is three forty-one until the *Salkeld* un-docks and breaks orbit later today. We've got to keep our life-support systems in balance, watch our mass distribution, and monitor the heat load. I can't have people going all over hell out here at their whim—"

"I don't think I understand you."

"Look at it this way, Doc. I've got more than three hundred people moving around LEO Base all the time. That's more than twenty-five tons of active meat whose movements change the torques and moments of LEO Base and make our attitude-control thrusters work like hell. I've got more than six hundred air-lock cycles per day—closer to eight hundred on some shifts—and I lose a little bit of oxygen every time a lock cycles . . . so my atmosphere losses begin to add up after a few days. Know where we get our attitude thruster propellant? Our makeup atmosphere? From the Jornada, that's where. At ten bucks a pound. And each person in LEO Base is equivalent to a hundred-watt light bulb in terms of heat input to the base—and the heat load on various parts of LEO Base has to be balanced out, or we've got problems, Doc."

"Okay, Mr. Day, I understand your problems, but the reason I'm here is to learn to live in space so Herb Pratt has a sick bay he can depend on in GEO Base," Tom persisted. "I can't be strapped. I've got to look around here, and then I've got to get back to Jornada as quickly as possible. If you restrict me, that means I'll have to stay longer, which means I'll use up more life-support consumables. And incidentally, suppose there's an accident while I'm here? Are you saying I won't be able to get to the injured persons because my Shift Two badge won't let me leave my sleeping module at that moment?"

Charlie Day sighed in frustration. "Tourists!" he muttered. "Okay, Doc, I'll have Traffic issue you an All Areas/All Times supervisory pass badge. But, dammit, please don't make my job any tougher than it is already! Don't go larking off all over the place. Matter of fact, I'd appreciate it if you'd check with me by intercom before you cycle through a lock; maybe I can integrate your cycle with that of someone else's within a few minutes, if you wouldn't mind the wait."

Tom's new pass patch helped, although the steward groused about having to relocate Tom to a supervisory billet—a one-sixth segment of a hex module six feet long with room enough for one person's sleep sack. In other words, Tom found himself in a private room that would permit him to come and go as he pleased without disturbing other occupants.

LEO Base was still new and growing, and Day's people had tried their best to keep up with the expansion while at the same time providing the continual stream of newcomers with directions on how to get from place to place. However, the directory service and the direction signs on the multitude of hatches and passageways were never really current. It was easy to get lost in the three-dimensional world of a space facility, especially when you were a two-dimensional person from Earth.

Tom got lost trying to find the First-Aid Center. Once he was lost, he discovered he had become completely disoriented. In fact, he was so disoriented that he lost what little up-down reference he had had in the first place. *Which way to the hub hex?*

He found himself with his arms wrapped around a conduit in a passageway. Naturally, this blocked the flow of traffic, and it wasn't very long before a base steward showed up to help him.

Tom Noels made several mental notes—later transferred to his dictated notes—on some very simple actions Dan Hills, Charlie Day, and Herb Pratt could take to prevent this sort of thing from happening.

The First-Aid Center to which the steward took him wasn't much, just one-third of a hex module no bigger than one of the communal sleeping compartments. Nobody was in the center; it wasn't intended to be manned continually, because John Curry's analysis had indicated that the expense of one person to handle First-Aid wasn't justified in terms of cost—lift cost, life-support consumables cost, cost of living space, etc. Tom had reluctantly concurred because he was primarily in-

terested in GEO Base and because the trip from LEO
Base to the Jornada seemed to be quick.

Tom discovered that the center had been stocked,
following his instructions, as a typical industrial first-
aid unit. The drugs and equipment would handle
superficial injuries or help keep a badly injured person
alive long enough to transfer him to the Jornada on the
next StarPacket—one of which was always docked at
LEO Base, unloading or loading people or light priority
cargo. In extreme emergencies, parachute-recoverable
ballistic-reentry lifeboats, reminiscent of the old Gemini
capsules, were available.

The setup looked good to Tom, but he fretted because, even though the unit was properly supplied and
maintained, he was concerned about how to handle certain kinds of injuries in weightlessness.

He found the cafeteria and got lunch, plastic packets
of dehydrated and frozen foods that he had to prepare
himself. He managed to add water to the dehydrated
foods without letting more than a few drops get away
from him; he was fascinated by the behavior of the water droplets in weightlessness. The frozen portions he
heated in one of the microwave ovens.

How long would it be before the LEO Base workers
began to complain about this food? he asked himself. It
was pretty uninteresting. Mostly, it was pasty, sticky
stuff, like puréed baby food, designed to prevent
crumbs from getting loose and yet sticky enough so that
natural adhesion or surface tension would keep it attached to the spoonlike eating utensil. No bones or skin
or pits had to be thrown away as garbage, only the
waste plastic that would be whisked down the disposal
chute and eventually returned to Jornada in a StarLifter.

GEO Base would require better food, he told himself, even if workers rotated to Earth occasionally.
Food was food, but if Tom knew the human working
person—and he did from his own New Mexico experience as well as from his service aboard the S.S. *Patrick
Miller*—better food than this would be required, or else
the workers would start bringing in their own. And that

might cause real problems with the rudimentary life-support systems.

He had just finished eating and was putting his waste food containers into the disposal when a loudspeaker called, "Dr. Noels, please report to the First-Aid Center. Dr. Noels, please report to First-Aid! If anybody knows the whereabouts of the doctor who came up from Jornada on the *Salkeld* this morning, please bring him to First-Aid."

Tom was oriented now. He knew how to get there. So he departed without trying to reply on the intercom.

Four people were jammed into First-Aid when he arrived, and the place was filled with a pink mist. All four people wore pressure suits, but three were without helmets. The exception was a short, stocky person whose utterly relaxed position, afloat in the compartment, spelled "unconscious" to Tom.

"Get that off!" Tom snapped to a young woman who was holding the man by his pressure helmet. "What happened here?" Then he saw that the right leg of the man's pressure suit terminated at the lower end of the calf, just above the ankle. So that was the source of the pink mist.

"Fred was working on the power-control junction and must have had a suit radio failure," the young woman remarked. There was no panic in her voice. "Some yo-yo was trying to mate the attach points of another submodule, and he didn't see Fred's leg in the way. When I saw it and yelled, Fred didn't hear me. His radio must have been out."

The man's foot was sheared through just above the ankle, and it had not been a clean severance. Somebody had acted fast out there, and the compartmentation of the pressure suit had saved the man. A rough tourniquet of electrical cable had been wound around his leg, the only thing that had prevented the pressure in his suit from pumping all his blood out into vacuum. Nonetheless, he had lost a lot of blood.

"You and you!" Tom snapped to the two men who had accompanied the woman. "Out into the passageway! Stay there in case I need help. Not enough room in here for everybody. Ma'am, are you up to staying to help me?"

"Damned right! Fred was one of my men! I'm Lucky Hertzog. This is Fred Fitzsimmons."

"Formal introductions later. I'm Dr. Noels. We've got to work fast."

That was easier said than done.

Moving in a hurry in weightlessness was difficult and bordered on the impossible because Tom wasn't used to it. Several times he pushed off too robustly and ended up banging hard against bulkheads or cabinets. The equipment he removed from cabinets wouldn't behave itself. Fitzsimmons was in shock, and it was important that Tom get oxygen and stimulants into the man immediately, but the hose on the oxygen mask wound itself all over the place. Finally, with Lucky Hertzog's help, he managed to get the oxygen mask securely in place.

There was no way that an IV was going to work, Tom discovered. Without gravity, it wouldn't drip. He thought of injection, then discovered he couldn't get the air bubbles out of the syringe in the usual manner. He ended up swinging it at the end of his arm and squirting most of the injection into the compartment before he felt it had been deaerated enough to prevent an embolism. Getting the IV working was strictly a lash-up, and he didn't have time to be neat. He had to start lactate of Ringer going right away, followed by whole blood—if there was any—followed by closing or cauterizing the severed blood vessels that, in spite of the tourniquet, were still seeping. He called in one of the men from the passageway and instructed him on how to inject the IV solution gently and slowly into Fitzsimmons' arm.

No whole blood was available in the First-Aid Center. Tom cursed himself for not specifying that there be some. It was, therefore, vitally important that he tie off the blood vessels as quickly as possible. Then he had a thought.

"Did anybody save the foot?" he asked Lucky Hertzog.

"It floated off somewhere while we were getting the bleeding stopped and moving him back into pressure."

When Tom couldn't find any sutures in the cabinets, he yelled for the remaining man waiting in the passageway. "You, get up to my quarters and bring back my flight kit. I don't know the compartment number—ask a steward. And hurry!"

After ten minutes passed and the man had not returned, Tom was in a bind. He had to stop the bleeding. "I've got to cauterize! Is there a welding torch around here?"

"Nobody in his right mind would do oxyacetylene welding here," Lucky told him.

"If I don't, this man's going to die from blood loss!"

"How about an arc welder?"

"Get it in here!" Tom didn't know how he was going to cauterize the stump of a leg with an electric arc welder, but he would try to figure something out. Unfortunately, there wasn't an arc welder within three hex modules of First-Aid.

Tom didn't panic, but he was slowly coming to the conclusion that his worst fears would be realized. He was going to lose this man because he hadn't been able to assess the medical requirements of a space facility accurately.

Lucky Hertzog released Fitzsimmons' head and moved toward the compartment door, maneuvering easily in zero-g.

"Where are you going?" Tom asked.

"You've got to seal that stump, right?"

"Right, but—"

"I'm going over to the beam builder three modules away. I'll bring back enough activated epoxy to cover that whole stump." And she was gone.

But the man returned with Tom's bag before Lucky did. Tom kept packaged sutures and needles in his kit, along with the necessary surgical tools. He always tried to go prepared to handle emergencies, a habit born from his life in the Southwest, where towns and doctors were far apart.

Tom was in the process of tying off arteries when Lucky Hertzog floated in, both hands full of a lump of curing epoxy.

"How long before that cures?"

"About fifteen minutes, Doc. It's got maybe ten minutes' working life left."

"Okay, I can get these arteries tied off by then. Stand by."

But doing so wasn't as easy as he had thought. Blood spurted everywhere. It was almost impossible to keep the working area clear of blood, which formed drops and globules, its surface tension making it creep along the exterior of every object it touched. But he managed to get the main arteries tied, then formed a base to the stump with the glob of epoxy.

The procedure worked. The blood flow stopped, and Tom was able to remove the tourniquet. It hadn't been sterile, and it hadn't been neat, but Fitzsimmons was still alive.

Then his heart stopped in shock from general loss of blood.

"CPR!" Tom snapped.

He quickly discovered CPR wouldn't work in weightlessness. When he punched down on Fitzsimmons' chest, he and Fitzsimmons flew apart.

Lucky quickly jammed Fitzsimmons' body into a locker along one side of the compartment and jammed herself in with him. With her back against one side of the locker and his against the other, she began CPR.

"Spell me," she gasped to Tom after about five minutes, during which time he had been trying to get the leads of the defibrillator untangled. One of her men moved in and took over, leaving Tom to his struggle.

But between Lucky Hertzog and her two workers, they managed to get Fitzsimmons' heart going again without the need for Tom to defibrillate—a risky business in the metal-walled compartment.

Tom and Lucky were still working on the man when

Charlie Day stuck his head into the First-Aid-Center. "Will he make it, Doc?"

Tom shook his head. "Not unless I can get him back to Jornada *fast*."

"I'll hold the departure of the *Salkeld*. It's ready to undock in ten minutes." The LEO Base boss disappeared.

Tom vented a sigh of relief. "Good. If I can get him on that StarPacket, he has a good chance."

"Your first time in zero-g, isn't it?" Lucky Hertzog asked.

"Yes, and I'm afraid I botched a lot of things."

She shook her red curls, obviously having adjusted to the disorientation brought on by rapid head movements that plagued newcomers. "Not as bad as some others I've seen. You're clumsy, and you're still gripping gravel. But you'll adapt. What the hell, I can't complain. Fred would be dead if you hadn't been here."

"Maybe," Tom admitted, "but I've got to do better than this at GEO Base. We won't be able to hop a Star-Packet and head for help out there."

"You're going to be the doctor at GEO Base?"

"If I don't accidentally kill myself in this screwy environment first."

"We'll teach you, Doc."

There was one helpful characteristic of weightlessness, Tom decided. It was possible to move the seriously injured Fitzsimmons easily without putting him under any additional stress. The two men who were bumped from their seats on the *Salkeld* didn't complain. As the stews were strapping Fitzsimmons next to Tom, the doctor turned to Charlie Day. "Get on the horn to Jornada. I want Dr. Vanderhoff and a paramedic team standing by at the edge of the runway when this bird stops rolling. And a medevac helicopter waiting to lift us all to Beaumont General in El Paso and a trauma team standing by there. This man isn't out of danger yet!"

"I haven't exactly been sitting on my can, Doc," Charlie Day told him. "They're already waiting. By the way, they found the foot." He took something out of a plastic sack—the severed right foot of Fred Fitzsimmons was still in the boot of the pressure suit. Tom took a quick look, then closed the sack and handed it to a stew. The foot had been completely dehydrated from its exposure to vacuum. "Stick this somewhere. Fitzsimmons may not want it, but I do. I'll need it to train my medical staff, if Fitzsimmons will let me use it for that, if he lives."

The next ten hours were a confused blur to Tom. The return flight and landing of the *Salkeld*, the transfer of Fitzsimmons to El Paso, the hours of surgery that miraculously saved the stump of the leg without necessitating a full amputation to the hip despite the fact that Tom had had to work without asepsis at LEO Base, and the moments when the injured man faltered, then recovered—Tom didn't remember exact details and was rather surprised when he woke up the next day, checked the record, and discovered he had forgotten almost everything he had dictated into the hospital record the night before. He went to see his patient.

Fitzsimmons was conscious, though heavily sedated, and was being maintained by two IVs as a plethora of instruments measured his vital signs. "You the doctor who saved me at LEO Base?" he asked haltingly.

Tom nodded. "With the help of Lucky Hertzog, who knew a lot more about how to work in weightlessness."

"Lucky's a good gal. Knows her stuff. Good person to work for," Fitzsimmons remarked. He managed to glance down at his right leg, then sighed. "Looks like I won't be going back up there to work for her again. Dammit, that was a good job."

"Don't worry about it now," Tom told him. "You've lost a lot of blood, and you've got to rest. Eden Corporation will take care of things."

"Who's going to hire a man with one foot?"

"You'll have a prosthesis. A year from now, nobody'll know. Besides, this is a big project. Eden Corporation has work for you here on Earth."

Fred Fitzsimmons shook his head slowly from side to

side on the pillow. "Doc, I quit my work here and took that job with Eden Corporation as an electronic instrument installer because I wanted to go into space. I've wanted to go into space ever since I was a kid. I saw Eden Corporation recruiting interviewers turn down experts who'd lost a finger or were handicapped. I *know* I won't get back into space again—and just because of some damned radio failure that I should have spotted!"

"Look, things will work out." Tom made a mental note to prescribe some neotriptyline antidepressant. Discouragement and feelings of inadequacy usually accompanied the loss of any part of the body, and Tom wanted to head off the problem with Fitzsimmons. The man would live, but he faced a major hurdle if his attitude didn't change. "I've got to report the accident to Owen Hocksmith himself, so I'll do what I can."

Fitzsimmons looked up at him. "Thanks, Doc."

Tom had heard that phrase many times in his career. In most cases, it was an automatic response from a patient. But there was something in the tone of Fitzsimmons' voice that made Tom realize the man really meant it.

For the first time in many years, Doctor Tom Noels felt good.

"That was probably the most valuable trip of my life, Smitty," he told Hocksmith after he had reported verbally to his boss.

"I hope so," Hocksmith replied. The two of them were sitting on the rail of the old ranch house, overlooking the valley to the north. "It was an expensive one for me, too."

"Sorry, Smitty, but I had to get up to LEO Base to find out what weightlessness was like."

Hocksmith shook his head. "I didn't mean it that way, Tom. It was just damned lucky you were there, or it would've been much worse."

"Smitty, the hospital and rehabilitation costs for Fitzsimmons aren't going to faze Eden Corporation."

"That doesn't bother me, either." Hocksmith gazed

out over the ponderosas to the valley, which was at a lower altitude and where only piñon and juniper grew. "I'm used to living with employee accidents and illness. Insurance premiums are figured into the budget. I expect some accidents and even some deaths on any big job. But the goddamn government doesn't. They figure I've got to run a completely safe show, and they're on my ass right now, T.K. They'll be backing you up against the wall within a few days.

"Is ISHA involved in Fitzsimmons' LEO Base accident?" Tom asked incredulously, aware that dealing with the Industrial Safety and Health Administration could prove to be a problem.

Hocksmith nodded. "And EPA. And Department of Health and Social Services. And a whole series of Washington bureaucracies that've managed to butt into the employer-employee relationship over the past several decades," Hocksmith growled. "It'd be different if I didn't look out for my people. But I always have. I've got more busted-up cowhands on the H-Bar-S than I can count, but just because they fell off a horse and broke something when they were chasing a Hocksmith cow through the bush doesn't mean that I'd turn them loose to fend for themselves. My daddy didn't get the loyalty of his hands by sending them into town and putting them on the dole once they'd dinged themselves working for him . . . and I won't throw away a man, either."

Hocksmith heaved himself off the wooden porch rail and began to pace slowly back and forth on the broad veranda, a sign to Tom that he was really upset. "But these bureaucratic bastards don't understand this, or that you can't make *any* job completely safe— especially a job in space where we don't know all the problems yet. They're trying to tell me how to treat my people! The ISHA crew's coming in tomorrow to investigate the Fitzsimmons case. You'll be involved, T.K. Sorry about that."

"Only thing I can do is tell them the truth," Tom said.

"That won't be enough for them. They'll want to know why Eden Corporation didn't take steps to anticipate the accident and eliminate its cause."

"Smitty, if we could anticipate accidents, there wouldn't be any. Nor would there be a need for doctors."

"You tell them, T.K. I've tried." Hocksmith sat back down on the rail, some of his tension gone as a result of unloading the problems on his friend.

"I will. And I've got a whole list of things that have to be changed or corrected or instituted up there in LEO Base and in GEO Base as well, Smitty."

"It's kinda late for changes, T.K."

"No, it isn't. Not if ISHA and the rest are breathing down your neck. And not if you really treat your people right."

"What have you got in mind?"

"First off, colors."

"Colors?"

"Didn't think about it until I got up there and saw for myself. You've got to use some color psychology not only in the StarPacket passenger cabin but also in LEO Base and GEO Base."

"Gawdamighty, Tom! You want me to hire one of those flashy interior decorators?"

"No, Smitty. Just listen, and you'll understand. First of all, everything up there's almost the same color—natural metal, some white or gray plastic coatings, a lot of anodized surfaces, and color-coding stripes on ducts and piping. That's strictly mid-Twentieth Century Industrial, often called Early American Esso Station. You feel you're trapped in a big tin can. The Navy learned about this back in the sixties, when it started making those long submerged cruises in the early nuclear submarines. I can dig up the references for you, if you want, but to make a long story short, they discovered that crew morale, effectiveness, and efficiency shot up when they started to use proper colors on the interiors of their subs. And we've got to do the same in orbit, plus a couple other little color tricks I dreamed up. Look around, Smitty. What do you see?"

Hocksmith waved his arm. "My land."

"What color is it?"

"Uh . . . browns, greens, blue sky, spots of red rock outcrops . . ."

"And the ranch house, what about that?"

"The same. Earth colors. But other colors, too."

"Smitty, the people you've got working up there were born and raised on Earth. They're not used to living in a tin can. Get Dan Hills and his people to come up with paints or other coatings to liven up LEO Base and GEO Base. Have them look into the research that's been done. In work areas, you want yellows and oranges and reds. In rest areas, use greens and Earth colors. That's all straightforward industrial psychology, Smitty. I know Dan's concerned about toxic outgassing of coatings under reduced pressure, but some of the new epoxy paints don't outgas at all once they've cured."

"Okay, Tom, go talk to Dan. He'll blow his stack, but have him bitch about it in my direction. You found other things up there, too?"

"Yes. For example, I became completely disoriented because I didn't know which side of the module was supposed to be the floor."

"There're no floors up there, Tom. There's no up or down in space. You know that."

"*I* know. But I can't convince my brain of that fact. And others up there are having the same problem. Until we get people born in zero-g who consider that state to be natural, I suggest we identify floors in the modules, even though it's physically unnecessary."

"How do you propose to do that? Put labels on them?"

"Just about. As far as our eyes and brains are concerned, a floor is always a dark color and a ceiling's a light color. It'll help people from becoming disoriented in the StarPackets if the deck is painted a dark color and the overhead is painted white. Same goes for the modules. That's only one new suggestion that came to mind when I was up there."

"You mean you've got a *list?*"

"You bet! And another list on top of that, dealing with medical equipment and facilities . . . because we all made the mistake, myself included, of deciding to put the medical facilities in weightlessness."

"T.K., why the hell didn't you or my engineers figure this out before changes got to be very expensive?"

"Simple. Number One: I didn't know about them because I'd never been in space, and neither had any of Dan Hills' people. Number Two: I couldn't even assign priorities to them until you had the StarPackets and LEO Base in operation so I could see for myself and learn what the problems of living and working in weightlessness *really* are. I told you this trip was a valuable experience, Smitty. Sure, it's going to cost you, but in the long run it may mean the difference between getting the job done or not. *And* you can use it in the ISHA affair."

"Oh? How?"

"The ISHA people haven't the foggiest notion of what it's like up there. Now that we do, we can handle them." Tom grinned at his friend. "After all, Smitty, as you taught me a long time ago on the Hill—if you can't convince 'em, confuse 'em!"

Chapter Six

"I am Dr. Ernst Gustav von Hesse!"

Tom Noels had been expecting a Teutonic, European-trained doctor complete with accent and Vandyke, and he wasn't disappointed because the visitor from ISHA matched his name perfectly. Tom shook a hand that felt like a dead fish—slippery and pliable. "Good morning, Doctor. Care to sit down so we can go over what concerns you?" He indicated the isolated grouping of chairs around a low table in one corner of the Eden Corporation headquarters' reception room.

"I would prefer a place where we could speak in private, Doctor. May we go to your office?"

"I don't maintain an office here, Dr. Hesse."

"Dr. *von* Hesse."

"Sorry. I don't have an office here."

"You don't have an office?" Von Hesse seemed incredulous. "How do you interview patients? Are you denied an office by the corporation?"

Tom shook his head. "I don't have any patients here, and I don't work for Eden Corporation. I'm a professional subcontractor. If I need a place to work, I borrow one of the cubicles with a computer terminal in it." He didn't try to explain that hardly anyone at Eden Corporation had an "office" with a desk and the other accouterments. Eden Corporation was totally computerized. Hence, a person's "office" could be any place with access to a computer terminal and a video telephone, which meant that an office was a private cubicle for those who required it.

"However, I'll find an unused cubicle if you wish to speak in private," Tom added.

"Please do so."

They were stopped from leaving the reception area by a door that remained closed. Tom put his palm against a plate on the wall alongside the door and announced into the grille of a speaker/microphone, "Dr. Tom Noels, contractor, with Dr. von Hesse of ISHA." Von Hesse's black attaché case—Tom knew Von Hesse was a specialist in bureaucratic medicine because he carried an attaché case in lieu of a black medical bag— was scanned quickly by a sensor and found to contain nothing but papers. The master computer, recognizing Tom's hand print and voice print together, as well as analyzing Tom's voice for any stress patterns that might be caused by duress, decided that everything was all right and silently opened the door.

Tom ushered his visitor into a private cubicle. "What can I do for you, Doctor?" he asked as they sat down.

Von Hesse placed his attaché case on the table and opened it. "ISHA regulations require that the proposed GEO Base hospital meet our basic standards for industrial medical facilities housed entirely within a building that is a work place."

"I didn't realize that the Industrial Safety and Health Administration had jurisdiction over hospitals," Tom remarked quietly.

"If said hospitals are an integral part of an industrial facility, yes," Von Hesse replied, taking out a multi-paged form. "I have been assigned the responsibility for reviewing and approving your plans. It shouldn't take more than a few hours to go through this interview form. Following that, I would like to see your plans, equipment list, and job descriptions. Then I'll leave this detailed background form for you to fill out."

"I was under the impression that ISHA had no jurisdiction over space facilities," Tom said, trying to keep his cool.

"Various UN treaties place all space facilities under the jurisdiction of a government, regardless of whether or not they're operated by private interests. Therefore, ISHA has jurisdiction."

Tom sighed. "Doctor, look, I'll be happy to provide you with any information you want, but I don't have several hours to spend with you, much less to fill out some long form you're expecting to leave with me."

"Do you want to have your facility approved?"

"Not really. As far as I'm concerned, if it's equipped and staffed to handle medical situations that I, in my professional judgment, believe could occur, I don't see that it requires anybody's approval, including Eden Corporation's—to whom I'm responsible under contract."

"That is not the case," Dr. von Hesse stated pontifically.

Tom leaned over the table and put both arms on it, looking Von Hesse straight in the eye. "Are you questioning my professional judgment, Doctor?"

"Federal regulations require ISHA approval of your facility."

Tom stood up. "In that case, I have nothing to say to you, Von Hesse. I suggest you look into the *Principles of Medical Ethics*, Chapter Three, Article One, because I believe you have absolutely no faith in my professional judgment."

"Dr. Noels, this is not a matter of faith in one's professional judgment; it's a matter of federal law. The principles of medical ethics have absolutely nothing to do with it. I strongly suggest that you read the applicable chapters of the CFR."

"CFR?"

"Code of Federal Regulations, which I have with me." Von Hesse pulled a thick booklet from his attaché case. "I also suggest that you cooperate voluntarily. Otherwise, ISHA will obtain the necessary actions from the federal judicial system to compel your cooperation."

Tom sat down. He sighed. "Okay, Von Hesse, what do you want to know?"

Von Hesse wanted to know everything, and he was disturbed when Tom didn't have all the facts neatly documented in file folders. Tom kept calling up data from the computer and displaying it for Von Hesse to see, in answer to the ISHA doctor's many questions.

"I am amazed, Doctor, that you don't keep records," Von Hesse remarked in an attempt to chastise Tom.

"What do you think these are?" Tom demanded. "I should cut down a living tree to make paper to print this information on when I can store it on plastic disks coated with iron oxide?"

Von Hesse, who was immensely proud of having been educated in Aachen, Germany, and having taught as a *Privatdocent* at Heidelberg, but who didn't dwell much on the fact that he hadn't practiced medicine at all in the United States, was visibly upset over Tom's GEO Base plans. "You have not followed the ISHA guidelines for in-house industrial hospitals," he pointed out importantly. "You do not have an adequate staff as required by Paragraph Four Thirty-one, subparagraph c-four-g. You do not have an on-site pharmacy as required by Paragraph Four Fifty-seven, subparagraph b-fifteen-g-two. You do not maintain an on-site medical library, and you do not plan a medical-records system that conforms with ISHA requirements for reporting."

"Dr. von Hesse, the regulations you're quoting were drawn up for large factory complexes here on Earth," Tom objected. "I'm dealing with a totally different medical and public health environment in GEO Base. I've got excellent communications, including an interactive computer link. And I'll be working with a population that's already been thoroughly screened physically and mentally."

"These regulations must be followed, and their compliance must be enforced," Von Hesse replied curtly. "GEO Base is an industrial facility, and there is no distinction drawn in the regulations that would permit a waiver for an industrial facility in space."

"Doctor, have you ever practiced rural medicine? Or shipboard medicine?"

"They have nothing to do with ISHA regulations regarding industrial medical facilities," Von Hesse insisted.

"Your ISHA regulations are totally inapplicable to the situation I'm going to find at GEO Base," Tom fired back. "Nobody's ever practiced medicine in weightlessness except Dr. Joe Kerwin, a few NASA astronauts with medical training, and myself—if I can count the limited experience I had earlier this week at LEO Base!"

Von Hesse tapped a well-manicured finger on the thick booklet. "These are the regulations, and you must follow them."

Seeing that this approach was having no success with the bureaucratic doctor, Tom changed his tack. Von Hesse was bound by the regulations he had to enforce and was a Civil Service employee who was obviously both procedure-oriented and promotion-motivated, so Tom decided to appeal to the man's self-interest rather than to his professional ethics.

"Look, Doctor, I've been out there. It's a totally different environment from the surface of Earth," Tom explained. "For example, we both take gravity and atmospheric pressure for granted here when we undertake even a simple surgical procedure. I can tell you from experience that it's not the same in orbit. I had a very bad time simply trying to stop bleeding caused by the severance of a foot."

"We've heard of that accident, and it's unfortunate I won't be on the board that investigates it."

"Yes, it's probably very unfortunate, because I learned a great deal about orbital medicine while working on that patient," Tom continued. "Let me tell you about it, and then I'd like to go over my analysis of possible injury modes in GEO Base operations along with my plans for handling each. We're pioneering a new field of medicine here, Doctor, and since I'll be working with you at ISHA for some time to come, I'd like to share my findings with you so that there'll be at least one orbital medicine specialist in ISHA—you. Until you and I train others, we'll be the only two experts in this new field of medicine."

Dr. Ernst von Hesse took the bait. Nonetheless, Tom ended up agreeing to meet some of the ISHA standards, which meant he would have to hire additional people.

His first telephone call after Von Hesse left was to Robert Eddy. "Bob, we've got to come up with some additions to my contract under that contingency clause we thrashed out. ISHA just landed on me, and I'm stuck with putting extra people and equipment up there that we didn't figure on."

The next call was to John Curry, the man who approved expenses and signed the checks. "Sorry, John, but ISHA got me, and I've already worked it out with Bob Eddy under the contingency clause of my contract. I'll have a revised budget to you as quickly as I can work one up. But I thought you'd want to know, since this development may affect your cash-flow situation."

The call to Dan Hills wasn't pleasant, either. Now they would have to figure on more equipment to lift to GEO Base, plus a lab technician and two paramedics who would be required to meet ISHA staffing regulations.

Then Tom Noels sat back in the cubicle, put his hands behind his head, stared at the ceiling, and started to think about the people he would need. He finally straightened up, punched a number into the phone, and waited until his party answered.

"Doña Ana Diagnostics." The image of a dark-haired young man who wore old-fashioned heavy black spectacles faced him. "Well, howdy, Doc!"

"Howdy, Dave," Tom replied. "As hot in Las Cruces as it is here in Duke City?"

"Hotter. How's your space clinic coming?"

"I'm putting it together. Are you still hanging in there with your lab?"

Dave Cabot nodded. "Yes, but just barely, Doc. I've been thinking of talking to you about getting some work out of the Jornada Space Port because things are slack here. All the new automated analysis equipment's so expensive that I'm having trouble justifying loans from the bank to buy the new stuff in order to stay competitive. We've always been a small lab, and I just can't meet the competition of the big national outfits. Nomad Corporation has just expanded its El Paso operation with a branch up here."

"I read about that and thought about you. Tell you what, Dave, how'd you like to operate as a subcontractor for lab operations at my GEO Base clinic?"

"What'd you just say?"

"I need a medical lab in my GEO Base clinic. I have the choice of putting one together myself, with very little time to get equipment and hire people, or I can turn to someone I trust who's already in the business. Do you want the job? You'll have to move to GEO Base, but it's going to be interesting doing lab work and pharmacology in orbit."

Dave scratched his head. "I don't know. I'm here by myself now, but—"

"Take tomorrow off. I'll have an Eden Corporation courier chopper stop for you on its way up from El Paso in the morning. Come have lunch with me and let me show you what's involved. If you're interested, we'll talk turkey. If not, you get a free trip to Albuquerque."

Dave grinned. "You know, I was thinking of taking tomorrow off anyway, Doc!"

Taking a page from Owen Hocksmith's own manual of management, Tom got his medical technology lab by putting David Cabot under contract to organize it.

Tom had to hire at least two paramedics or medical technicians to assist him. He couldn't afford to hire a doctor, nor did he want to until he had learned considerably more about the problems that are an integral part of space medicine. He didn't know where to place an ad for a paramedic, so he passed the word among his medical colleagues and to the personnel managers of most of the hospitals in New Mexico, Colorado, and Arizona.

Only one person surfaced: Stanley Allen Meredith, a thin young man with a full beard who showed up at

Eden Corporation headquarters with everything he owned stuffed into a backpack. When Tom interviewed him, there was no doubt that Stan Meredith was a very intelligent individual who was mostly self-educated. He had just spent a four-year hitch in the Navy as a pharmacist's mate on a guided-missile destroyer, which meant that he had been the only medical man aboard—the ship's doctor in name if not in professional qualifications.

"This sounds like a great job, and I'm really turned on about it," he told Tom. "I'd like to get it because it'll give me the sort of experience nobody else has yet. I want to be a writer, but it's tough for a beginner to break in. So I've got to hang in there as a paramedic until I get the breaks."

The lack of respectful attitude didn't bother Tom, because Stan Meredith not only exhibited an outstanding knowledge of the paramedic's job but possessed what Tom immediately sensed was an extreme sensitivity to people, the ability to empathize with others that was so much a part of medicine and was yet so often ignored by many in the medical field. Meredith's obviously informal manner was, Tom realized, a superficial cover-up for this sensitivity. Not many men who served as pharmacist's mates aboard a destroyer received the Navy's Distinguished Service Medal. Tom offered Stan Meredith the position as paramedic at GEO Base.

"I'll let you know in a couple days, Doc."

Meredith accepted the next day.

Tom had real trouble making the telephone call that would hire his primary assistant, his nurse. He put off the decision as long as he could, watching the days tick by on the ironclad schedule that Dan Hills had supplied him. Finally, he had to make a choice. The problem was, all three applicants for the nursing position were well qualified, but none had had experience in rural medicine. All came from large urban areas on the East Coast and in the Midwest. Not a Westerner among them. He thought he knew why; medical personnel were at a premium in the western states and would remain that way as long as the region continued to expand so explosively.

Tom would never reveal to anyone the mechanism by which he made his choice. He had his usual vivid dream one night. It was the Julie Lea dream, but without Julie Lea again. However, a new personality appeared. The next day, he telephoned Angela Mae Gordon and told her she would be selected for the position if she was still interested.

On the same day, he received a videophone call from El Paso. It was Fred Fitzsimmons.

"You're looking good, Fred," Tom told him.

"Feeling good, too. They're discharging me today. I'll be on crutches until they fit me with the prosthesis and teach me how to use it," the spaceman replied. But the grin on his pudgy face quickly disappeared. "Doc, I don't want to sit on my ass the rest of my life, living off the disability payments. And I'm having one hell of a time convincing people to hire me."

"Well, why don't you talk to some of the rehab people and get them to retrain you for a new trade, using your instrument tech background as a foundation?"

"That's not what I am," Fitzsimmons replied frankly. "I knew enough about it so that Eden hired me, but my background's in electronic medical instrumentation, especially the gear associated with intensive care and trauma. Uh, look, Doc, I want to get back into space in the worst way. In fact, worse than ever now, because down here I'm a guy without a foot and considered to be handicapped. But in weightlessness, that condition doesn't make a damned bit of difference."

Tom sighed and shook his head sadly. "Damn, Fred, I wish I had an opening for an instrumentation man, but I don't."

"Can you use a paramedic?"

Tom nodded. "I do need one more."

"I'm your man," Fitzsimmons stated bluntly. "Look, Doc, to qualify to wire up patients in trauma, I had to go through paramedic training in Los Angeles. And believe me, Doc, a paramedic doesn't have to have both feet on the ground in weightlessness!"

"Fred, grab the next corporation courier and haul up here to Albuquerque." Tom was happy that he'd completed the search for his paramedics, but he was elated that he would have one who had been in orbit and understood the environment.

Tom's staff selections met with the official approval of Doctor Ernst Gustav von Hesse, M.D., *Privatdocent*. But John Curry had fits over costs and cash flow for the medical facility.

Dan Hills was upset and somewhat surly.

"Dammit, Doc, you're becoming part of the problem rather than part of the solution," the engineering chief told him. "Three more warm bodies, which amounts to more than five hundred pounds of additional humanity. That means you've cut into my contingency life-support reserve factors by twelve pounds of food per day, six pounds of oxygen per day, and twenty-seven pounds of water per day—not to mention such cute little items as having to recycle the additional waste products, plus getting rid of about five hundred watts of additional heat load . . ."

Tom let the engineer ramble on, getting his complaints off his chest. "I empathize with your problems, Dan," Tom finally said. "The recitation of your afflictions grieves me deeply. Never before have I encountered an engineer with as many problems as you have. Let me give you the telephone number of the ISHA representative who laid these additional three people on me. You can tell him all about your problems, and he may be sympathetic."

Hills remained silent for a moment, appearing to fume. Tom knew this was part of the man's makeup, the way the engineer relieved personal stress. "Never mind, Doc," Hills finally replied. "I've had the course trying to reason with those idiots in Washington about lots of other things. Welcome to the club. This all goes to prove the validity of Murphy's Law, Corollary

Forty-three, Part Seventeen, Paragraph One-Oh-Four, otherwise known as Eiffel's Law—"

"Okay, Mister Bones, what's that?"

" 'In any design where a parameter such as weight or volume is critical, the value of the critical parameter will increase exponentially as a function of time, regardless of the efforts of engineers to reverse the trend.' In other words, if it looks easy, it's difficult, and if it looks difficult, it's damned near impossible. I'm going to take the afternoon off. Want to shoot eighteen holes with me if I can get us tee time?"

Tom was an unusual doctor; he didn't play golf. He had never had time—and he didn't have time that day, either. He had assembled his staff in Albuquerque and was running short of time in which to train them in what little he knew about orbital medicine. He was really counting a great deal on Fred Fitzsimmons, who had already had four weeks of work in LEO Base with Lucky Hertzog. Fred was the only member of the team who had had any experience living in zero-g.

The first order of business had been a complete two-day physical exam at the Lovelace Clinic. This was not intended to uncover potential physical or psychological problems of his staff, nor to cover himself or Eden Corporation in case of unforeseen physical problems connected with working in space. Tom knew he was pioneering a new field. He had NASA data on physiological changes all the way back to the Mercury program, plus the long-term information from the later SkyLab, Free Flying Module, and Space Park programs. And he had what little he could get of the Soviet data, which covered much longer durations in weightlessness. He was unable to insist on full physicals for the hundreds of Eden Corporation space workers; that would have taken too long and been too costly. He therefore had to limit his statistical universe to the five people—himself included—of the GEO Base clinic. The Lovelace information would serve as a base line against which he could compare data from future physical exams at Lovelace made during Earth furloughs.

In addition to the routine exam at Lovelace, Tom personally gave each team member a physical exam, using techniques he had learned on the S.S. *Patrick Miller*. Many of the procedures were considered fraudulent, meaningless, or worthless by American physicians. But Tom knew better because he had learned and practiced the techniques in places where the AMA and the FDA didn't exist.

"Acupuncture?" Angela Mae asked incredulously.

"Don't sneer. It works," Tom told her.

"I know it works as a supplement to anesthesia, and I've seen it used there," she admitted. "But this testing for the balance of acupuncture meridians sounds a little bit like something, well—"

"Like something a quack might use, Nurse? Sorry, I put words in your mouth. You're quite correct in questioning the procedure, but I also expect you to learn something about it because it does indeed work . . . along with some other strange and unusual techniques you'll find me using."

Tom used the laser acupuncture and meridian balance instrument that he had had to purchase in Switzerland. With the device, he took measurements at various locations on the skin of his team members. Angela was skeptical, Dave Cabot less so, and both Stan Meredith and Fred Fitzsimmons were completely receptive.

"Hell, Doc, I've seen stranger things in Hong Kong and Subic Bay," Stan Meredith said. "Bothered the hell out of me at first. But then I started to use some of them—until the captain caught me and told me to follow the Navy manuals. But I went ahead anyway and used Tibetan humor balance and herbal medicine when the skipper wasn't looking."

"You want to give me a hand on the humor evaluation tests, then?" Tom asked him. "It would be valuable to have a second person's opinion."

"Sure, if you'll teach me the kinesiology evaluation technique you just tried on me. That's unbelievable!"

Tom called his team together for the first time, and after introductions and a brief rundown on the background of each member, he told them, "We've got three weeks—twenty days, to be precise—to put this team together before we're scheduled to lift for GEO Base. In view of the shortness of time, I must presume that each of you is current and needs no additional work to bring you up to speed on what you've got to do in GEO Base. However, I'd be interested to know if any of you think you'd like to hone your edge a bit by some special work you might do here in Albuquerque within the next twenty days."

Stan Meredith raised a finger. "Doc, I've been out of the Navy for two months now. I could be rusty as an old chain, and I'm not really up on non-Navy paramedic techniques. Think you could arrange for me to spend a few days with the Fire Department's paramedics here?"

"Not a bad idea," Fred Fitzsimmons noted. "It's been nearly a year since I went through paramedic training in L.A. I could use a refresher, too. Besides, I'd like to spend a few days at Bernalillo County Hospital to get updated on the new equipment and techniques."

"I can arrange that," Tom said. "And it's probably a good idea to transition directly from active medical work in Albuquerque to GEO Base."

"Doctor, may I ask you a question?" Dave Cabot put in.

"Shoot!"

"I'll be able to do most of the medical lab tests, and at your request I'm also handling the pharmaceutical department." The young medical technician had a worried tone in his voice. "You've specified some strange equipment to run tests that I don't understand, and you've asked me to stock herbal medicines that are not only damned difficult to find but—excuse me if I seem blunt here—straight out of folk medicine . . . mushrooms, herbs, various types of soil, strange plants, pollen spores."

"You're right," Tom admitted, "but I'm the doctor. I've never been chained to accepted techniques or the fads of the moment. I learned a long time ago that the people in this part of the country—Anglos, Chicanos, and Indians—had acceptable and workable empirical procedures and remedies. I learned a lot more about that sort of thing working on a freighter for three years. There'll be no county medical society looking over my shoulder at GEO Base, and I seriously doubt if we'll ever see Dr. Ernst Gustav von Hesse of ISHA. Dave, you may have to go to Juarez for some of the stuff I asked for, or you may have to travel to Switzerland, Cairo, or Singapore. Wherever you have to get it, get it and don't waste time. And don't worry about it. We're going to have to use *all* the medicine known to the human race mainly because we're facing some real unknowns. Don't be at all surprised if some of the procedures we use aren't 'approved' here in America or are completely new and different."

Angela Mae Gordon spoke up. "I will need to go over some of the procedures you intend to use in GEO Base. I have no experience in weightlessness, Doctor. But I can see that weightlessness will make a lot of our ordinary procedures impossible."

"Not just the practice of medicine, Nurse, but living itself," Tom pointed out. "All of us will be going through a transition period during which we'll have to adapt to GEO Base living, plus learn how to adapt medical service to its restrictions. The latter will probably occupy our attention for the rest of our professional lives. On the other hand, we should be able to adapt to GEO Base conditions within days—or weeks, at most."

"Doctor, we've found out that a person adapts within two days—or he doesn't adapt at all and must be sent home," Fitzsimmons said. "That's in regard to the immediate physiological adaptation. We haven't been out there long enough yet to find out whether or not any long-term physiological or psychological adaptive problems exist."

"Fred, you've logged more time in orbit than any of us," Tom observed. "You've got a lot to teach us in the next three weeks. My experience was brief, so you're the expert in weightlessness. All of us will meet around this table every morning at eight o'clock for two hours of seminar," Tom announced. "I'll go over the equipment and facilities we'll have in GEO Base, and we'll consider some of the medical problems we're likely to encounter. Fred, I want you not only to amplify on the latter, based on your own experience, but also to enlighten us all about the little day-to-day aspects of living in zero-g. Dave, you and I have already discussed some of the problems of handling pharmaceuticals, so I want you to cover how we plan to handle solids such as capsules and liquids like IVs and injections. Stan, you've been involved in isolated medicine aboard the U.S.S. *Sherwood*; I want your input on procedures. After the seminar every day, each of you will be free to undertake whatever medical updating or refreshing you want; I'll arrange whatever you need."

"What about me?" Angela asked.

"You, Nurse Gordon, are my assistant and Number Two on our totem pole." Tom knew he was perhaps being somewhat too stiff and formal with the nurse, and he didn't exactly know why. She was, of course, extremely attractive, which disturbed Tom but which he also managed—thus far—to keep out of the way of their professional relationship. "If *I* can't adapt out there, or if my pressure suit springs a leak, *you've* got to run the show until a new doctor shows up. Remember, this is frontier medicine, and you'll be a doctor in fact, if not by approval of the State Medical Examiners."

Angela suddenly looked very serious. Always, there had been a doctor around or on call, and she had been able to count on that doctor to make decisions. She wasn't certain whether she would be able to do the same on her own. The thought frightened her, but she did her best not to let it show.

The effort worked, of course, because Angela Mae Gordon knew precisely how to get what she wanted any time she wanted it.

Tom Noels should have spotted that character trait in

Chapter Seven

Nobody came to see the GEO Base medical team off except Senator Owen Hocksmith.

Tom reflected that the small turnout was typical for the sort of people he had chosen for his team. They had friends in many places but were loners at heart—yet they seemed capable of working together as a team. They were pioneers capable of leaving behind everything in their pasts.

At least, Tom hoped so.

He voiced his sentiments to Owen Hocksmith as they sat together after dinner in Tom's Spartan room in the ETO Passenger Terminal. "Well, the die is cast, Smitty, as Caesar once said."

"He wasn't the first to say it, T.K. He was repeating a common proverb," Hocksmith pointed out. "And don't ask me why it's one of the things I remember from old Major 'Daft' Taft's class in Ancient History, but I do. I liked history."

"I would've flunked the course if you hadn't threatened to beat my ass with a broom every time I got a low grade on a test," Tom reminded him. He glanced over at his old friend. "But if I fail on this one, Smitty, you won't be able to beat my ass."

"Not if you're belly-up," Hocksmith said wryly.

"And not if I'm dead. That's a deadly place up there. Dan Hills figures he'll lose a hundred fifty people building the pilot SPS. I've got to cut that number down. I'll do it," Tom vowed, "if I don't blunder."

"You won't. You're a good doctor," Hocksmith told him.

"Maybe I won't goof up directly, but my people could—and I'm responsible regardless."

"You worried about your people, T.K.? You picked them."

"That I did. And yes, I'm concerned. I'm not the manager you are, Smitty. I could've made the wrong choices."

"Who are you shaky about?"

Tom knew, but he couldn't admit it for several reasons. "Maybe I'm just edgy about the whole thing. It's just so damned new, and it's got me stretched out more than anything I've done since med school."

"Good! A person works better when he's afraid of failing."

"Speak for yourself, Smitty. How's it going on your end?"

"Nothing that a billion dollars wouldn't fix."

"Only a billion? Why, a man with your connections should be able to swing that on an unsecured note." Tom was trying to relieve Hocksmith's obvious tension, which was, Tom saw, far greater than his own.

"I could swing it with no sweat if I wanted to deal with New York, Frankfurt, and Bahrain, but I'm trying to stay away from that circle because those people have played loose and free for a couple of centuries, and they haven't exactly behaved with long-term consequences in mind—or else they realized what those consequences might be and ignored them or hoped something would change. Oh, sure, they've managed to do a lot of beneficial things. But they've also managed to screw up some very important matters that affected the lives of millions of people—and I can't afford to screw up this venture. Or bring anybody into it who could. Too damned important."

"Smitty, I always thought the financial people made their livelihood by betting on the future and counting on a positive outcome—otherwise, we wouldn't have things like credit or, even, loans."

Hocksmith nodded. "Bankers and financiers will always bet on a sure thing, T.K., or at least on a deal with the lowest possible risk and with some security backing up their bet. You're a prime example. Banks have always been a soft touch for a doctor because the loan office knows damned well that a doctor's going to make the grade. How many M.D.s have you known that have gone belly-up?"

"Not many. Professional people generally manage to cut the mustard."

"Some of them, but not all of them. As a financier, I wouldn't loan a professional writer a penny, even though he might be the world's greatest, with a Pulitzer and two books on the *New York Times* bestseller list." Hocksmith leaned back in his chair, stretched his long legs out in front of him, and put his hands behind his head. "Sure, the money boys bet on the future all the time; you're right in your assessment as far as it goes. But too often, financiers also try to shape the future to minimize risk and work because, like most people, they're lazy. Look at space and energy, for example. Less than a decade ago, the bankers were telling the world through their flunkies that space was a waste of money and resources, because they thought the ultimate consequences would screw up the way they had things arranged on Earth . . . which is true, so I'm going to have to do battle with them sooner or later. But I want it to be on *my* terms! And that's why I've *got* to succeed with the SPS—and why *you've* got to succeed with your part of it—and I know you will, or I wouldn't have called you last winter."

"You'll hack it, Smitty. And thanks for the vote of confidence, friend."

"Okay, Mister Christmas, let's see how well you remember your ancient history. How did Zeno define a friend?"

Tom grinned. "Another me."

"Close, but not precisely correct. Look it up, mister, and report to my room with the right answer. And bring your broom." Hocksmith smiled.

* * *

The passenger cabin of the StarPacket SP-03 *Layton* looked different from that of the *Salkeld*. They had taken Tom's advice about color and interior decoration.

To Fred Fitzsimmons, it was just another lift. But he left his crutches on the ramp and smiled because he knew he wouldn't need them in orbit.

Stan Meredith observed everything carefully, exhibiting no evidence of anxiety. He was making mental notes against the day when he would write the great modern space novel.

Dave Cabot, born and raised in Las Cruces, had been around rockets all his life. He was excited because he had wanted to ride in a space vehicle ever since that long-ago day when his father had taken him to Cape Kennedy to watch the last Saturn 5 boost SkyLab into orbit.

Only Angela seemed a little apprehensive, but Tom couldn't tell whether it was real or whether she was playing out some role. He found himself seated next to her in the webbed seats of the *Layton*. She looked pale, but her fair skin always appeared that way to Tom. Even during her stay in sunny New Mexico, she hadn't picked up a tan, only a series of painful sunburns. Her genes obviously came from the cool, shady forests of middle Europe. She was, Tom decided as he gazed at her, a modern Valkyrie, at least in appearance. There was no question in Tom's mind: Angela was a beautiful woman.

The announcement came without warning as usual: "Up ship!"

As the lift acceleration began, Tom discovered Angela's hand gripping his in a sweaty, trembling grasp. She was frightened. But by the time the *Layton* went into free fall, she had relaxed her grip. Tom saw a smile on her face.

"Just like going over the top of the roller coaster!" she said to him in a small voice. "Except it just keeps right on going over the top!"

"You okay, Angela?"

She reacted to the use of her first name by grasping

his hand again. "Yes! This is going to be fun. There're lots of things we're going to have fun trying out in weightlessness!"

LEO Base didn't look the same, either. It was no longer just cans in the sky. It had floors and ceilings, even in zero-g, because of the new color scheme. It was busy, and it was hot. A lot of people were working at LEO Base or passing through to GEO Base. Obviously, the additional transient bodies were adding to the heat load, causing peaking that the radiators weren't totally capable of handling.

Tom had no time to look for Charlie Day; the Pot-Vee *Edison* was loading for LEO departure, and the five members of the GEO Base medical team were immediately shunted from the StarPacket docking module to the Pot-Vee docking module.

"Except for fewer people, it's just like changing planes at O'Hare," Angela observed.

"Little Chicago in the sky," Stan added. "I guess there'll always be a place to change transportation—trains, planes, or spaceships."

There were few amenities on the Pot-Vee *Edison*. But since the transition to GEO Base took several hours, the craft did have a bathroom of sorts—nothing more than a simple adaptation of the proven technology of the SkyLab "waste management system," as the old NASA circumlocution labeled it. The Personnel Orbital Transfer Vehicle itself was just a double-decked cylindrical cabin section eighteen feet in diameter and fifty-five feet long with a control compartment, docking air lock, and tunnel forward. On its aft end was the cylindrical hydrogen-oxygen propulsion module, the common orbital propulsion module used for both Pot-Vees and Cot-Vees.

There was one flight attendant, a short, wiry young man with his head shaved smooth as a ball bearing. As he helped Tom into one of the net-mesh seats, the doctor remarked, "Excuse me, but as a doctor, I'm curious why you shave your head. Is there some reason for doing it here in space?"

The steward didn't nod. "There's a very good reason, Doctor: No barbers at LEO Base or GEO Base, plus another factor few people took into account. If you think shorn hair goes all over the place on Earth, try cutting somebody's hair in orbit. I can keep it shaved smooth in orbit. Just makes it easier, that's all. And I wear a cloth helmet to protect my scalp if I have to move around a lot."

Tom glanced over at Angela, who looked back at him and said in a low voice, "Don't you dare!"

The pilot of the Pot-Vee *Edison* turned out to be Ross Jackson. He recognized Tom when he came through the cabin on his way to the flight-control compartment. "Howdy, Doc! How's my favorite sawbones? Going to make the big jump to GEO with me, huh?"

"I thought this flight went to Acapulco."

"You can have it! Just water, sand, humidity, and gravity." The older astronaut saw Fitzsimmons. "Fred, you're coming back?"

"Hi, Ross!" Fitzsimmons called to the pilot. "This time, I'm one of Doc's paramedics."

"Can't keep you out of space, eh, Stumpy? Welcome home." Jackson's nickname for Fred Fitzsimmons stuck—but it was used only by those who worked with him in the weightlessness of space. It was Ross Jackson's verbal recognition of the fact that a man without a foot wasn't handicapped in space.

"Thanks, you Ancient Astronaut," Fred shot back.

"Easy flight today," Jackson remarked. "Three hours, fourteen minutes dock to dock. Relax and enjoy."

"Pretty short time for such a high lift, isn't it?" Stan Meredith asked. "Planning on high boost?"

"Naw! This flying sewer pipe is boost-limited to point-one-five gees because of its structure," Jackson explained. "Besides, we don't need the boost that's required for Earth-to-orbit. You'll hardly notice it now—

but, man, it'll feel like a rock dropped on you after you've spent six weeks in weightlessness!"

The Ancient Astronaut was right. There were some bangs, clanks, muffled clunks, and gentle jolts as the *Edison* undocked from LEO Base. And when the thrust of the oxygen-hydrogen rocket engines came on, there was the gentlest of accelerations, accompanied by a slight vibration and a damped shaking.

"Combustion noise being transmitted through the thrust structure, plus a little bit of damped pogo oscillation," Fred Fitzsimmons explained.

"Why didn't they get the pogo out of these ships before they put them into operation?" Dave Cabot asked. "Didn't pogo oscillations give the engineers all sorts of trouble on Saturn and the Space Shuttles?"

Fred smiled. "Welcome to private-enterprise astronautics! There's worse vibrations in an airplane. It costs so much to get all pogo oscillations out of a design under all sorts of load conditions—and these Pot-Vees operate with all kinds of loads—that it's more cost-effective to let them shake . . . within reasonable limits, of course."

"But won't this thing eventually shake apart?" A note of anxiety entered Dave's voice.

"Nope," Fred replied. "Never had a Pot-Vee crumple yet. The engines are de-rated so much that the pogo doesn't affect them, and the engines themselves are modernized versions of very old, well-proven designs that never gave a bit of trouble."

"RL-10s," Stan put in.

"Right you are. Dave, you've gotta remember that this is *not* government astronautics, where everything's built to tight specs and then tested to death."

"A mouse built to government specs," Stan muttered.

"Huh?" Dave queried.

"The old definition of an elephant," Stan told him. "The *Edison*'s a mouse built to industrial specs—and there's a world of difference."

There were no cabin windows in the Pot-Vee, so it was a three-hour flight without a view. The feeble ac-

celeration lasted for several minutes, followed by free
fall. The door to the flight deck opened, and Jackson
came floating out, announcing, "We've got a couple of
hours of free fall now. Passengers may unstrap and
move around at will."

The bald steward and the Ancient Astronaut moved
in what was obviously a very special manner as they
proceeded through the cabinful of people—they maintained an orientation with their feet pointed toward
what would normally be the deck. Tom knew why. If
anyone aboard was disoriented by weightlessness, it
wouldn't help his welfare a bit to see his confidence
models, the pilot and the steward, floating around upside down.

Fred was already unstrapped and floating about six
inches off his seat. Jackson stopped by in the aisle.
"Checking out the old reflexes, Stumpy?"

"Yeah, but so far the loss of the mass of my right
foot doesn't seem to pose any big problem."

Nobody in this load suffered from disorientation, and
Tom was thankful of this because it would give him
some time to become acclimated to zero-g himself before having to administer to drop-sick passengers.

As a result, within a quarter of an hour the double-
decked cabin of the Pot-Vee *Edison* was full of people
having the sort of riotous fun available only in zero-g.
Years earlier, the fine art of astrobatics—plain old ac-
robatics performed in weightlessness—was the private
sport of astronauts. The motion pictures and TV trans-
missions they had made from SkyLab and the shuttles
had been fun to watch. It had been obvious from those
pictures that the astronauts were having a ball. Now,
SPS workers on their way to GEO Base had a few
hourse of astrobatic tension and boredom relief.

There were a few bruises and contusions as people
collided with one another or with the unpadded walls,
bulkheads, and furnishings of the cabin. But the injuries
weren't serious, and both Fred and Stan got in a little
practice as Tom watched.

At one point, Stan floated up to Tom and quietly

asked, "Uh, Doctor, it seems that weightlessness opens up all sorts of possibilities for medical research. You wouldn't happen to know if, uh, any research has been done to date on human sexual activity in weightlessness . . . ?"

"Yes, there has."

"Nuts! I was hoping I might be the first to publish!"

"Found a suitable pair of experimental subjects?"

"Not yet, but there are possibilities. Uh, any prudes in this outfit?"

"Not that I know of," Tom told him.

GEO Base was totally different from LEO Base.

Whereas LEO Base was a pass-through transportation hub and an SPS module subassembly facility, GEO Base was the big, well-equipped, complex, final assembly construction site. Neither Tom nor the members of his team had the chance to see GEO Base as they approached for rendezvous and docking. Although the interior of the Pot-Vee docking terminal appeared identical to the one at LEO Base—it was, because the terminal at both locations consisted of identical hex modules—GEO Base was obviously bigger and more strung out. Not even Stumpy Fred Fitzsimmons knew his way around GEO Base, though he had been there once during the very early days of its development a few months ago.

There were no guides, human or computerized. There were no directories. Once the medical team had collected its personal baggage, there was no one to tell them where the medical module was or where their living quarters were located.

Ross Jackson came to their rescue. "Everybody out here has a job to do on SPS construction," he explained. "Can't afford tourist guides. I'm not even sure I know where your med module is, but I can take you to the base engineer's office. You met Herb Pratt on your first boost, didn't you, Doc?

"Big, tough-looking, construction-boss type? Sure, I remember Herb."

Herbert Karl Pratt, P.E., was just as Tom had remembered him. Except that here at GEO Base, where Pratt was in charge, the engineer appeared to be even more dictatorial. He looked up from the control consoles of GEO Base Central as Tom floated up to him. "Well! Our doctor and his team have finally arrived! I needed you day before yesterday, but nobody was around to help. Lost a man to a slow leak in his P-suit. Time my gang got him back to pressure, he was unconscious and they couldn't revive him with first-aid."

"Sorry, Pratt, but we couldn't have gotten our lift reservations changed under any circumstances." Tom was curt. "Besides, if everything went according to schedule, my med module wasn't hard-docked until yesterday. I trust it's in place, isn't it?"

"Hills and Day may get away with schedule slippages, but I don't tolerate them," Pratt snapped. "Yes, your module's in place."

"Good. Where is it?" Tom asked.

Pratt punched a keypad, and a diagram appeared on the display in front of him. He punched a few more keys. "Come over here," he told Tom, "and I'll show you where you can find it."

"How come you haven't got directories posted in critical spots around GEO Base?" Tom queried as he moved to where he could see the display.

"Because GEO Base is changing day by day. Once we get the first unit on line and gear GEO Base up to the two-per-year rate, the place'll become static enough so we can post directories," Pratt explained. He pointed on the display. "There you are, at the end of this support structure."

Tom peered over the man's shoulder, trying to make the display snap into perspective in his mind. When he did, and when he saw where his module was located, he said quietly to Pratt, "I understood that the med module was supposed to be sited in a more central location."

"Had to move it. One of Hills' boys miscalculated a

moment arm, so I had to shift some modules around to keep things in balance for a while."

Tom shook his head. "Pratt, it's got to come back to where it's supposed to be. I can't handle a medical emergency when my facility's a couple kilometers from the other end of GEO Base. Please see to it that the med module's moved back as soon as possible. In the next few hours."

Pratt leaned against the straps that were holding him to the chair's cushions. He folded his arms across his massive chest. His little gray eyes peered at Tom from his craggy face. He opened his mouth only enough to say, "No."

"Why not?"

"One: because I don't have the crews and the tugs to do it right now. Two: because it'll screw up the mass and moment distributions if I do it now. And, three: It's a support element with second priority to construction elements."

Tom stared at the GEO Base engineer for a long minute. "May I use your phone?"

"To go over my head and call Hills? No." Herb Pratt had been worried about the doctor's arrival for several days. He didn't know the medical man, but his own experience with doctors had led him to believe they were autocratic, often capricious, and generally prima donnas who didn't take well to working as a member of a team. Therefore, he had prepared himself by putting up several defenses against this new doctor. His first action, he had decided, would have to be an immediate confrontation to establish his ultimate authority at GEO Base. Pratt felt he couldn't afford to let the doctor get the upper hand, even from the first moment. The engineer's way of setting up a showdown had been to move the med module—he knew he could have moved a storage module or a living module instead—and then to exert his authority by refusing to move it back. Otherwise, Pratt believed, the doctor would move in with no problems and then start to cause them.

"Doc, there's one thing you've got to get into your head right away: This is an engineering job, and it's the reason we're all here in the first place. I'm the GEO Base boss—Base Operating Engineer, if you want my official title—and it's my responsibility to see to it the job's done as planned, within costs, and on schedule. You're a support element, and you'll take your orders from me just like any rigger out there running final assembly. If you understand that simple fact of life, Doc, we'll get along fine."

Tom decided the best way to handle this totalitarian would be in the same manner he had handled the martinet second skipper of the *Patrick Miller* when the replacement captain had assumed command in Manila. "Mister Pratt, I hope you'll understand something, too. I'm here with my crew to become a part of your team . . . which means working *with* you. I'm your medical and health expert, your brains in an area where you have no expertise. I have every intention of working *with* you. I have no intention of questioning *your* expertise. As a matter of fact, I wouldn't have your job under any circumstances, and that's not totally because I'm not qualified. But as your medical expert, I *am* here to protect you."

"*Protect me?*"

Tom nodded, then immediately wished he hadn't. Rapid head movements aren't recommended to newcomers, not if they want to maintain their orientation. "Dan Hills tells me Eden Corporation's planning to lose over a hundred men on this job. You tell me you've lost one already. It's my job to reduce that problem. I'll do it. If I can cut your manpower losses by fifty percent or more, you'll look pretty good, not only to Dan Hills but also to John Curry and even to the senator, won't you?"

Pratt didn't say anything. Then he turned to his keypad and began to run his fingers over it as he studied what came up on the display as a result. He finally turned back to Tom. "The med module will be resited in fourteen hours. Why don't you have a look at it and let me know if everything aboard arrived okay?" He paused, then added, "Since you're unfamiliar with GEO Base, I'll have one of my junior engineers show you how to get to your module."

The interior of GEO Base was like Grand Central Terminal in New York City, with two exceptions: The passageways were smaller, and it was in weightlessness. GEO Base was a warren of connected tubular and hexagonal passageways lined with ducts, piping, conduits, and handrails. Lighting came from only one "wall" of the passageways, a concession to the fact that the space riggers were still Earth-born and used to up and down.

"How are we ever going to find our way around this place?" Dave Cabot asked in amazement as a young engineer led them through yet another pressure-seal door. All modules were safetied by a circular pressure-tight door that had to be opened to permit transit and that automatically closed and sealed unless its autocontrol circuits were temporarily disabled. People normally passed in both directions through such hatches, but occasionally one had to be left open in order to move a large piece of equipment through.

"Easy," Fred remarked. "If it's anything like LEO Base, you'll find your way within days, and then you won't even think about it until some morning when you find they've changed something and you've got to find a new way. You'll start thinking in three-dimensional terms. You'll adapt surprisingly fast."

"Adapt or die," Stan Meredith muttered.

"Huh?"

"Never mind. Paraphrasing Darwin."

The door to the med module was sealed as it had been since Tom and Dave had checked it out as JSP before its transportation into space. As Tom moved to break the seal and open the door, Fred stopped him.

"Uh, Doc, I wouldn't, if I were you," Fred said.

"Huh? What's the matter, Fred?"

"You and Dave sealed that module at JSP how long ago?"

"Let's see, about three weeks ago, wasn't it, Dave?"

"Yeah."

"How do you know it doesn't have a leak?" Fred wanted to know.

"Sorry to sound stupid, but this space living's new to me," Tom remarked. "So it has a leak? So what?"

"Do you know there's pressure on the other side of that door?" Fred asked.

"Why, there's bound to be! We sealed it pressurized," Stan said.

"Doesn't mean it still has pressure," Fred explained. He moved to the door and to the control panel next to it. "Look, the secret of living to a ripe old age out here involves a firm belief in Murphy's Law. *Never* take anything for granted, especially when your life may depend on it. *Always* assume that something's malfunctioned until you *know* it hasn't. Suppose the med module sprung a leak during boost to LEO Base, or when they were transferring it to a Cot-Vee, or when they unloaded it here and docked it to GEO Base. What would be the consequences?"

"We'd have lost a lot of our equipment, to say nothing of most of the pharmaceuticals and lab reagents in there," Dave ventured.

"Plus your life if you managed to get that door opened with vacuum on the other side of it."

"It's not supposed to open with vacuum on the other side of it."

"Hell of a lot of people got killed out here because something was 'supposed' to be fail-safe, Dave. Everybody, look here at the little panel alongside the door. There's one of these at every hatch. If you ignore it, you're likely to kill yourself by what we might call 'traumatic abaryia,' which is a word I just made up, Doc, and that you can steal if you want. Crack that door with vacuum on the other side of it, and the pressure in this module would drop in less than a minute to a level that would kill you. The automatic door on the inboard end of the living module would automatically seal. Hell, Pratt can't afford to let everybody in GEO Base get killed just because some damned fool forgot to look at the tell-tale alongside the door before he tried to open it. Sure, it's supposed to be fail-safe—*but don't you ever believe it!* You stay alive out here by placing absolutely no trust whatsoever in safety devices that were designed by engineers sitting down on dirt. They aren't going to get killed if it doesn't work. Fired maybe, but they're still alive. You all listen to me. You're part of the same team I'm on, and we can't afford to lose a single one of you. Especially you, Doc. I may not be able to keep you from getting shortened a foot or two, but I may be able to keep you alive."

The pressure indicator showed there was indeed pressure in the med module, but Fred told them not to believe even that. "It could be frozen or have malfunctioned in sixty different ways. Next step is to check the test port in the door."

Fred showed them how to crack the test port on the door and listen for the whistle. Every door and hatch had such a test port, a very simple device that couldn't fail: a small opening that could easily be opened and just as easily shut and sealed again. Any pressure differential across the door would cause the test port to whistle.

"We're in luck. The pressure held," Fred told them.

The hospital portion of the med module proper was docked closest to the rest of GEO Base and occupied half the length of the module. As the med team swarmed in, they found everything had not gone well during the boost because some of the equipment holddowns hadn't held during the acceleration of a Star-Loader or a bit of rough handling during transfer at LEO Base or docking at GEO Base.

"CAT scanner's gone," Dave told the doctor. "Ripped right off the bulkhead and whanged the Diagnostic Ultrasound unit. So we lost that, too. Hope you've got insurance, Doc."

"If that's all we lost getting it here, it's a small miracle," Tom admitted. "I want everybody to thoroughly check every piece of equipment you are familiar with, even though somebody else may have checked it, too. If anything's busted, I want to know stat so I can get new stuff on its way."

"Yeah," Stan remarked, "sure as hell the first bad case we have will require that Diagnostic Ultrasound unit."

The living quarters were on the outboard end of the med module. In accordance with Tom's requests— made on the basis of his earlier experience in LEO Base—each member of the team had a private sleeping sector. None of these "cabins" was spacious, each being a one-sixth sector of the hexagonal cross-section of the module, minus the hexagonal tunnel down its middle, and eight feet in length.

"Good heavens! We're supposed to live *here?*" Angela asked, aghast at the cramped aspect of her cabin and its 24-inch sliding pressure door.

"Well, I had about as much room in a destroyer," Stan remarked. "And some people had even less room on the smaller nonnuclear submarines."

"Actually," Fred Fitzsimmons remarked, "we've got it plush, gang. We've got our own cabin. Most of the construction crews have to work on the hot-bunk system and can use their cabin only during their sleeping shift."

"But it's so *small!*" Angela pointed out.

"What do you mean, 'small'? It'll get much bigger as you learn how to live in zero-g, Angela," Fred commented. "You've got more than a hundred-fifty cubic feet of space. A coffin's only about thirty cubes, and that's all it takes to hold a human being."

"Oh, thanks for the comparison!" Dave remarked.

"We're all spoiled," Tom pointed out to his crew. "This is sheer luxury compared to the way most people on Earth live. Take Southeast Asia, for example—"

"You take it, Doc. I've been there," Stan pointed out.

Each cabin had its own lighting system, its own emergency life-support system in addition to the air ducts leading to the main GEO Base life-support system, a sleeping sack, and lockers to hold clothing and personal effects. Each cabin door could be closed and sealed from within and from without, but could be opened in an emergency from the main module control center panels.

"Well, at least you don't have to worry about somebody being able to slide open the hatch when you're sleeping in there," Dave remarked to Angela. "You've got privacy if you demand it."

"I don't always demand it," Angela said.

The sixth sector of the module was a lavatory. The living quarters themselves occupied only eight feet of the length of a fifty-foot hex module. Eight more feet of length were occupied by a stand-by lavatory in addition to two segments devoted to dedicated module life-support and power-distribution equipment. The remaining nine feet of the outboard half of the module was an open common room. The common room had a feature not present in any of the living cubicles: a 12-inch triple-glazed port.

Tom found Stan gazing out this window on the universe.

"The problem with all this space stuff is you can't see very much of what you're actually in," the protoauthor remarked. "Everything's sealed up in a tin can."

"Ports cost money."

"Then why do we have one here?"

"I thought the reasons for putting one in the old NASA SkyLab were still valid, so I talked Dan Hills into it. After all, there's more to working and living in space than the task of staying alive," Tom explained.

Chapter Eight

We've been at GEO Base for a "day" now, but the only way we can keep track of time is by the clock, although our circadian rhythms tell us when it's dinner time in Albuquerque. I don't know how our circadians are going to shift around under these conditions.

Naturally, I'm keeping precise medical records on everything we do at GEO Base Clinic. They're stored in GALEN *somewhere on Earth below. But because of what we're doing here, I'm keeping this independent journal that will, for now, be my private diary. I thought about starting this while I was still on Earth, but the rush of schedules set by somebody else never seemed to leave enough time for me to do it. And maybe I didn't need to do it then. Maybe what I needed then was to keep so busy that I didn't have time to think about what had been, only about what was coming. Now, I probably need it for many reasons, not the least of which is to document for my own later study and, perhaps, amusement the things I was thinking about and the way I was thinking about them during what is undoubtedly another turning point in my life.*

I hope this one won't be as traumatic as the last one was.

I think my people are good. I've yet to find out for sure. Once I get a better handle on them, I'll know how to set up our team rotational schedule back to Earth. My paramedics seem fine, and I know my med tech's competent. I worry a little bit about my nurse. She seems competent, but she's a beautiful woman, and the natural instincts originating in my cerebellum may be warping the judgments that come from my cerebrum. I haven't felt as attracted to a woman since Julie Lea.

I also think I've got to record the sort of things I will in this GALEN *journal. I've always been taught that one stands on the shoulders of those who've gone before and must, therefore, provide a foundation for those who will follow. The obligation is always forward to the future, since I can never repay the obligations I incurred in the past. Someday this may be an important document or contain some tidbit of valuable data for those who will follow me, but perhaps I'm being presumptuous. However, I don't belittle myself and what I'm doing; I'm pioneering, and I know it. But I also know the risks.*

Dan Hills and Herb Pratt have planned on losing a hundred fifty people. I've vowed to reduce that number. As of today, the count is eight. And they've brought up only ten of the two hundred fifty-six solar array modules.

I'm so very far away from everything now.

I'm used to being isolated—in the Southwest or on the old S.S. Patrick Miller. *But this is isolation of a totally new sort. If it weren't for* GALEN *and the outstanding communications we have with Earth, this would be lonelier than the Antarctic bases.*

"Med module, this is Base Central. Medical emergency!"

Angela touched the reply button on the intercom. Concurrent with her actions, Stan and Fred came to life, Stan switching off the library computer terminal, where he had been reading, and Fred securing one of the positive-pressure IV units in his paramedic bag.

"Central, Med here. Go ahead," Angela responded.

"Meteorite penetration with injuries, Sector Charlie Victor, Module Four Seven."

"Ask if they've got pressure there," Fred put in quickly.

In anticipation of his question, the voice from GEO

Base Central continued. "Module is under pressure with a patch on the hole."

"Get details!" Stan snapped.

"Central, Med. Do you have a report on the extent and nature of injuries?" Angela asked. She wasn't writing things down; with the computer power available in their local systems plus GALEN when needed, everything went into the keypad before her.

"One life-support-systems installation technician apparently hit when the meteorite broached the module," Central came back. "Just our luck: One chance in a hundred billion, and he gets hit when it comes through the bulkhead! Meteorite size unknown, but it left a fifteen-millimeter hole in the module wall."

"Where's Doc?" Stan asked, strapping his paramedic kit on his back.

"Sleeping this shift," Angela reported. Then, to Central, "Any further information on the extent of the injury, Central?"

"Negative, Med. Just get there. Somebody reported it's like a bullet wound."

"That tells me what I need to know," Stan muttered. "Fred, grab Bag Delta in addition to your usual kit. Now, where the hell's Charlie Victor, Mod Four Seven?"

Angela had it on the display.

"Wake up the doctor," Fred told her as the two paramedics sailed out the hatch. "If the meteorite left a fifteen-millimeter hole in the wall, it's probably less than five millimeters in diameter. If the meteorite's still in the guy, we'll be bringing him back here for surgical removal."

Angela found Tom sleeping in his cubicle with the light on. She hadn't been able to sleep without some sort of light, either, lest she wake up from the classic falling dream to find herself actually falling in the dark. Seeing him sleeping peacefully there in his sack, she overcame a very powerful urge and merely reached out and touched him. "Doctor, wake up."

* * *

Stan and Fred discovered that it took almost nine-teen minutes just to get to Charlie Victor, Mod Four Seven. There were a lot of hatches to go through and a lot of modules to traverse. "Fred, if we don't find some faster way to move around this rabbit warren, a lot of people are going to be dead before we reach them," Stan pointed out, finally opening the hatch to Mod Four Seven.

Fred was right behind him through the hatch. "I'll ask Doc to see Pratt about getting us an Eff-Mu."

"What's that?"

"Extra Facility Maneuvering Unit. A scooter to any-body but these acronym-happy engineers. Boy! Looks messy!"

Four people were clustered around a fifth who was writhing in agony. In zero-g, it was almost impossible for the four men to hold the agonized fifth one.

"Paramedics!" Stan announced as he fought his way into the group. "Let me in here!"

"He's hurt bad," somebody said.

"We can't hold him."

"Turn him loose, then," Fred ordered.

"He'll hurt himself if he bangs into something."

"Got any strapping?" Fred asked.

Somebody came up with twenty feet of a three-inch web strap of the sort used to tie around loads to tow them or affix them temporarily to a hold-down ring.

"Where's he hit?" Stan asked, and then saw for him-self the red stain spreading across the left anterior abdo-men.

"Stan, wrap this strap around his chest, under his arms," Fred snapped, handing him the bight of the strap which he had folded in the middle of its length. In less than five seconds, the webbing had been secured around the injured man's chest, below his arms. Fred tossed a free end to one of the onlookers, ordering him to "get over by the bulkhead and just hold this—not tightly, just enough to keep him from drifting. You, take the other end and get over on the other side of the module. Take a strain on it, but just enough to keep him from drifting around."

The injured man was safely secured in the middle of the module, but was still writhing in pain.

"Med clinic, Stan here," the paramedic reported over his wrist radio unit.

"This is Dr. Noels, Stan. What have you got?"

"Subject has sustained a puncture wound in the left anterior abdomen approximately ten centimeters below the rib cage and five centimeters from the medial line," Stan replied. "Those numbers are estimates, Doc. Bleeding is profuse. Subject is semiconscious and in obvious pain. Vital signs are—" He looked at Fred.

"Going into shock," Fred reported. "Pulse one hundred, weak and thready. BP one-ten over sixty and dropping. Subject is hyperventilating, now unconscious. Extremities cold and clammy. Definitely cyanotic."

Stan repeated this information to Noels.

"Start him on one hundred percent oxygen with positive pressure," Tom told them. "Start a positive-displacement IV with both sodium bicarbonate and lactate of Ringer. Stand by to insert an airway if needed. You can't do much about the blood loss, so wrap him in a thermal blanket and transport him immediately. We'll be standing by in the surgical area."

Because of the weightless condition, Stan and Fred had to insert an airway to prevent the man from choking on his own gastric juices and swallowing his tongue in the reflex action caused by his own saliva. They didn't try to halt the bleeding from the abdominal wound, but wrapped him in the aluminized plastic thermal sheet from their kit. Transporting was easy in zero-g, but getting through all the hatches while continuing to monitor his condition and maintain the positive-displacement IVs was difficult. It required almost a half hour to bring the man back to the med module.

Tom and Angela were ready and waiting, having already donned sterile surgical suits and scrubbed with pads premoistened with antiseptic. This was the first time Tom had scrubbed for zero-g surgery, and he didn't feel right using the premoistened pads. He was accustomed to having copious amounts of water and surgical soap flowing over his hands and arms. Such a routine was impossible in zero-g, and he had spent a long time figuring out how to scrub effectively in weightlessness.

The surgical sector of the med module had been shifted to operational mode with slightly increased oxygen content and ten millimeters' positive-pressure differential with the rest of the module. Tom had adapted clean-room techniques such as the positive-pressure differential. The life-support system for the surgical sector was also equipped with half-micron filters.

Even before the injured man was transferred to the narrow surgical table, Tom ordered the paramedics to strip him down. Angela was to get the patient wired to the monitors as quickly as he was stripped, and Dave was to take a blood sample and type it stat.

There was no trouble getting the man onto the table and strapping him down securely so that Tom could begin work on him. Fred and Stan floated out to change into surgical suits and scrub.

"Looks like a bullet wound," Angela observed.

"Projectile wound's the same whether it comes from a bullet or a meteorite," Tom muttered. "We don't have to worry about tetanus here, but we'll give him some tetanus antitoxin later, just to be sure."

"I can't think of anything more sterile than a meteor in space," Dave remarked, taking his blood sample.

"We don't take chances. We don't know what it might have picked up when it slammed through the side of the module. And we don't know what kind of strange and screwy things might have been on it in space, things just waiting for a little heat or atmosphere in order to revive. I've got to get the shock under control and make sure this guy's anesthetized." Tom reached over and removed a six-inch stainless-steel needle from the sterile rack that held his surgical instruments. Feeling with his fingers, he located the proper site and gently inserted the needle just below the collarbone on the left side. Selecting another, shorter needle, he placed it in the man's neck just below the left ear.

Angela was astonished. "What are you doing, Doctor?"

"Acupuncture," Tom replied curtly, inserting yet another needle. "Learned how in Shanghai, Hong Kong, and Singapore. Hand me those two electrical leads, Nurse."

"I didn't think that was accepted practice, Doctor."

"If it works in China, it'll work in GEO. Remember, I'm the county medical society here and the sole member of the OMA."

"OMA?"

"Orbital Medical Association. Acupuncture and a lot of other techniques are perfectly acceptable to the OMA." He clipped the electrical leads to two of the needles. "Give me three volts at fifty microamps."

The procedure halted the shock condition, and respiration returned to normal. Blood pressure was 130/70 and pulse was down to 65 by the time Fred and Stan returned, gowned and scrubbed.

Dave Cabot stuck his head through the waving plastic curtain that partitioned off the surgical sector. "Doc, I think he's got type AB, Rh negative."

"What do you mean, you *think?*" Tom snapped.

"First time I've ever tried to type blood in zero-g," the med technician admitted. "Liquids spurt all over the place!"

"I warned you about that in Albuquerque!"

"I believed you, but believing and experiencing are two different things."

"This man's lost blood," Tom told him. "AB negative's pretty rare. Any in the blood bank?"

"We haven't been here long enough to get more than twenty quarts from donors, and we haven't got a drop of AB negative," Dave told him.

"Get GALEN to tell you who's at GEO Base with AB-negative blood—and then get them down here!"

"I'm AB negative," Stan put in.

Out of habit, Tom shook his head and became momentarily disoriented, even though he had already spent several days in GEO Base. "Nope. I may need you, Stan, and I can't have you out of action. Get on the GALEN terminal and find out from the med records who else is available."

All the while, he was working on the man strapped to the table. The meteorite must have been a slow one. It had apparently lost most of its velocity and kinetic energy penetrating the side of the module, because it hadn't gone all the way through the man's abdomen. There was no exit wound on the man's back.

"Stan, move the Diagnostic Ultrasound unit in here. I've got to locate that meteorite. It's too deep to probe for, and it may have punched through the kidney . . . which means we're in trouble."

"Diagnostic Ultrasound's busted, Doc."

"Damn! I forgot! Get the X-ray unit in here. I'll have to probe utilizing videoradiology." Tom preferred to use Diagnostic Ultrasound because he could more easily locate organ boundaries. Without it, he was forced to revert to old techniques which wouldn't give him the sort of contrast he really wanted. If the meteorite was a chondrite, he might have trouble with a precise fix of its location. Then he remembered that he had a computer available.

"Fred, you're the electron pusher—get on the horn to GALEN's central office, have the videoradiology output plugged into our communications down-link, and tell GALEN's people to give us computer enhancement of our signal on the up-link."

"Right away!"

"Doc, we've got two with AB negative aboard. Only two. Ellen Adele Hertzog and Herbert Karl Pratt."

"Lucky Hertzog!" Fred said with surprise. "Are you sure she's in GEO Base?"

"Computer says she arrived two hours ago with the last subassembly to dock."

"Dave, get in touch with them both. Ask them if they'll donate blood. And put out the call for all Rh-negative types to come in; at least we can get them to donate plasma. This guy's lost a lot of blood. And he's going to lose more before I can get that rock out."

The videoradiological scan showed the meteorite to be just above and slightly in front of the left kidney. Tom sighed. "If I had to rely on straight radiology, I would've assumed the object had penetrated the kidney. It's that close."

"Shock wave probably did some kidney damage," Angela volunteered. "We used to see remote tissue damage from shock wave in a lot of shooting cases."

She would have seen plenty of gunshot cases in Philadelphia and Washington, Tom told himself. In addition to being a decoration, Angela was turning out to be a real asset.

"We've got to repair damage in there," Tom mused, studying the video screen. "I'll have to go in. Angela, Fred, we've got to keep the blood under control or it'll be everywhere. Lots of sponges and pads. Dave, you're not scrubbed; you keep a sponge count on GALEN and stand by the keypad for other inputs."

"Roger. I'll tape the video so we can play it back at any time to locate sponges and pads."

"I don't want that radiology transmitter in my way."

"I'll pull it back, and we'll get GALEN to zoom the video signal. We can also use very low dose rates since we have computer enhancement available."

The meteor had torn up some of the small intestine but had missed the spleen and the liver, coming to rest just short of the left kidney. It was messy battlefield-type reconstructive surgery. Tom had just secured the little four-millimeter rock between his forceps when he heard a voice on the other side of the surgery-area curtain call out, "Hello, Fred! Hey, it's good to see you back, even if you had to lie your way in as a paramedic."

"Hi, Lucky! Hell, I'm the best paramedic around, next to Stan here," Fred's voice resounded. "And lie, hell! Do you know how hard I had to study in that El Paso hospital?"

"Is this doctor the same one who worked on you in LEO Base?"

"The same. And he's good, Lucky. Hi, Pratt! Glad you could come. You've both got the same rare blood type as our meteor victim."

"Can you make it fast, Fitzsimmons? I've got to get back to Central. We've got another module ready to be docked," the base engineer reported.

"Right away. Come over here, both of you, and we'll get started. Dave, can you give me a hand?"

"Roger."

"Okay, make a fist. Now, grab this rod and open and close your hand on it. Good. Hey, that's a good vein, Pratt! We'll have you out of here in no time with that flow rate."

"Fred, you're as clumsy with that needle as you were with a voltage probe!"

"Sorry, Lucky! Your vein's small and hard to find. There! Got it!"

"They've always claimed you were bloodless because of that red hair, Lucky," Pratt added. "Now we know."

"Shove it, Herb. Ten bucks says I'll fill my blood bag before you do."

"Still the gambling type, huh?"

"You bet, Fred!"

Tom had the meteor chunk out. "Keep that," he told Angela. "If this guy doesn't want it, we'll use it as the first exhibit in the Museum of Orbital Medicine. Let's get out and close. Dave! Coming out! Stand by for sponge count!"

"You've got fourteen to worry about!"

"That's a lot," Angela remarked.

"We had to keep the field clear," Tom pointed out. Actually, zero-g surgery hadn't turned out to be as difficult as he had anticipated. The capillary action of sponges and pads kept blood and other fluids out of the way, but Tom discovered he had to have himself firmly anchored to the bulkhead or the table. It was like trying to work floating underwater.

Tom left an abdominal wick through the peritoneum

to equalize any possible pressure buildup and to drain off internal fluid. The wicking action of surface tension was probably the most effective method he had worked out for slow transfer of fluids.

"Okay, let's secure him right here. No reason to move him," Tom said. "I'd rather have him stay under these clean-room conditions anyway; it'll simplify our asepsis procedure."

"Right," Angela agreed. "Shall I keep monitoring him against the possibility of post-op shock?"

"Always. But we can do it from the med monitoring panel. Leave him wired up. And let's get whole blood into him as quickly as possible. Those acupuncture blocks won't work forever."

He pulled himself out of the curtained OR and into the main med module, stripping his gloves and mask as he did so. Lucky Hertzog and Herb Pratt were still strapped to the bulkhead, but their phlebotomy bags were nearly full. Tom greeted them. "He'll be okay, Herb, if we can get that whole blood into him. Thanks for donating. Hello, Lucky, good to see you again. I presume you were joking about Fred?"

"Does it really make any difference? Don't tell me he's not a good paramedic," the red-haired power engineer replied.

"He's a good paramedic," Tom told her, noticing for the first time that Lucky Hertzog was a trim, attractive woman, even in the almost shapeless jump suit that was commonplace attire.

"Well, don't worry. I was kidding him—and you," Lucky admitted.

"Testing, you mean," Herb Pratt growled. "Noels, look out for this one. She's one of the bitchiest engineers I'm forced to work with, and no pun intended."

"Good old Herb Pratt!" Hertzog fired back. "Your same old lovable self. Doc, don't let Herb get to you. At Georgia Tech, they must teach their engineers that the whip is more effective than the carrot. Aha! Pay me, Herb! I'm finished bleeding!" Fred had moved in and removed the needle from her arm.

"There wasn't a bet."

"You nodded," Lucky reminded him with a smile. She had a nice smile, showing small, straight teeth behind small but well-formed lips that bore no makeup. "You mean I'm going to have to spread the rumor that you're not only a slave driver but a welcher, too?"

"You do that, and I'll boot your undoubtedly attractive ass right out the nearest lock to vacuum. Hertzog, you may be able to push Charlie Day around when you're in LEO Base, but you aren't going to do the same thing out here with me. Get that through your scarlet head for a change."

Tom could see that there was no love lost between the gruff base engineer and the red-haired power engineer. Actually, Tom wanted to cheer her on for being able to hold her own against such a formidable adversary. Lucky Hertzog obviously had what used to be called "pluck"—she was confident, sassy, and apparently exceedingly capable in her job.

"Go screw a heat pipe," Lucky told Pratt quietly, rubbing her arm as Fred put a piece of tape over the spot where the phlebotomy needle had gone in.

"How do you feel?" Fred asked her.

"Okay."

"Take it easy for at least eight hours," Tom advised. "I wouldn't put on a P-suit and go into vacuum if I were you. Your body needs time to rebuild its blood supply. You might have trouble if you subjected yourself to the reduced pressure of a P-suit."

"Okay, I'll work the video monitors instead," Lucky said. "Much as I'd like to take the shift off, they need me on Module Ten's integration. Besides, there's nothing much else to do up here in Pratt's Plant for Prudes except watch TV from Earth or sleep—usually alone, too."

Pratt changed the subject as Fred moved in to remove the phlebotomy needle from his arm. "Who was hit with the meteor, Doc?"

"I don't know. I thought you'd be able to tell me from your records. He didn't have any ID on him."

Pratt rubbed his left arm, below the puncture wound of the needle. "I'll give you a call from Central and tell you who he is. Damn! What a long shot! Gotta hand it to you, Doc. Without you and your team, I would've lost him. I've got to get back to Central and make my accident report to Albuquerque."

"Look, what I told Lucky also goes for you. Take the rest of the shift off and give your body time to rebuild its fluid volume. Neither of you is in any condition to make decisions, and you shouldn't subject yourself to any stress for eight to ten hours."

"Don't worry about me, Doc. I can handle myself," Lucky put in.

"I'm sure you can. But just knock off the competition with the men around you for a few hours, okay?"

"Competition? Why, Doc, I gave that up years ago," she told him with a smile. "No male can compete with what I've got! This equality stuff's for the incompetents."

"I wish I had the authority to fire you!" the base engineer snarled as he undid his straps and moved quickly toward the hatch at the end of the med module. He pushed off, got halfway there, then threw his hands out and went into an uncontrollable tumble.

By the time Fred, Lucky, and Tom reached him, he had lost what was left of his last meal.

"Whoozy," he managed to whisper.

"I told you to take it easy, Herb," Tom chided. "Fred, let's get him back and strap him down to rest for a few hours." He shot a glance at Lucky Hertzog. "You, too."

"No, I'll be a good girl, honest," Lucky told him. "More comfortable in my quarters. Better yet, come on down to the wardroom with me, Doc. I'll buy you a bag of coffee. After performing surgery in orbit, you oughta be able to take a coffee break, right? Or was med school any different from engine school? We used to run on coffee and mazindol. How about you?"

"Well, you're right, but as doctors, we could get our hands on stuff more potent than that." With a doctor's typical postoperative indication of tension release that involved the nonchalant turning over of the rest of the small details to his subordinates, Tom announced, "I'll get Miss Hertzog back to her quarters via the wardroom. Fred, make Mr. Pratt comfortable until I get back; tell Central where he is. Angela, you and Stan start transfusion with that whole blood, both quarts of it. If any other donors come in, take care of them. Dave will help you. Angela, you can reach me in the main wardroom if you need me." He stripped off his surgical coveralls, leaving himself dressed only in the singlet and shorts worn by most people in GEO Base who stayed in pressure all the time. The blood-spattered coveralls went sailing through the module toward the waste receptacle. "Let's go," he told Lucky. "You'll have to show me the way because I still get lost in this rabbit warren."

"Got news for you, Doc," Hertzog said as she took his hand and half led him and half let him lead her toward the far hatch. "It may be a rabbit warren, but all the people in it don't act like rabbits."

Wardroom was another name for cafeteria, but because it served a diversity of functions, its volume was more like that of an assembly hall, seven hex modules grouped together in a honeycomb with large openings cut through the module walls. The wardroom was in operation around the clock because of the three eight-hour shifts. Somebody was always eating. Others used the wardroom as relief from the tiny living quarters or as a place to stay while someone was sleeping in their joint quarters.

Tom had been so busy making sure the med module was working properly that he hadn't had time to do more than visit the wardroom for meals. Even at that, he had usually had one of his team bring meals to him in the med module because he was so busy. Now he realized he hadn't taken advantage of one of the prime features of GEO Base: the Rest Shift recreational facilities.

GEO Base might be 22,400 miles from Earth, but it was in instant communication with the ground. All the major network TV programming was fed up to the base, along with additional channels devoted strictly to news, sports, education, or movies. There was interactive video for gaming with several computer nets below. One could also use any of the terminals for interactive educational studies. Another honeycomb of modules adjacent to the wardroom housed the zero-g spa and gym, where one could work out with springs and bungee equipment to maintain muscle tone, or participate in any number of almost continuous games of space hockey, racquetball, or astrobatics.

Tom realized he would have to take some time to work out regularly, lest he lose all his muscle tone.

Lucky removed two bags of hot coffee from the dispenser and punched in her charge code. "My treat, Doc. Least I can do for saving Fred Fitzsimmons."

They found a table. Each tucked his knees under it. Tom still preferred to strap down, but Lucky had enough weightless experience that she was able to stay put without the seat belt. "Yes, Fred's a good man, and he's helped me out a lot. But, as I recall, you had something to do with saving him, too, Miss Hertzog."

"You haven't been in GEO Base very long, have you? In spite of our glorious leader, Herb Pratt, there's very little formality. If you call me 'Miss Hertzog' again, Doc, I'll take your favorite scalpel and—never mind." Her blue eyes twinkled, and she took a sip from the coffee bag.

"Have it your way," Tom replied carefully, "since you seem to manage it anyway, Lucky. Where did you pick up that nickname, by the way?"

"You haven't guessed?"

"Are you inordinately fortunate?"

"You might say that," she replied demurely. "All the recreation in LEO Base and GEO Base isn't confined to the wardroom and the spa—or to the computerized games Eden Corporation's provided. That's all very nice, and we appreciate it. But sometime I'll introduce you to the longest continuous floating crap game in space."

Tom grinned. "Seems to me that's a line from an old Broadway play."

"Could be. Probably is. But this is a real floating crap game. And there are a couple of continuous poker games going on, too." Lucky sipped her coffee. "I picked up my nickname in engine school. The macho male engineering students couldn't admit to themselves that a woman could crack a quiz with a higher grade than most of them, so it was easier for them to attribute my success to luck. When I showed a few of them how to make ten straight passes in a row—that's with dice, Doc—down in the pit of the electric-power lab, the nickname stuck."

"I take it you don't like 'Ellen Adele' as a pair of given names?"

She bristled. "Not only no, but hell, no! When my mother was alive, she used to call me by both names and tried to bring me up like a flossy little doll she could dress up in frilly dresses and the like—when all I wanted to do was to go out with Dad on emergency and house calls." She calmed down, took another sip of coffee, then looked levelly at Tom. "Don't you *ever* call me that again, Doc!"

"The name's Tom."

"But I like 'Doc.' "

"Damned few doctors do, but we put up with it because we have to. With you, I don't have to."

Lucky Hertzog didn't reply for a moment, then brushed her flaming hair out of her face and remarked, "You like to live dangerously, don't you?"

Tom felt he had a handle on the fiery engineer's personality. "Look who's talking! I don't know anybody else around here who's bold enough to lip-off to the base engineer and tough enough to get away with it, too. As a matter of fact, I don't see too many women out here doing this risky kind of work, either."

"Doc—uh, sorry. Tom, life's too short and sweet not to savor all of it that's possible. I like it in big, juicy chunks. I'll leave propriety, sobriety, and security to those of my sex who'd rather exist without taking chances. A homebody I'm not."

"That's pretty obvious."

"Really? Well, Tom, someday I'm probably going to take a permanent liking to some man, and I may yet turn out to be the best damned homebody you've ever seen. Matter of fact, look out; I might even go after you. But you'll never know it if I decide to—not until it's too late, that is." Suddenly she put her head in her hands.

"Feeling okay?"

"Sorry. A little disorientation."

"You just parted with over a quart of blood," Tom reminded her. He reached over and took one of her wrists, feeling for pulse.

She shook her hand out of his grasp. "I'll be all right."

"That's true—because I'm going to see to it that you get to your quarters right away. And if you try to fight back, I'll slug you and put you out for ten hours of enforced rest," Tom told her sternly. "Come on, show me where your quarters are."

"No good. Helen's on her sleep shift there right now. I've got no place to doss out. Why do you think I wanted to come to the wardroom with you? I need to kill about two hours before I can get into the sack."

"We've got room in the med module."

"Along with Pratt? Not on your life, Tom!"

"I said, come along. I've got a ten-bed hospital there, and the individual beds—well, beds they're not, but they're private. The caffeine helped you a little, but you still need a few hours' rest. Come on."

Tom showed her to an empty room; it comprised two sectors of the hex module and was considerably larger than the standard private quarters because it required room for equipment and possibly two or three medical personnel as well as a patient. He told Lucky to crawl into the sleep sack and rest, then added, "I'll bring you something to drink. It'll help. You'll need to replace fluids for a few days, anyway."

Lucky was too exhausted at that point to object. When the loss of blood hit her, it hit her hard, Tom noticed. She was now almost docile.

Fred and Stan were busy monitoring two more people who had come in to donate blood, and Angela was monitoring their surgical patient. So Tom had Dave concoct eight ounces of fruit juice with neonitrazepam added. But when he got back to the bed bay where Lucky was, she was already sound asleep.

Chapter Nine

From the Galen Journal of Dr. T. K. Noels:

Three weeks now. And the Grim Reaper Count is fourteen because we couldn't get to them in time.

In one case, it wouldn't have made any difference, anyway. In spite of the fail-safe design of the P-suits—so loss of pressure in one part of the suit won't result in a total loss of suit pressure—we lost a rigger yesterday for a stupid reason.

Riggers working in P-suits are required to use the Buddy System—checking each other's gear before cycling to vacuum. But this crew was in a hurry to get on the job. So the buddy didn't check both of the helmet pressurizing lines where the fittings go into the helmet. From what Pratt determined by studying the P-suit later, neither line was inserted in the fitting past the detent. I've got to admit, it's difficult to tell when you've twisted the fitting past the detent, especially if you're already wearing P-suit gloves.

Out in vacuum, the guy snagged one of the lines and pulled it out of the helmet fitting. The check valve closed when the line left the fitting, just as it's supposed to do. But when he heard the line come out of the fitting, he turned, caught the other line on the same beam element, and pulled the second line far enough out of the fitting so it blew most of his back-pack oxygen supply out into space . . . and at the same time failed to come out of the fitting far enough to activate the check valve. He lost helmet pressure in a few seconds. By the time his buddy got to him, he died from what Fred termed "traumatic abaryia," or rapid and terminal loss of pressurization.

Contrary to what we once thought, it wasn't messy. He didn't explode, and his blood didn't boil because the rest of the P-suit was still pressurized.

At the autopsy I discovered Angela doesn't like to participate in them. The alveloae apparently started to collapse but the alveolar capillary membranes hemorrhaged before they could. The man drowned in his own blood. See my full medical report in the formal GALEN file for the rest of the details.

This was the first man lost to traumatic abaryia. In general, the post-mortem results matched the animal test data from vacuum chambers on the ground.

They're right: Pioneering amounts to discovering new and more horrible ways to die.

Until the manufacturer comes up with a kit to revise the fitting and the check valve, Pratt's had to have a P-suit inspector check everybody going into vacuum. We got the word in the med module and had to run through a revised emergency suiting drill.

Another case was perhaps worse from our point of view because, although the man was alive when we got him, he was too far gone to save. Writers often talk about the "primordial cold of outer space." But we lost this man to hyperpyrexia—overheating.

P-suit backpacks are designed to get rid of the metabolic heat generated by the individual, plus the environmental heat load from outside. There's a limit to the backpack's capability. Everybody's trained to recognize the symptoms of potential overload—a rise in P-suit temperature, hyperventilation, headache, et cetera. When it starts to happen, you slow down, rest, relax— or you're dead very quickly. This poor guy never had a chance, and it was a genuine industrial accident that finished him.

Again, it happened in Lucky Hertzog's power-control crew. Lucky doesn't like the reputation she's getting. This was the second member of one of her *power-control crews to become injured while on duty. Fred was the first, of course.*

While a photovoltaic power module's brought up from LEO Base, where it's assembled, it converts sunlight to electricity, which is used to power the electric thrusters which propel it to GEO Base. The structure isn't metal; it's a carbon-reinforced composite plastic.

The riggers had docked the new module to the main array, and Lucky's crew moved in to make the electrical switchover. Supposedly, it's impossible to create an electric arc in a vacuum, but GEO Base is surrounded by a halo of escaped life-support-system gases, outgassing products from materials, and other things that make the vacuum less than perfect. This is a construction site, and I've never seen a clean construction site anywhere.

During one of the switchover sequences, part of an insulator failed and an arc jumped across the rest of the insulator to the structure. It vaporized the carbon-composite plastic, which in turn vapor-deposited on everything within fifty feet, including the P-suit of the man who was nearby. It blackened his P-suit within a fraction of a second. He was in full sunlight at the time. Within ten seconds his suit and backpack were too hot for the backpack system to handle. He practically fried in less than thirty seconds.

When Stan and Fred got him here, his pulse was already 160, blood pressure 140/60, respiration 30, and body temperature 105.6. His pupils were dilated, he was in convulsions, and he was almost drowning in his own vomit. He went into profound shock and circulatory collapse. He died almost at once.

That sort of thing bothers me. We must have a way to get to these people faster. I'll talk to Pratt about getting an Eff-Mu so we—

"Doctor? Oh, I'm sorry! I didn't mean to disturb you." Angela peered through the hatch into Tom's quarters and found Tom floating quietly in lotus position at the opposite end of the compartment.

"You didn't," Tom told her. "Disturb me, that is. What's up, Angela?" He keyed the interrupted private-journal entry into GALEN's disk file on Earth, cleared the display, and put the terminal into standby mode.

"Do you have a minute, Doctor?"

"Sure. Let's go to the main compartment."

"I'd like to talk with you privately."

"Uh, okay. Come on in. There isn't very much room in here, but it is private."

The nurse floated into the sleeping compartment, tucked herself into the opposite end of it, and pulled the sliding door closed.

Tom saw tears in her eyes.

"This is very unprofessional of me, Doctor," she began, trying to maintain control of herself. "A nurse should be able to work in a professional manner no matter where."

"This is different from what you thought it would be, isn't it?"

"Yes."

"Do you want to go back?"

"No."

"What's the problem, then?" Tom asked, knowing full well what it was.

She was silent for a long moment before she replied. "Doctor, it's so *lonely* up here!"

"Lonely? We've got eight hundred people around us, Angela. Do you feel this way because all your life has been spent in large cities where there's a lot more action?"

"No, there's plenty to do in off hours," she admitted, "but we really don't have any off hours. We're always on call, like residents."

"Uh, look, we've had a number of patients in here, mostly cuts and bruises and minor complaints, plus our three major cases thus far," Tom pointed out. "I can't say that we've been as busy as an emergency room in a town the size of Truth or Consequences, New Mexico. We haven't been that busy yet. If you're not getting

enough off-duty time, I'll figure out something, because
I don't want to burn you out."

"That isn't exactly it."

"Oh? What, then? The thought that you might be
called to duty at any moment?"

"Partly." She sighed, sort of wrung her hands, and
continued to look teary-eyed. The tears refused to run
down her cheeks, however. In the weightless environment, they simply welled up in her large blue eyes. "I
said it's lonely. The men out here are—different.
Rough. Uneducated. 'Coarse' is maybe the word."

"They're engineers, riggers, construction workers—
people who're here to do a difficult and dangerous job,
Angela."

"But there's no one I can talk to," she almost wailed.
"I'm just a nurse and a woman, and they're interested
only in the latter . . ."

Tom pulled a tissue from a holder, floated across the
narrow compartment, and handed it to her. "Blot the
tears out of your eyes so you can see. Angela, when I
interviewed you, I was worried this would happen.
Your life's been spent in the big urban areas of the
eastern United States, places where there were always
interesting men around. You're very intelligent, and
you demand intelligent male companions. You're also a
very beautiful woman—don't think I haven't noticed
you, because you know I have!—and my professional
judgment tells me that you must have strong drives."

"Why don't you do something about it, then?" she
suddenly asked with surprising directness.

"That's why you came here, isn't it?"

"What's the matter with you, Tom Noels? I'm here,
and you know why. The door's closed. There's nothing
between us but air. Yes, I'm lonely. I'm lonely for *you!*
I have been for weeks! *What's the matter with you?*"

"It's a long story, Angela, and it happened a long
time ago."

"I know."

"Who told you?"

"Never mind. I know. Tom, she's gone and she isn't

coming back. But there are others who'd love you just as much if you'd only let them. Live in the present. There are only two of us out here."

"Angela, I can't just turn on like *that*." He snapped his fingers. "I don't care how beautiful you are or what emotions are stirring back in my brain. I have a dysfunction and I know it, but there's not much I can do about it."

"There's something *I* can do about it," she told him softly.

Tom's movement toward her to hand her the tissue had continued with a smaller residual motion that brought them closer together in the weightless confines of the cabin. Inches separated them now. In a single motion, Angela pulled away the net holding her hair in place and off her face; her blond mane exploded into a halo of shining curls floating like a wispy golden wreath around her face, over her shoulders, and down her back. Another quick motion produced the tearing sound of a velcro seam separating, followed by another. Her white blouse and slacks floated gently into a far corner of the cabin.

Only a man with a severe sexual dysfunction caused by a serious psychosis would have been immune to the enticements Angela used to full advantage in the weightless cabin. The basic sensual nature of this woman had disturbed Tom from the first moment he had met her, and he had spent months fighting what he, as a doctor, knew must be the inevitable.

Tom was inwardly surprised. There was precious little time to feel guilty or even to think about Julie Lea. Angela wouldn't permit it. All her education hadn't taken place in nursing school and the wards of the big urban hospitals; much of her vigor Tom recognized as coming from a genetic link to the rustic Viking life of her forebears.

Much later, she whispered, "Thank God there were no medical emergencies!"

"As far as I'm concerned," he told her gently,

"you're one . . . and any time in the future you want to be, too."

"In spite of Lucky Hertzog?"

"What's Lucky got to do with it?"

"You didn't think I was going to let another woman get away with you, did you?"

"Is *that* what motivated you, Angel?"

She snuggled. "Partly. Sometimes a girl has to be a bit aggressive when competition looms."

"Yes," he said with a sigh, "we rarely admit our debt to Darwin."

"Are you worried about the others finding out?"

"Angel, who are we to deny what seems to be common knowledge about relationships between doctors and nurses?"

"I like that."

"You like a lot of things. What in particular this time?"

"Being called Angel."

"That's your name."

"Yes, but you're the only one who's realized that and used it."

"I don't think there could be a better place for an angel than in a place in the sky."

"Did you expect to find one here?"

"No, I hired one to be here."

"I knew you knew," Angela exclaimed.

Later, it was only Stan who sensed something had happened. "Doc, you're acting spry. First time I've ever heard you humming."

Tom stopped what he was doing. "I was taught not to whistle, so I hum instead."

"Look, you should know that Fred and I don't think we're doing our jobs properly," the paramedic told him.

"You want an Eff-Mu so you can get around GEO Base faster."

"Right. We lost the hyperpyrexia case because we couldn't get there fast enough. It takes forever to go through all the hatches and corridors of GEO Base."

"Stan, I agree on both counts," Tom replied. "You need an Eff-Mu, and all of us need to be able to get around GEO Base faster in emergencies. But do you think a standard two-man Eff-Mu will really do the job?"

"Why not?"

"Why don't Earth-bound paramedics use motorcycles?"

"I see what you mean. We need room for the patient."

"Roger. Eventually maybe not, but right now we've got to provide that, too. Is there any Eff-Mu type that'll handle the two of you plus a patient?"

"I'll ask Fred."

Fred said no. "We'll have to have Pratt make one for us."

Dealing with Herb Pratt was another matter.

"Not only no, but hell, no!" Pratt snapped when Tom approached him in GEO Base Central. "Sure, I've got a shop here, Doctor, but it's fully scheduled with work relating to the assembly of the pilot SPS. I haven't got the time or the funds to come up with a special ambulance vehicle for you. Matter of fact, we're so tight that I don't even have a two-man Eff-Mu I could give you."

"Pratt, I'm going over your head on this one," Tom declared.

"You can't. I'm GEO Base boss."

"I can. I don't work for you. My contract's with Eden Corporation," Tom reminded him.

"I might get an Eff-Mu freed up next week after Module Twenty gets here."

"No score, Pratt," Tom stated firmly. "I told you what my problem is. You refused to help after I tried to cooperate by coming to you about it first. And I've informed you of my intention to go over your head. I've got to get my ambulance, or people will die. So I'm going to go get it."

"Dammit, Noels! I've told you I intend to cooperate with you," Pratt fired back from his main control console, trying to keep one eye on the display and the other on his visitor. "But you've got to learn how to cooperate with me!"

"Groveling isn't one of my strong suits."

Back at the med module, Tom tried to get Dan Hills on the net. Line busy. He tried John Curry. No channel available. Then he realized the childish trick Pratt was playing from Central. Tom fumed for a moment.

Pratt was the sort of boss engineer needed to ram through a difficult new engineering project like the SPS pilot plant. The man was result-oriented. And with Hocksmith running on a thin thread, Herb Pratt was probably one man who could save him.

On the other hand, Tom recalled the Hippocratic Oath. He had never taken the Hippocratic Oath; contrary to popular belief, no doctor ever stands up, raises his right hand, and repeats that ancient Greek statement of the basic medical ethic. The Hippocratic Oath is simply accepted by the profession in tacit agreement on the manner in which physicians should behave.

Not all of them accepted it, of course.

But Tom felt a sense of *noblesse oblige* in the matter of medical ethics. The job of getting the first Solar Power Satellite completed on time and within the tight budget was one thing. But, as a doctor, he couldn't stand by and permit people to die because of inaction.

There was one GEO-to-Earth circuit Pratt didn't control. Tom sat down at GALEN and called GALEN Control. Within minutes, he had a videophone channel working through his GALEN terminal.

Dan Hills was in a meeting in Washington. John Curry was in Phoenix and unavailable. Reluctantly, Tom tried to reach Owen Hocksmith and got through to him at the H-Bar-S Ranch.

"Howdy, T.K.! Glad you called. I've been trying to reach you, but the circuits have been busy," Hocksmith's image on the terminal told Tom. "I thought we had plenty of channels to GEO Base!"

"Oh, we do, Smitty. But every once in a while they get preempted by the engineering types," Tom replied.

"How'd you get through?"

"We're talking on my medical computer net. It doesn't care whether the data are voice or computer codes, as long as they're digitized," Tom explained. "Any particular reason you wanted to talk to me?"

"Only to cry on your shoulder, as usual." Hocksmith sighed with exasperation. "You wouldn't believe what those idiots in Washington are doing to me! Tom, I want to warn you that Von Hesse plans to make an on-site inspection of your facility."

"We'll handle him, Smitty."

"Good. He's coming up sometime in the next few weeks with an inspection group."

"Things could be worse," Tom stated.

"Pratt says you're doing one hell of a good job up there."

"We could do better."

"How?"

Tom told him, feeling somewhat reluctant to discuss the details of his conversation with Herb Pratt. But he discovered he didn't have to.

"I knew you'd tangle with Pratt, and I figured you'd handle it the way you have. But why'd you come to me about it, T.K.?"

"Because I couldn't get to anybody else. Hills is in Washington, obviously trying either to convince or to confuse DOE, depending on what the subject matter is and the extent to which DOE understands it. Curry's in Phoenix, obviously working on financial matters with the ValSun National Bank or Arizona Gas and Electric. Sorry, Smitty, that I had to dump this in your lap."

"Well, nothing another billion dollars and a hundred employees wouldn't solve. That's what I get for trying to do this job the private-enterprise route," Hocksmith said with a growl.

"I thought it was *free* enterprise."

Hocksmith shook his head, a response that had become strange to Tom after only a few weeks in orbit, where it wasn't done. "Never has been free. Had to work like hell to keep it private. Someday I'd like to try free enterprise. It might work the way Friedman said.

In the meantime, I'm going to handle your request personally, T.K., not because I need something to do, but because I need to perform a little engineering job to save my sanity. Day after day, I have to deal with the Alice-in-Wonderland world of finance and government bureaucracy. I need your little project so I can work with the real universe for a few precious moments. Feed me your requirements, T.K., and I'll see to it you get your orbital ambulance."

Hocksmith was true to his word, but not before the GEO Base medical team had to handle another problem.

Four riggers showed up at the med module. Rather, two riggers towed two others. Even the two who could move didn't look very well. In spite of weightlessness, they managed to stagger.

"Sweetie, we don't feel so damned good," one told Angela as they entered the module. They rebounded from the edge of the hatch as they did so. "Kin ya give us somethin' to make us feel better? Ol' Jim here—and Al, too—passed out on us. And I'm about to pass out, if I don't heave first."

Angela managed to get a plastic bag to the man before he threw up. But the other conscious man beat her to it.

Fred was the second team member on the scene. He didn't pay any attention to the conscious men, but started checking one of the unconscious ones. "Angela, he's comatose—cyanotic or acidotic. I can't tell without a blood check. Same with the other one."

"They've all been drinking," Angela noted.

"You betcha! Hell of a party!" one of the conscious ones muttered thickly.

"Alcohol poisoning?" Angela ventured to guess.

"Nope," Fred put in. "I'll bet they got a load of orbital moonshine, and what we're seeing are the effects of methanol."

"Dr. Noels!" Angela called out, but Tom was already out of his quarters and into the med module, having been attracted by the commotion. "Possible methyl alcohol poisoning!" she told him as he came up to her.

Tom took one look and acted fast. "Get them down. Angela, Fred, start positive-displacement IVs with sodium bicarbonate on the two who've passed out! Dave, shag it out here stat! You, too, Stan!

"I need blood analysis as fast as you can get it," Tom told his med tech. "Blood-alcohol level, along with pH and electrolyte balance. Accuracy second to speed, because if it's methanol we haven't got much time. Angela, Fred, Stan, we treat for methanol poisoning first! If it's something else, it'll be less serious."

They strapped all four into med module treatment units and started the IVs.

"This guy's going fast," Stan remarked. "Acts like traumatic shock, Doc. Hypotension. BP down to seventy over forty!"

"Gastric lavage!" Tom snapped. "Get it started on the others, too. Whatever is in there, pump it out of them!" He turned to his conscious patient. "Any headache? Leg cramps?"

"Uh . . . naw—but my gut hurts somethin' terrible!" And he passed out.

"What were you drinking?" Tom asked the remaining conscious man. "Tell me fast! It could save your life!"

"Aw, we was just havin' a li'l party with some stuff Al made from raisins and breakfast cereals we took from the cafeteria. Pretty good moonshine, too . . ."

"It could be anything," Stan pointed out.

Tom didn't say a word. He was thinking. He ran through the symptoms of the various alcohol poisonings. He knew he was doing the right thing when it came to wood alcohol ingestion: sodium bicarb IV with gastric lavage. He wouldn't know whether or not to try rebalancing electrolytes until he got the blood work-ups from Dave, who had drawn his samples and was working rapidly in the med lab section of the module.

Dizziness. Discoordination. Gastroenteritis. Hypotension. But no cramps. Obviously no convulsions . . . yet. The unconscious ones were in a stupor with falling blood pressure, but the condition didn't add up to methanol poisoning.

Gastric lavage produced a brownish liquid smelling of alcohol.

"See what Dave can do with it," Tom told Angela.

The initial blood report from the comatose man showed pH in the normal range but various departures from normal in electrolytes. There was also evidence of hypoglycemia.

"All four of them can't be diabetic!" Tom muttered to himself as he looked over the scribbled note from Dave. "They'd never have gotten past the medical check at JSP! What the hell is it? I've never seen this before. Angela, have you?"

"No. Botulism, perhaps?"

"Not from a liquid as loaded with ethanol as their drink was," Tom observed. "Well, this is what I've got GALEN for!"

He pushed off to the med module treatment-bay terminal and got on line. He keyed in the symptoms and requested analysis and most probable diagnosis. The computer worked it over on Earth and shot back the sentence that flashed across the display screen: INCOMPLETE SYMPTOMATIC REPORT. CHECK FOR RETINAL INJURY AND REPORT FINDINGS.

Tom's first peek through the ophthalmoscope into the eyes of the man still semiconscious revealed normal eye grounds. He typed into GALEN: NO RETINAL INJURY. EYE GROUNDS NORMAL.

As quickly as he had finished typing that, the reply appeared: PROBABLE DIAGNOSIS: ISOAMYL ALCOHOL POISONING. SIMILAR TO ISOPROPYL ALCOHOL POISONING. INGESTION OF 8 FL OZ STRAIGHT ISOAMYL ALCOHOL PROBABLY FATAL. OTHERWISE, PROGNOSIS FOR RECOVERY GOOD. TREATMENT: GASTRIC LAVAGE, IV GLUCOSE, CORRECT DEHYDRATION, AND ELECTROLYTE CHANGES. DIALYSIS IF POSSIBLE.

"Isoamyl alcohol. *Fusel oil*," Tom said, snapping his fingers.

"We can handle it," Stan remarked.

"I know these guys," Fred added. "Hard drinkers. All of them. Probably tried to smuggle hooch up but got caught. And the limited ration that Pratt permits everyone every week wasn't enough for these boozers. So old Al here—he's from Georgia—I'll bet he figured he'd make himself some moonshine instead. Ten to one, they've got a vacuum still rigged somewhere outside a convenient lock."

The semi-conscious one mumbled something and finally got out, "Damned good stuff! Grow hair on your toes."

"You bet, chum," Fred told him. "Damned near grew lilies on your chest, too."

After they had pumped all four dry, restored BPs to near normal, injected replacement electrolytes by positive-displacement IVs, and strapped the men into rest racks, Tom looked around at the mess that was the med module. "These are Pratt's boys," Tom growled. "Damned if we're going to clean up all their mess!" He shoved off for the intercom panel and got the base engineer on the screen.

"What the hell do you want, Doc?" Pratt asked. He wasn't happy about Tom's call to Hocksmith.

Tom told him. "Pratt, four of your assembly gang came in here fresh from a drinking bout with their own moonshine. There's a vacuum still in operation somewhere in GEO Base."

"Oh? Who are they?"

"Come on down and identify them. Bring six people with you to help us clean up this mess. Oh, don't worry; we saved them. They were full of fusel oil. Why don't you put some bread in the cafeteria so anybody else who tries this will at least be able to filter it through a loaf of bread first? Bread won't take out all the fusel oil, but it'll probably keep the concentration below the lethal limit."

Pratt pondered this information for a moment. "Doc, you should have let them die. Now I've got to go to the expense of shipping them back to JSP and terminating them."

"I've got to presume you're kidding, Pratt."

"Not about firing them—after they tell me where the vacuum still's located. Doc, I'm going to make an example of them. Maybe it'll save some lives and keep your med module clean. And, uh, Doc, I'd appreciate any advice you might be able to give on how to keep this from happening again . . . and what to do if it does."

Tom refrained from raising his eyebrows in surprise. Maybe he was finally getting through to the GEO Base boss. He knew he was when, a few days later, Pratt called him. "Doc, your special ambulance is coming up in the next Cot-Vee supply ship. Should be docking in six hours at Portlock Foxtrot. We're also putting a docking collar module on the free end of your med module, so don't be disturbed when you hear noises. You'll be able to dock right to your sick bay."

"Thanks, Herb. To what do I owe this unanticipated cooperation?"

"Let's just say the word got passed, Doc." There was no rancor in the GEO Base engineer's voice, but there was a touch of respect. "Or maybe I can put it this way: You told me you were going around me, and you did. So it didn't bother me. But, brother, you went *all* the way around! You can expect full cooperation with future requests because the med department's priority's been bucked up to the Special category." He didn't bother to explain what that was.

But Fred knew. "Special Priority is only two steps lower than an order from a disembodied voice on high. Who do you know? The colonel himself?"

"Yes. But I never asked for any special priority, Fred."

Fred shrugged. "One thing you learn out here: If your fairy godmother waves her wand over you, don't argue with her. It beats riding home in a pumpkin."

And that was how the GEO Base paramedic ambulance received its nickname: "the Pumpkin."

The Pumpkin turned out to be a masterpiece of

quick-and-dirty engineering. It was half a hex module outfitted with a StarPacket vernier engine as its main propulsion system and a series of electric thrusters for maneuvering. It had no direct view to the outside universe, only an array of video displays—large windows in space were a constant trouble source because the state of the art couldn't keep them from leaking, and the Pumpkin's life-support consumables were limited to twenty-four man-hours with no recycling. The unit sported a universal docking collar on the end of the hex module opposite the StarPacket vernier engine.

Tom went with Fred and Stan to take delivery of their new gadget and bring it around to the med module dock. Pratt's men had latched the half hex of a docking port and pressure lock to the med module a few hours earlier in an operation that took only twenty minutes. GEO Base had been designed like an Erector set with plug-in modules; there was no time to build pretty or permanent space facilities on this job.

"Know how to fly this beast?" Stan asked as Fred slipped into the pilot's seat while the paramedic and Tom looked on.

"Doesn't seem that much different from a Pot-Vee or an ordinary Eff-Mu," Fred mused, scanning the panel.

"Don't screw around," Tom told him. "Let's find an instructor and get qualified to operate it."

"I'm qualified in Eff-Mus," Fred pointed out. "And the instructors are all down at the LEO Base training site. Besides, Doc, the Pumpkin's the only one around. We're going to have to learn to operate it ourselves."

"Not without P-suits and extra oxygen aboard," Tom ordered. He looked over the panel. "Attitude indicator. Four relative velocity indicators linked to eight search radars and three lidars at will. Beacon transponders. You know, this really isn't that much different from flying airplanes on instruments."

And it wasn't. They returned for their P-suits, loaded another twenty-four man-hours of oxygen aboard, then checked out the Pumpkin—propellant load, battery-charge level, life-support-system consumables level, and the rest of a three-page checklist that someone had managed to put together for the Pumpkin when it was assembled at LEO Base. The controls had been highly simplified and were like those of a helicopter, with two sidearm controllers and two foot pedals to provide control in roll, pitch, yaw, and translation in six degrees of freedom. The StarPacket vernier engine offered enough thrust to get the Pumpkin moving for fast sprints, while the electric thrusters—the same kind used to propel the SPS array modules from LEO Base—permitted the gentlest of velocity changes.

"I think I can fly her," Fred declared.

"With that stump?" Stan said incredulously. "How you gonna get to the left pedal?"

"With my right foot, dummy. You can push only one pedal at a time. Right?"

"Uh . . . yeah."

Fred reached out and plugged his suit comm system into the panel. "Get yourself plugged in here, then faceplates down and pressurize suits. We'll get clearance to undock and maneuver."

Tom and Stan did so and heard Fred's voice in their helmet speakers. "Central, this is the med ambulance at Portlock Foxtrot. Request permission to undock, run test maneuvers, and redock at the med module. Also request that the call sign Pumpkin be assigned this vehicle."

"Med ambulance, GEO Base Central. Stand by." There was silence for a moment, then the voice came back. "Med ambulance, your call code is Pumpkin. Transponder squawk normal will be zero-seven-zero-seven. When on an emergency mission, your squawk will be seven-seven-seven-seven."

Fred repeated it.

"You've got it, Pumpkin. GEO Base Central clears Pumpkin to undock from Portlock Foxtrot at minus-x velocity one meter per second, portlock reference. Stand by for vectors to a safe test area."

Chapter Ten

From the Galen Journal of Dr. T. K. Noels:

    Ten weeks and the Grim Reaper Count: Nineteen.

And everything from popping off a P-suit helmet to getting crushed when two heavy array components drifted together. There may not be weight up here, but mass and momentum still exist. I'd classify most of these deaths as ordinary industrial-type accidents, albeit in a new and different environment. Although I'm keeping records on all of them, I'm going to speak in this Journal only of the most interesting ones, those specifically related to working in the space environment.

The Pumpkin's saved a couple of people already. Three of us have learned how to operate it: Stan, Fred, and myself. Now I understand why space pilots are people who are instrument-rated airplane pilots and also own their own boats. "Flying" the Pumpkin is like flying an airplane by instruments; you must believe what those gauges are telling you, and you can't pay any attention to the inputs from your vestibular apparatus or from kinesthetic senses. Docking and undocking the Pumpkin is like bringing the S.S. Patrick Miller alongside and gently docking to a pier; the Pumpkin has far less momentum, however, and is probably more like docking a row boat. There isn't anything difficult about it provided you aren't in a hurry.

That's going to be the biggest problem with the Pumpkin. When Fred and Stan are on a call, they're in a hurry. I expect to get reports of hard docks. I hope they don't crumple too much stuff until they learn how to handle the Pumpkin under the stress of an emergency. I'm not too worried about them crumpling the Pumpkin; all the stress is column loading on that hex module, and it'd take a big bump to make the structure fail in that mode.

If I'm beginning to sound a little like an engineer, it's because I'm surrounded by a massive engineering task. Outside our med module, engineering and construction jargon is all I hear unless I've found some time to watch TV from Earth.

I might add there's been little time to watch TV. My personal life has taken a turn for the better. I'm learning that Angie—but she likes me to call her Angel—is quite different from Julie Lea. I expected that. What I did not expect was the fact that I could possibly become attached to someone else, especially a woman who's so totally different. Angie's all business and professionalism on the job; the façade collapses when we're together. I know there's a change taking place in me; my sense of humor's coming back. Maybe the Greeks were right after all; they maintained that the purpose of humor is to preserve one's perspective. On the other hand, how does that jibe with the humor of a pratt fall? (No pun intended.) Or "gallows humor"? Have to think about that sometime.

This work is becoming very satisfying. In spite of the extremely Spartan conditions under which we're living, I'm enjoying this because Smitty was right: It's a challenging new field of medicine.

We've had our expected quota of minor industrial accidents. Cuts, bruises, contusions, a few broken bones, some cases of exhaustion because a rigger worked beyond his limits in vacuum and zero-g, a couple of burns, but nothing really serious until we ran into "vac bite."

The safety compartmentalization of the P-suits hasn't always been a safety measure, although it's undoubtedly saved many lives from traumatic abaryia. Nobody thought about secondary effects. The cuff latch on a man's glove failed yesterday, and the glove blew away. "Vac bite"—which is what we're calling it colloquially until I can figure out a suitable Greco-Latin term —is the result of exposure of the extremities to vacuum conditions.

The extremity—hand, foot, arm, etc.—doesn't explode; connective tissue's strong and the human skin's remarkably tough. But the extremity swells up in the Kittinger Syndrome, first experienced by Captain Joseph Kittinger during a stratospheric parachute jump back in 1960. The absence of atmospheric pressure causes vasodilation and edema, which becomes very painful. The swelling also inhibits movement. If the abaryic condition prevails for several minutes, it can cause aneurism and rupture of the capillary walls followed by hematomas. Unless there's a cut or other opening in the skin, there's little chance of blood loss. But if the abaryic condition continues, tissue's destroyed. The course of the affliction begins to parallel that of frostbite, which is the reason it got its vernacular name. It's painful as hell and immobilizes the extremity. Right now, the only way we know to treat it is with cold packs or hypothermic immersion, along with analgesics and mild diuretics. I'm thinking about the possibility of trying a hyperbaric chamber, but we haven't got one here yet. Maybe in a year or so.

No bends yet. Everyone flushes the nitrogen out of his system for thirty minutes by breathing pure Oh-two before cycling into vacuum. But if there were an explosive decompression of any of the living spaces in GEO Base or with my paramedics on an emergency, we'd get bends because we're running an oxynitrogen atmosphere.

The SFO satellites—Solar Flare Observatories—running unmanned in a different part of geosynchronous orbit have detected activity that normally precedes solar flares. So we've been operating in the Flare Watch mode. If we go Flare Alert, we'll have no more than ten minutes to get into P-suits and make it to the caisson, our storm cellar.

Seven hex modules in a circular honeycomb make up the caisson. It's surrounded by the water tanks of GEO Base: twelve hex modules nested in honeycomb around the caisson. There are seven half-hex modules on each end of the caisson, and they're water tanks, too. We've never had to worry about water in GEO Base for several reasons, not the least of which is the fact that every human in the station puts about seven quarts of water per day into the system through metabolism and urine. However, that's only a small part of the GEO Base water supply, which amounts to over 3700 tons of water. We'll never use that much in GEO Base. It's here for the primary purpose of radiation shielding.

Dan Hills had once asked me to check his figures on the mass of water required to knock down the radiation of a solar flare to something that would give a person in GEO Base less than a twenty-five-rem exposure from the largest solar flare recorded to date—the one of 23 February 1956. Well, if we get another one like that, we'll all have to be shipped back to Earth . . . and that will be the end of our space traveling. However, the average solar flare will give us less than a single rem inside that caisson.

Dan's a bright one. All the pre-Eden studies of space habitats assumed extraterrestrial materials for shielding. We aren't that far along. But we always need water, and water is handy to have around to break into hydrogen and oxygen for propellants. It's nontoxic and easy to transport. Only problem is that it weighs eight pounds per gallon. But it's easily moved around by piping and pumps.

My med team has its own duties inside the caisson if the alarm goes off. We all wear dosimeters during the Watch. In the course of the emergency, we'll be prepared to handle radiation sickness, although there isn't much we can do if a guy shows up with more than four hundred rems in him.

Stan came forth with a statement that deserves to be remembered, at least in my journal: "If God had meant *people to live in space, He would have coated them with lead."*

We'll just play it cool and see what happens. The Flare Watch could be canceled. This could be just a false alarm. After all, solar-flare prediction is still an arcane art, I'm told.

He was driving the Pumpkin down Interstate 25 in Albuquerque, heading for the Bernalillo County Hospital. Julie Lea had returned! She wasn't exactly the same as she had been. Death did some strange things to people. But she was back. He got there terribly fast and found himself in Emergency. Angela came out to meet him and seemed to be vague about everything. She led him into one of the hospital rooms, and they got into bed together. It was warm and comfortable and erotic. But he suddenly found himself falling out of that warm bed . . . and falling . . . and falling . . . and falling. Lights flashed in his eyes and someone was screaming at him, "Alert! Alert!"

Then it was the reality of weightlessness, the wan light of his tiny sleeping quarters, the flashing emergency light on the bulkhead, and the all-call loudspeaker blaring, "Flare Alert! Flare Alert! All personnel to the caisson! Flare Alert! Flare Alert! Nine minutes and counting! Flare Alert! Flare—"

He was out of his sleep sack immediately, out of the tiny cubicle, and into the main med module, moving toward his P-suit locker. He had the lower half on and was ducking his head into the upper half and helmet when Angela and Stan arrived. Fred and Dave were not long behind them. Nobody said anything. Tom turned to Angela and checked her helmet hoses, the backpack fittings, and the waist seal. With a sharp tug, he tested the glove and boot seals. While he was doing that, Fred was checking him. Pure oxygen was flowing into his helmet as he finished checking Angela's suit and moved to check Stan. It would take thirty minutes or more to flush the nitrogen out of his system, but there was little chance of a decompression.

It took two minutes for five of them to suit-up and check each other. Tom didn't stop moving. He pulled his emergency medical kit from its locker. The others were doing the same thing. Then, ready, they moved to the module hatch.

Tom keyed his radio on the special med frequency. "Radio check. Angela?"

"Here!"

"Fred?"

"Loud and clear! How me?"

"Five by. Stan?"

"Yo!"

"Dave?"

"With you!"

"Five minutes!" came the warning over the all-call frequency.

As they moved rapidly through the corridors of GEO Base, they joined a river of P-suited figures heading in the same direction. Tom detected a vibration of GEO Base as he grasped handholds and pulled himself along. Tons of water were being pumped by computer control into the tankage surrounding the caisson.

They were on station with two minutes to spare.

It was a human sardine can.

P-suited figures were stacked in honeycomb cubicles that were just big enough to hold a single person in a P-suit—a volume of thirty-six cubic feet. The med team wasn't much better off, except they were in the middle of the honeycomb and able to move anywhere in the caisson for medical purposes. And they had the luxury of a tiny emergency surgical volume not much larger than Tom's sleeping quarters.

Caisson stewards, chosen not only for their ability to keep cool but also because they were big and brawny, moved quickly among the hundreds of people stacking up like cordwood. They shifted P-suit supply hoses from backpacks to the caisson supply system and plugged the comm system into each person.

"Nice work," Tom told his crew over the med net.

"Lots of time to spare. Plug into the caisson supply and comm net; no sense in using up your backpack."

"How bad is it?" Angela asked.

"I've heard only what you've heard," Tom replied.

"These usually don't last more than twenty-four hours," Fred volunteered.

"All personnel, this is Base Engineer Pratt," the big man's voice boomed through their individual helmet loudspeakers. "Relax. We'll know in a few minutes if everybody made it. Sorry we don't have channels enough to allow you to talk to one another. There's music on Channel B. If you're short on sack time, I'd suggest you use this period to catch up. Under all circumstances, stay quiet and keep your activity to a complete minimum; we have limited life-support oxygen and regeneration in flare emergency mode. If you don't cool it, I guarantee one of the stewards will be around with something to send you beddy-by fast. If you're in trouble, press your call button. If you didn't get a chance to hook up your urine and fecal bags, do it now while we've still got pressure in here. If we happen to lose pressure for some reason, and if you're not hooked up, you'll just have to stew in your own juices."

There was a pause, then he went on. "This is a Class One flare. Solar proton flux should peak in five hours. With luck, we'll be out of here in fifteen hours. Sorry about the lack of room, but better you're alive in thirty-six cubic feet than dead with all of space to roam in. Hang in there!"

There was a click, and Pratt's voice came through the med net. "Doc, are you here?"

"Roger, Herb."

"We're missing fifteen riggers. They may have been out on the far array subassembly. If they get here in the next thirty minutes, they shouldn't have picked up more than twenty rems outside. I'd like you to check them and their dosimeters when we let them in."

"Right. We're ready. Anybody else?"

"Don't know. LEO Base is auditing the count, since

it's below the Van Allens and not as vulnerable as we are. We'll know in an hour or so the status of other people outside."

In their positions in the emergency med section, they were ranged around the wall and could see one another. Tom peered at each of his team members, checking their expressions. "You okay, Dave? You're sweating."

"Uh, Doc, a little claustrophobia."

Stan, who was next to Dave, plugged his monitor into Dave's suit. "Respiration up. BP normal. Pulse normal. Body temperature normal. Did you put on your woolen socks, Dave?"

"Come off it, Stan!" Fred snapped. "I'll bet your vital signs indicate you're scared, too."

"I'm cool, Fred. I've got my bags attached."

"Scared, Dave?" Tom asked.

"Uh . . . yeah, Doc. When I think we're surrounded by seven million pounds of water and are more than twenty thousand miles from anything, it's weird. And there isn't a damned thing we can do about it, either! That's what bugs me most."

"Want a meprobamate?" Angela asked.

"Yeah."

"Is it all right, Doctor?" Angela asked, checking first.

"Sure. Take one yourself if you feel you need one, Angie. Same goes for anybody else. Won't affect your performance in the clutch, and may help you, in fact."

"Good, stiff drink would do wonders," Stan put in.

"Opposed as I am to my personnel drinking on duty, I do happen to have a small bottle of rather good stuff in my quarters," Tom remarked lightly, trying to relieve tension. "And I'm planning a little party—not large, mind you—to celebrate our first flare alert when we get back to the module. And, Fred, the stuff won't have to be filtered through a loaf of bread; I brought it up in my black bag. Medicine."

Angela popped the meprobamate through the pass valve into Dave's helmet; he caught the capsule on his tongue and swallowed it without using the helmet's water nipple. "I think I can add a bit to the festivities," the med tech said. "Not everything in that pharmacy is U.S.P."

Tom didn't take a meprobamate.

In any event, his medical team didn't have time to get bored and start crawling up the walls, since eight hundred people were crammed into space that would normally be occupied by only two hundred. And most of those eight hundred people had little to do except stare at the web netting of their honeycomb, looking at the back of the P-suit of the person "above" them. Few had had time to bring things to read. A combination of carefully selected music against a background of pink noise played through their helmet loudspeakers, but even this didn't keep all of them calm.

Although there were some housekeeping and support staff in GEO Base, most of the workers were involved with the final assembly and testing of the SPS itself. As such, they were the space equivalent of the high-iron men, riggers, offshore oil drillers, and electrical-transmission-line builders. They were hard and tough, and they were used to living dangerous lives. However, the space experience was new to all of them, and some reacted uncharacteristically. The strangeness of the environment, the constant awareness of death near them or around them, the invisible specter of ionizing radiation, and the relative isolation of GEO Base got to a few of them. Tom and his crew didn't have time to become bored; they were busy sedating or tranquilizing frenetic, disturbed people. They had to do it fast to prevent sympathetic reactions from others nearby who were probably just as scared. This meant that the med team often couldn't be tactful, gentle, or highly selective. The prime objective was to quiet the person and help preserve the tenuous control of the situation.

It got worse when the fifteen riggers showed up from the far end of the assembly, where there hadn't been any fast Eff-Mu transport available back to the caisson. Tom checked each dosimeter as they filed past him into the hands of his team. "Two-ten rems . . . Two-oh-five rems . . . Two-thirty rems . . ."

Everyone had picked up between two hundred and two hundred sixty rems.

They could be saved, but it wouldn't be an easy job. Nearly all of them were nauseated. Most of them had filled their fecal collection bags, and one man was nearly drowning in his own vomit-filled helmet.

Dave's primitive blood-analysis equipment wasn't really up to doing full work-ups on all fifteen men, but it was good enough for Dave to be able to confirm the usual symptoms of acute radiation syndrome. "Leuko-cyte count is down. Some electrolyte imbalance."

Tom looked at the numbers on the report pad Dave had handed him. "Standard," he remarked. "Okay, let's start IV with lactate of Ringer on all of them and ad-minister two hundred fifty milligrams of oxytetracycline through the IV channel. Give each of them twenty-five milligrams of promethazine IM; that'll make them feel a little better." He turned to one of the riggers whom Fred was cleaning up. "You're going to be all right. None of you got enough dosage that we can't treat you."

"Well, I don't much give a damn at this point," the rigger replied listlessly. "Never felt so lousy in my life."

"You'll feel better soon, and you'll all be going back to Earth on the first ship," Tom told him They would have to transport them; Tom didn't have the facilities to handle fifteen people with acute radiation syndrome. The riggers were in for two to three months of intensive hospital care.

After ten hours of hard work in the caisson, Tom and his med team were fatigued beyond comprehen-sion. "Hot food and coffee," Tom told all of them. "Dave, lock up the amphetamines and methylphena-date. Stay off the uppers, all of you! We're past the peak, and we'll probably be out of here in another eight to nine hours, according to Pratt."

But they hadn't peaked out. Pratt himself came look-ing for Tom. "Doc, the seven people riding Subassembly Twenty-three up from LEO Base have arrived. They collided with the array, but the safety circuits shut down the affected portions. Uh, Doc, they're in bad shape."

"What's the radiation level out there? Can we go out and get them?" Tom asked.

"If you don't stay too long. You'll pick up about fifteen hundred millirems per hour out there right now."

"I'll go," Tom snapped decisively. "Fred, Stan, will you volunteer to go with me, maybe pick up a rem or two in the process?"

Stan reached for his life-support backpack. "Right with you, Doctor."

Fred reached over and grabbed his paramedic kit. He didn't say anything.

"Angie, you're in charge until I get back," Tom told her.

"Doc, there're seven of them," Pratt pointed out. "The three of you won't be able to handle them. I'll get some volunteers and go along with you."

Tom turned and looked at the base engineer. "Herb, I won't ask you to risk it."

"Have you ever handled people with heavy radiation doses before? I have. You'll need help."

"Where the hell did you get experience with radiation-overdosed people?"

Pratt hesitated. "Shouldn't tell you, because it's still classified. The only accidental meltdown that ever occurred was Groom Lake, Nevada. That's all I'm gonna say. I was a young civil engineer just out of Cal Tech. My first job. I went in with the medical team because I'd helped build the containment structure . . ." He paused again, then went on. "Until you've done it, you don't know what's involved. And after you've done it, you hope to hell you never have to do it again. But I guess I wasn't lucky. You'll need help, Doc."

The base engineer was right. If it hadn't been for Pratt and the four men he got to volunteer, Tom and his two paramedics couldn't have done it.

The dosimeters in the personnel module of Photovoltaic Array Subassembly 23 showed a total dose of 6570 rems over a period of ten hours.

Information on human reactions, symptoms, and effects of massive doses and dose rates of ionizing radiation is sparse. Tom knew there had been only thirty documented cases of serious exposure in over fifty years; obviously, because of what Pratt had admitted, there had actually been more. Still, the number of fatalities had been less than a dozen, which is a remarkable industrial safety record. The data from Hiroshima and Nagasaki were questionable because of the amount of time that had passed between exposure and the arrival of doctors trained in nuclear medicine, which was still a very primitive field at that time. The only data of any reliability and repeatability had come from animal tests, and nobody really knew if the results could be extrapolated to human beings. But it was all there for Tom to see and eventually record: seven more cases of extreme radiation exposure.

The five men and two women had taken such a heavy dose that the cerebral syndrome had struck them full force within an hour. By the time Tom and the others reached them, the seven were already suffering from tremors, ataxia, and convulsions. There was also ample evidence of the gastrointestinal syndrome of intractable vomiting and diarrhea.

None of the seven had been in P-suits when the radiation hit, and they had neither the strength nor the will to get into P-suits afterward.

But Tom, Pratt, and the others didn't open their faceplates. In fact, Tom knew they would have to leave their P-suits outside the caisson when they returned, because there was no way any of them could avoid the human waste that floated everywhere in the personnel module.

"Herb, they're pretty far gone," Tom remarked over the suit-to-suit radio channel.

"They are."

"I don't think we can save them."

"Not with more than six thousand rems in them. Best you can do, Doc, is put them out of their misery."

"Pratt, I won't perform euthanasia!"

"Best thing you could do for them."

"We'll sedate them. Fred, Stan, a hundred fifty milligrams of meperidine hydrochloride IM."

Neither paramedic did more than acknowledge the order before starting to administer the injections while Pratt's men held the dying.

"When we get them quieted down, we'll bring them back to the caisson and make them as comfortable as we can," Tom said.

"I wouldn't," Pratt objected. "Knock them out with drugs and leave them here."

"The hell you say, Pratt! Even if they're dying, they deserve to die among people, not out here all alone in a tin can! I'm a doctor with respect for humanity!"

"I thought they drained most of the milk of human kindness out of you doctors in med school," the engineer shot back.

"Not all of it. But we learned how to restrict its flow."

"Well, now's the time to do it." Pratt paused, then put his gloved hand on the shoulder of Tom's P-suit. "Look, Doc, I may act like an inhuman slave driver, but, believe me, that's just a mask. I've been through this before, and I dislike it intensely. I feel for these seven people, but they're too far gone to realize what hit them, no matter what I do. They may be alive, they may be semiconscious, but they don't know what the hell is happening. The situation is going to get worse, and you'll have a decreasing ability to handle the total loss of sphincter control. They have maybe three hours left." He sighed, and the sigh was very evident over the radio link. "If you take them back to the caisson, they won't know it. But eight hundred people will, and those eight hundred people aren't prepared to deal with their condition. Look, we have enough problems in the caisson as it is. For God's sake, don't make it worse."

Tom had to agree with the engineer.

"I'll stay with them," Fred volunteered.

"No, you won't," Tom said as they got ready to leave the module. "We're picking up fifteen hundred milli-rems per hour here. If you stay another three hours, I'll probably have to send you back to JSP to keep your total exposure under industrial safety standards, Fred. And I need you."

Cycling through the lock of that personnel module as the last person to leave the seven radiation victims was one of the toughest things that Tom Noels had ever had to do. His training and education told him he should stay on and administer to the sick until they died. But if he stayed, he would pick up a radiation dose that would retire him forever to the ground, and that would mean he'd abandon eight hundred people in GEO Base—and Owen Hocksmith as well.

He couldn't resist taking a final look before closing the hatch and starting the lock cycle. Afterward, he wished he hadn't done it. The grim scene would remain in his memory for the rest of his life.

He felt someone tug on his P-suit sleeve. "Come on, Doc," Stan's voice said quietly through his helmet speaker. "Pratt's right. You've done all you can."

Fred's voice came in atop Stan's. "Doc, we've got ten minutes before we'll pick up fifteen hundred millirems. We've got to go back *now*."

All of them peeled out of their P-suits before enter-ing the caisson. Once free of his helmet, Stan floated quietly to a corner and was sick.

Tom had steely control over himself after years in hospitals, but it took everything he had to keep from becoming nauseated himself—and he knew the cause wasn't the gastrointestinal syndrome of radiation expo-sure.

Angela was concerned and solicitous when the three of them returned. "Can I get you anything, Doctor?"

"No."

"We heard," Dave put in.

"The P-suit radios carried into here?"

"There's the antenna," Fred pointed out.

"Pratt was right, Doc," Dave said.

"Maybe."

"What do we tell those who ask?" Angela wondered.

"Nothing. Doctors should never hold press conferences about their patients, particularly without the permission of the patients," Tom replied. He was subdued as he went on. "If Pratt wants to make some sort of announcement, that's his privilege. But I suspect he won't say anything about it until this emergency's over, even though some of them had friends here."

After seventeen hours, the ionizing radiation from the solar flare dropped to the point where the GEO Base personnel could leave the caisson. They were a disheveled lot, and not the least disheveled were the five members of the med team. Everybody needed a bath, but it took some time for Pratt's people to get the caisson water back into the ordinary plumbing. When there was water in the system again, the demand was so high that it was beyond the capabilities of the pumps to maintain the pressure.

Tom, Stan, and Fred borrowed fresh P-suits from stores—their own suits were still awaiting decontamination—and, with help from a dozen of Pratt's service personnel, went about the grisly duty of returning the bodies to the med module.

"Tom, do I really have to?"

"Yes, Angie, you have to dress for autopsy."

"Haven't we been through enough already?"

"Angie, very few people have died from such a massive overdose of radiation," Tom explained. "And these poor unfortunates are the very first people to be killed in space by radiation from a solar flare. It's important that we autopsy all seven of them, especially the women—because I don't think there's any solid data on what happens to women with such massive doses."

She followed Tom's orders, but he sensed that something of the spark had gone out of his nurse. Granted, there had been considerable stress in the last twenty hours. But doctors and nurses were supposed to be stress-resistant, particularly under emergency conditions.

Stan and Fred helped, especially when it came to assisting Dave with the microtome mounting and staining tissue samples. Tom worked while a videocamera viewed the scene for GALEN's central files. After three hours' work showed no appreciable differences among the morbid physiologies of the men, he started the autopsies of the women who had been in the personnel module.

Even Tom had to admit to himself that the work was pretty bad, and it wasn't made any better by the fact that the first young woman they worked on was a pert technician in her early twenties whose face had undoubtedly been a picture of youthful health and beauty before the pain and convulsions had twisted it into a ghastly mask.

As Tom was dissecting the reproductive organs, Angela silently turned and disappeared from the surgical area.

"Stan!" he called. "Step in here, please!" Gritting his teeth, he carried on without his nurse.

When he had finished, he knew he'd found some new data, but he was so exhausted that he didn't try to evaluate it then. Asking Fred and Stan to sew the bodies into shrouds for shipment back to Earth, he went looking for Angela. She was huddled in her tiny personal cubicle, her body racked with uncontrollable sobs.

Tom rushed to the pharmacy and mixed twenty-five milligrams of amitriptyline in a bag of drinking water. Then he returned to Angela's cubicle. "Angel?"

"Go away. Please go away."

He put out his hand and touched her. "Angel, have something to drink."

"No. Go away."

She wouldn't look up at him.

"Angel, listen, I want you to get eight to ten hours of good, solid sleep—and you'll feel a lot better. Come on, drink this."

"And what happens after ten hours of rest?" she asked sharply, looking up at him as tears spread in all directions over the fair skin of a face drawn with exhaustion.

"What do you mean? We've got a job to do here," Tom reminded her.

"Day after day after day! Work, sleep, respond to emergencies! There's no end to it! There's just no end to it! There's no end to the work! There's no end to the cans and pipes we have to live in! There's no end to the crowding! There's no place to go off and watch the clouds and listen to the breeze and dangle your feet in the brook!" The words began to tumble out of her in a rush. "Even cities have parks! But there's no park here! Just walls and tubes and modules—and not a green thing anywhere! Day after day after day!"

"Nobody said this is a picnic, Angel."

She seemed to brace herself. Grabbing a tissue, she began blotting her face dry. Then she looked intently at Tom. "Doctor," she said with heavy emphasis on the formality of the title, "I can't do it anymore. I'm through. I'm finished. I'll be no good to you or anybody else here."

"Nurse," Tom replied, trying to reinstitute some discipline, "I want you to rest, and then we'll talk about this. You're exhausted. You're in no condition to engage in a rational discussion."

"Oh, yes, I am! I told you once I was lonely. Well, I'm still lonely—but not for you, because nothing's gone wrong with our relationship, Tom. Far from it! But I'm lonely for *home!* I can't take another day of living in these cans with death outside their walls. I can't take another day of not seeing the sky and feeling the ground beneath my feet. Tom, I'm sorry. I'm leaving. Doctor, I'm resigning, effective immediately. Please have Herb Pratt arrange to get me on the next ship down."

Tom put out his hand to her. "Angel, please think about this. I'll see you when you've had the chance to get some rest." His professional manner had fled him now. He suddenly found himself pleading with a woman he was beginning to love. His own fatigue echoed in his mind; he knew what was happening, but he was powerless to stop it. "Angel, please don't leave me."

She shook off his touch, and her tears and sobs returned. She looked at him with an expression of complete distress and wailed, "*I just want to go home!*"

Chapter Eleven

From the Galen Journal of Dr. T. K. Noels:

The Homesick Angel has left.

Angela meant it. There was no way I could talk her out of it. I had a sneaking suspicion in the back of my mind from the time I first interviewed her that there was something wrong about hiring her to work in GEO Base, and now I know what it was: She's a good nurse, but she's an Earth person.

Because she'd come apart on me, it was impossible for me to keep her around until I'd found a replacement for her. If a person's heart and soul aren't in this work, it's dangerous for him to be working with the sick and injured, whether it's on Earth or in GEO Base. I put her on the next Pot-Vee heading down to LEO Base. And I wrote an outstanding recommendation for her.

The departure of the Homesick Angel has caused me severe problems professionally and emotionally. Let me talk about the latter first and get them off my chest. Then perhaps I can more rationally discuss the professional problems.

If I had had any tendency toward paranoia, I probably would have succumbed to it when Angela left. Looking back, I find that every woman in my life has left me—my mother, dead when I was nine; a series of women in my dad's life; Julie Lea; and now Angela. It's not sane to believe this is a pattern in my life. It's probably just the breaks.

I've got to clench my teeth this time and carry on. Too many people in GEO Base are counting on me, and I can't let Smitty down, either. Especially, I can't let Smitty down a second time, because he had the guts to put his trust in me even though I'd walked out on the original Albuquerque clinic when Julie Lea left me. I can't face up either to betraying the trust of a friend or to doing something that I'd now consider to be a breach of what they taught me at the Institute in Roswell: personal honor.

That's why it wasn't impossible for me to do what I had to do in the case of the Homesick Angel. Although it wasn't impossible, it was indeed exceedingly difficult . . .

Damn, Angela was a beautiful woman! I was growing very fond of her, and that was a mistake. I know now that in her case I let my gonads do the thinking for me. But since I have to accept the responsibility for having hired her and brought her to GEO Base, I have to accept the consequences, too.

I talked to Smitty about it, and he pointed out that it probably could have been any woman, because I was still on the rebound from Julie Lea.

Dammit, how long is this rebound going to last, Noels? Can't you get a grip on yourself?

Physician, heal thyself.

Professionally, I'm short-handed. I'm fortunate in having Stan, a fine medical assistant with abilities and understanding far above those of a mere paramedic. He has an empathy with the sick and injured, but not to the extent that it incapacitates him or warps his judgment. In med school, Osterhoff once termed this the essence of the classical bedside manner. Stan knows, as I do, that the best doctors are con artists—but honest con artists because they require the confidence of their patients in order to engage in the give-and-take that's the foundation of the doctor-patient relationship.

With only four of us here and one required to be on duty, and me always on call as the only doctor, it's been a heel-and-toe situation for the past several days. I knew I had to get a new nurse as quickly as possible.

There haven't been many accidents or injuries pecu-

liar to the space environment. We haven't seen any head colds, upper-respiratory-tract diseases, allergies, or any of the other afflictions that keep otorhinolaryngologists busy on Earth. Nobody's permitted to get as far as GEO Base with a head cold. And we haven't had many GI upsets; the food's been good, and the public health measures keep this place much cleaner than Earth. We've had a succession of cuts, bruises, minor burns, and the sort of thing you'd expect to find on any construction job. There've been a few fights; again, this was to be expected among the kind of people who do this sort of work. But there haven't been any deadly fights or murders. I don't know why. When you jam eight hundred people into the pressurized sewer pipes called GEO Base, you'd expect to get the same ratio of murders per thousand population as on Earth. But we haven't. Perhaps it's because the SPS crews work every day in a very dangerous environment. They have outstanding TV and communications to occupy their spare time. They also know they'll be rotated back to Earth every sixty to ninety days for R & R, so they know they're not stuck out here forever, though some are beginning to say they really don't want to go back and are willing to sign on for extended stays.

As a result, we've expanded our weightlessness watch on physiological changes to encompass not only the med team but also some of the long-duration Eden Corp. people and others working for subcontractors. I've been carefully watching the forecast changes in bone calcium and blood fractions. But since everyone's encouraged to exercise during his off-time shift, I haven't seen any real muscle atrophy yet. I wouldn't expect it among those whose jobs require them to work in P-suits. In spite of a couple decades of design progress, working in a P-suit is still like wearing an inflated inner tube.

We stay busy, and we're getting busier all the time as more and more people learn they can't successfully be their own physicians. With trust in our med team has come an increase in the number of daily out patients.

Actually, if this keeps up—as it will—I'll have to add another M.D. to GEO Base before six months have passed. It's not because the number of accidents has increased, but because the pace of activity is growing here in GEO Base. When the pilot SPS proves out—as it will—and Smitty starts building two SPS units per year from this GEO Base site, things are going to get very busy indeed.

I couldn't go back to Earth to interview a new nurse, but I didn't have to. I did it all by two-way videophone in full color. I've never interviewed by remote control before, and I wasn't sure it was going to work. On the other hand, why shouldn't it have?

I've got my new nurse coming up on the next Pot-Vee.

Dorothy Helen Urton, R.N., is certainly a contrast to Angela. She's been involved in industrial nursing on the big electric-power projects in Arizona and California, basically the same thing we're doing here: the practice of medicine on the industrial scene in semi-isolation. She's five years older than I am, attractive, but not the disturbing beauty Angela was.

Reaction to Angela? Maybe. I don't know. Time will tell. But I wanted competence, professionalism, dedication, and that intangible pioneering attitude I can't describe yet in words.

Urton seems to have it. At least, it came through 22,400 miles of videophone link. If it can manifest itself under those conditions, it must be real and it must be powerful. I hope so, because it would be doubly difficult to go through another incident like that of the Homesick Angel.

"It's compact, Doctor, but it's adequate," Dorothy Urton commented after she had seen her cramped living quarters. "I know weightlessness permits one to use all the volume in a room. Please let me put my bag in the locker, and then I'll need to know where the equipment's located."

"Does the zero-g bother you?"

"Not at all," the nurse replied in a matter-of-fact tone. "However, I think I'll have to switch to contact lenses; I'm a bit afraid of these rimless glasses coming off and floating away. May I ask why your former nurse left this situation?"

"She got homesick," Tom answered simply.

"That's what you told me during our interview," Dorothy remarked in a perplexed tone of voice. "But I don't understand it. The facilities here appear to be adequate. Was she a claustrophobe?"

"Partly."

"That would explain it, Doctor. But I also suspect this would be difficult for anyone not used to working out in the boondocks." It was apparent to Tom that Dorothy Urton possessed considerable insight.

Tom toured the med module with his new nurse and had Stan, Fred, and Dave brief her on their equipment and where it was kept.

Dorothy was definitely a no-nonsense type. She was pleasant, but not fawning; friendly, but not intrusive; capable of radiating competence without being overbearing. "I can see I've got some learning to do," she observed. "All of you have been up here in weightlessness for almost two months now, and you've unconsciously adapted. You follow a lot of procedures that're strange to me but solve the problems involved with weightlessness—and you don't even realize you're doing them. Doctor, have you some curriculum set up to acquaint me with the little tricks you've learned?"

"I didn't really think about it, Nurse. We've been so busy just taking care of the day-to-day problems that I haven't had time to do anything like that."

"Consider me your first student, then, Doctor. You're going to get more people like myself up here. This is going to be a training ground for all the orbital medical people to follow. May I suggest that I spend my spare time working with Fred and Stan here, then move on into Dave's medical lab? I need to learn how you handle routine procedures such as IVs and blood work-ups."

Tom left Dorothy working with Fred, the team's expert on weightless procedures. Three hours later, he wondered why he hadn't heard from his nurse. He looked out of his cabin to see her practicing the positive-displacement-IV technique with normal saline solution on Stan while Fred stood by and advised her.

It was a slow day for a change. Tom spent most of it working in his quarters, thinking about what Dorothy had said about training. He powered-up GALEN.

"Hi, Stumpy, how are you doing?" A familiar female voice carried through the med module.

"Hi, Lucky! Meet our new nurse," Fred replied.

Tom powered-down and went out to see Lucky Hertzog. "Where'd you materialize from, Red? You're usually out flying an array subassembly."

"Hi, Tom! You're right. I just brought one up from LEO Base. How'd you survive the flare storm?"

"Not too well, I'm afraid."

"We heard about the seven," Lucky said somberly, but brightened again. "Angela's gone?"

"Got homesick," Tom replied. "Meet Dorothy Urton, our new nurse."

"I know her. We met on the Palo Verde Extension job. I'm surprised to find you here, Dorothy—then again, I'm not."

"It's a small world," Dorothy agreed.

"Only seems that way. The world's full of bodies, but they're just automatic pieces in the game. There are only a few real people," Lucky noted.

"I know all about that," Tom told her. "All I have to do is take an aspirin, and you'll all go away."

Lucky perked up and smoothed her coverall. "Well! Now that I've done my duty and said hello to Stumpy here, how about it, Tom? Got a few minutes? If so, entertain me!"

"Coffee in the wardroom?"

"Why not? Unless you had something else in mind."

"Just coffee, Lucky. It's been a hard day."

Soon they were sitting at a table in the wardroom.

Lucky unclipped her ID tag from her neck chain, tossed it in the air, and caught it. "Heads or tails?"

"Always betting! What are we betting on this time?"

"Paying for the coffee."

"It's my turn, Lucky. Besides, I do my gambling with higher stakes in the real world."

Lucky made a pout. "Spoilsport!"

Tom got two bags of hot coffee and returned to the table. "Tell me something. You're in a risky job, so why do you continue to gamble even when you're not gambling with your life outside?"

"Because life's a gamble, and I like to stay in practice," Lucky explained. "It's not like sex, where constant practice isn't necessary."

"Well," Tom observed, "we used to be told sex involved organs, not muscles, so exercise wasn't required."

"Do you believe it?"

"You brought it up for discussion."

"Speaking of sex, which we are," Lucky continued, "I'm glad you got rid of that sexpot nurse."

"I thought you liked competition."

"Did I say she was competition? And who says I was competing for you? Tom, you're getting a swelled head."

"Then why are you glad Angela's gone?"

Lucky didn't say anything for a minute, but played with the bag of coffee in her hands. Then she looked at Tom. "Because she wasn't one of us."

"I'm not sure I know what you mean, Lucky."

"Oh, sure you do, Tom! I called her a sexpot. That she was. Maybe a good nurse, too, but I don't know about that. I do know—and any other woman out here will tell you the same thing—that she *had* to have people around her and depended on them to maintain her ego. She was different from us."

"What makes you think everybody here's different? We still depend on each other, Lucky."

"Not the same way. We don't *use* other people. We work with them. We're individual members of teams

doing things together that individuals can't do alone."
She let the coffee bag float free in front of her as she threw
up both hands and exclaimed, "Tom, I don't know exactly how to say it, but you do know what I mean?"

"I think so, and I haven't been able to put it into
words yet, either . . . and I've been trying to."

"Writing a book about all this?"

"You might call it that. I'm going to have to train
others to do the things we've learned the hard way. If
we're to make progress out here, we can't afford the
luxury of reinventing the square wheel."

"Amen, brother!"

"Incidentally, since we're such rugged individualists
and don't need nobody nohow no time, as the old saying goes, how come you drop by the med module every
time you're in GEO Base?" Tom asked offhandedly.

He was surprised by Lucky's answer. "Do you think
I'm dropping in just to see you? Damn, you've got an
ego, Doc! Or a warped sense of humor—"

"Hey, cool it! You talk of a sense of humor, and I
was only trying to rib you," Tom said, backing off.

"Don't kid me that way, Tom! Honest to God, some
of you macho types still don't realize we women are
human beings and capable of doing a lot of things you
do!"

Tom put up his hands in the face of this outburst.
Obviously, Lucky Hertzog had her difficulties in a profession that was still dominated by men even after several decades of sexual equality. "Sorry. I won't do it
again."

"Listen, don't think I believe in female equality, because I don't. But I won't get stuck with the dirty end
of the stick, so I demand, and I get, all the traffic will
bear! Woman are not equal to men."

"Right. We differ by one little chromosome."

"Thank God for that little chromosome! That makes
us *superior* to men!"

Tom sighed. Lucky had a short fuse, and he had
made the mistake of lighting it. "Okay, I won't argue
with you. In fact, I *refuse* to argue with you. Lucky,

I'm a doctor. I know both the physical and the psychological differences. Believe me, I do indeed enjoy the differences."

"So do most other men!"

"I don't know how this conversation got out of hand . . . Well, I do, but I won't dwell on it. After this, I'll just consider that you came by the med module to say hello to Fred Fitzsimmons."

Lucky unstrapped herself from the chair and tossed her half-empty coffee bag toward a waste receptacle. "*If* I come by at all anymore!" she shot back.

"Please do," Tom told her. "You've got spirit, Lucky. Sass would be a better word. I kind of like that."

She hesitated, then said curtly, "Thanks for the coffee." She pushed off and headed for an exit without a further word.

Tom sat there for a moment in silence. He had managed to hold his temper under control; it had been a long time since he had lost his temper with a woman.

With a start, he suddenly realized he had never really lost his temper with *any* woman except Julie Lea. A host of recollections inundated him, memories he had shoved to the back of his mind, remembrances of the monumental fights they had had as teen-age steadies, as adult lovers, and as man and wife. Disagreements had been part and parcel of the only real love of his life. He had forgotten them, remembering only the sweet, succulent times. And then he realized that most of those wonderful times had occurred after he and Julie Lea had had one of their incredible emotional battles.

He sighed, unstrapped, pushed off for the waste receptacle, recovered Lucky's half-empty coffee bag— which had missed its target—and put both used bags into the disposal.

Lucky Hertzog was a fascinating woman, he decided, but in a different way than Angela had been. He realized he had developed a latent fondness for her—not a hotheaded roaring sexual attraction, as with Angela, not the sweet lifelong love he had shared with Julie

Lea, but a desire to know Lucky, to be with her and to share with her a few moments of the precious off-duty time he managed to squeeze into his busy days.

"Be reasonable, Tom," he told himself. "She's got a redhead's temper that'd be the bane of your existence. Well, maybe that's a generalization. Maybe a redhead's temper is an old wives' tale."

He discovered he had been talking aloud. One of the riggers sitting at a nearby table looked at him with a strange expression. Tom waved at him and pushed off for the exit.

When he got back to the med module, he sat down before the GALEN terminal and acted in a nonprofessional manner. He called up Lucky Hertzog's medical records, as was his privilege. He didn't admit to himself that he was doing it to find out more about her. What he discovered confirmed much of what he had deduced. Yet there were other factors he hadn't suspected.

She had been born and raised in Fairplay, Colorado, ten thousand feet up in the Rocky Mountains and a hundred miles from almost everywhere. Her father was a doctor, the only one who remained in Fairplay after the mines gave out and the only one there when the huge water-diversion and hydroelectric projects pumped thousands of people and billions of dollars into the area. Lucky's mother had died of exposure, reason not given in the records. But her death occurred when Lucky, an only child, was seven years old.

Tom couldn't tell from the medical records why Lucky had elected to pursue a career in electrical engineering. Perhaps it was because she had been raised by her father, or perhaps because she had been surrounded by civil and electrical engineers on the power projects during her teen-age years. Her degree was a B.S.E.E. from the University of Colorado in Boulder. Her father was still alive and residing in Fairplay, because she gave his address as that of her nearest relative to be notified in case of accident. Whether her father was still practicing or not wasn't noted, but Tom suspected he was, because doctors in remote areas normally didn't retire; they kept right on working until they, too, took that final ride to whatever medical facilities existed nearby.

Tom saw that Lucky had absolutely no medical anomalies—except that she was blood type AB, Rh negative, and had an unusually high hemoglobin value: 17 grams/100 milliliters. Perhaps her history of birth and development at an altitude two miles above sea level had something to do with that.

"Good afternoon, Doctor." A familiar voice broke into Tom's perusal of the GALEN data on the display screen. He turned to find Dr. Ernst Gustav von Hesse floating in the doorway to the cubicle. The ISHA doctor didn't look well; he was pale, and he gripped the edges of the opening with white-knuckled hands.

"Von Hesse! What are you doing here?" Tom asked, clearing the screen and floating over to his visitor. Tom knew exactly what was going on, so he approached Von Hesse in an inverted position relative to the medical bureaucrat.

Obviously, his doing so bothered Von Hesse greatly. "I have come to conduct an ISHA inspection of . . . Doctor, would you please turn right side up?"

"I am right side up," Tom said. "You're upside down."

"Uh . . . Doctor, would you happen to have fifty milligrams of cyclizine you could give me? I am experiencing a slight amount of disorientation."

"In my professional opinion," Tom replied, spinning himself around so that he had the same orientation as his visitor, "you're suffering from Borman's Syndrome."

"I am not familiar with that," Von Hesse admitted, turning slightly more pale as Tom spun around to the inverted position again and slid through the doorway past the ISHA doctor.

"Well, you've got it, so you'll be familiar with it from now on," Tom told him, taking his arm to lead him into the med compartment. "Look it up sometime. It's named after the first astronaut to experience your malady. Dave, get me fifty milligrams of cyclizine, please. We've got a disoriented visitor."

Von Hesse had trouble swallowing the capsule, even with water sucked through a straw inserted into a water-bag. He objected mildly when Tom insisted that he be secured in a rest basket. "Look, I don't want you to get sick. Up here, it's a three-dimensional problem, and my people are busy enough with professional work."

"I will feel better soon," Von Hesse insisted. "I must continue my inspection."

"Well, you're certainly welcome to stick around and watch what we do, but when we get busy, we won't have time for you."

"On the contrary, the regulations require that an inspection be given the highest priority."

"Von Hesse, you've been here—what, five minutes? This is the first five minutes of inactivity we've had in a long time. There's always somebody coming in the hatch. Or we're out on a call."

"Med Unit, Central!" the intercom rasped. "Accident in vacuum! Reported P-suit fire! Location Array Subassembly Module One Zero Seven. Repeat: One Zero Seven!"

Fred shouted back at the intercom, "Central, Med! Array Subassembly Module One Zero Seven! We're on our way! Clear traffic for the Pumpkin!"

"Fire in a pressure suit? How?" Von Hesse asked.

"I don't know." Tom snapped, "Fred, I'm going out there with you! Stan's in the sack, and I want him to get some rest. Dorothy, make the doctor comfortable until I get back. Prepare for burn therapy."

"That should be easier to accomplish in weightlessness," Dorothy remarked as Tom dived for the P-suit locker.

Tom wasn't as fast as Fred when it came to donning a P-suit, but then Fred had had more practice. It took Tom forty seconds. Fred buddy-checked him, then Tom returned the favor. They were out the far hatch and through the air lock to the Pumpkin ninety-three seconds after the call had come in.

Fred settled in the left seat, Tom in the right. "Checklist!" Fred called.

Together, they went through the power-up checklist. Total time, forty-two seconds. Less than three minutes after the call, Fred retracted the docking latches and backed the Pumpkin away from the med module on thruster power. While Fred was doing that, Tom interfaced the ship's computer with the one in GEO Base via radio link; he called up a three-dimensional display of the current GEO Base configuration and had the computer call out the location of the accident site.

"Computer has fed course parameters to the guidance system," Tom reported. Fred slued the ship and coupled the autopilot.

"Roger! Autopilot locked on. Stand by for thrust."

Tom spoke over the radio. "Traffic, Pumpkin. Emergency. Departing med module under primary thrust for Array Subassembly Module One Zero Seven. Are we clear to boost?"

Fred held his finger over the abort switch in anticipation of a possible Traffic delay. But it didn't come. "Pumpkin, Traffic. Clear to boost."

The boost came with a little fishtailing. "Dammit!" Fred swore. "Doc, this autopilot doesn't warm up fast enough. We'll have to go manual follow-up."

"I'll take it, Fred." Flying the Pumpkin wasn't as hard as flying a light airplane on instruments through an overcast at night. In this case, with the course already plotted by the computer, all Tom had to do was keep the marker bugs centered on the attitude-situation and relative-velocity displays. With the sidearm controller in one hand and the thruster and vernier throttles in the other, Tom didn't let the red Xs of the marker bugs deviate from the center of the display.

They picked up the group of P-suited figures on video long before the computer called for retros. To keep the thruster and vernier discharges away from the P-suited workers, Tom slued the Pumpkin in yaw and applied retro thrust by vector.

"Nice rendezvous, Doc," Fred remarked as the

Pumpkin came dead in space twenty feet from the work party.

"Save the compliments for later, Fred," Tom told him, and switched to the all-call channel. "This is Pumpkin at Module One Zero Seven. If you hear me at the accident site, reply and wave."

Two of the suited figures waved as a voice replied, "Read you five by, Pumpkin."

"Let's go see how bad it is and get him aboard as quickly as possible if we can. If the injury's inside the P-suit, we'll have to bring him back to pressure."

The paramedic didn't say anything, but reached over and activated Tom's P-suit backpack. Tom did the same for Fred. Only then did they disconnect from the Pumpkin's life-support system.

"Dump pressure, Fred."

Tom felt his suit pressurize as the atmosphere of the Pumpkin was dumped into space through spill valves that equalized the thrust produced. Normal procedure wouldn't have permitted dumping of pressure, nitrogen being the one gas that had to be brought up from Earth. In addition, the venting created a gas halo around the ship that might have permitted arcing of electrical equipment on the SPS array. But in an emergency where the Pumpkin had to be depressurized rapidly, there was no alternative.

Fred braced himself in the open hatch and fired the line-throwing gun. The foam plastic projectile sailed slowly across the void, trailing the line it pulled from the container on the gun. A P-suited figure reached out and caught the slow-moving plastic blob as it sailed past. Fred snubbed the line on a cleat inside the hatch as the other person whipped it through and around a beam of the array. Tom had his running safety line snapped around the main line as quickly as it was secured at both ends. He pushed off and sailed down the line. Fred was behind him.

Tom hit feet-first, absorbing his momentum by bending his knees. He felt the jar as Fred stopped beside him.

One of the P-suited individuals was obviously unconscious. Tom surmised this from the limp, rag-doll pos-
ture and random small movements of the limbs of the
P-suit. He looked at the faceplate and discovered that
the inside surface was covered with a brownish-black
deposit. The injured man was no longer being supported by his own backpack. It had been disconnected,
and he had been buddy-coupled to another individual's
pack.

"What happened?" Tom asked.

"Fire in the backpack," somebody announced on the
radio.

"Jed hollered that's what happened before he
choked," another voice cut in. "Pete got him hooked up
buddy-style in about twenty seconds."

"Is his backpack still burning?" Tom queried.

"We don't know. Dutch shut it down after Pete made
the buddy-couple."

"If there's a fire still in the backpack, I don't think
we should take it back aboard the Pumpkin," Fred said.

"We'll have to take the chance," Tom decided. "We
haven't time to get the thing off. I want to get this man
back in pressure immediately. We can't do a thing out
here in vacuum. Let's transport him right now. Pete,
come along with your buddy-couple until we get back
under pressure."

It didn't take more than thirty seconds to repressur-
ize the Pumpkin. Then Tom opened the faceplate of the
injured man's P-suit helmet. The man had had a beard
that had been singed off. There were first- and second-
degree burns on his face. The most severe burns were
in the vicinity of the oxygen inlet couplings from the
backpack to the helmet. Tom had no way of knowing
the nature or extent of possible burns in the lungs or
airways.

Fred immediately placed a blood-pressure and pulse-
rate sensor on the man's right carotid. "BP eighty-five
over fifty-five and dropping. Pulse weak and thready
. . . I can't get an exact rate, Doc. Respiration
seventy-two."

"Start an IV with Ringer's. Don't bother getting his P-suit off! Put it in his neck!" Tom snapped, opening the man's mouth and shining a flashlight in to check the mucosae. "Hyperemia of the oral mucosa. Haven't got time to check his larynx. I want hundred percent Oh-two, stat! And insert an airway just in case."

As quickly as they had accomplished this, Tom added, "Fred, boost us back to the module! Be gentle, but make it fast. We've got to get this man back where we have more facilities!"

It wasn't a gentle ride, but it was fast. Back at the med module, they pulled the P-suit off the man.

"No burns except around the head," Tom noted. "But there are bad tracheal burns, and maybe some lung damage. Dorothy, you concentrate on stabilizing his condition. Dave, get the Diagnostic Ultrasound unit over here; I want to check his lungs."

The five members of the med team succeeded in stabilizing the man's condition, and Dave jury-rigged a respirator with gentle suction action to remove the fluids created by pulmonary edema. To stop a sudden onset of violent coughing, Tom gave him a bronchodilator and started him on massive doses of corticosteroids.

For two hours while they worked on the burned man, Dr. von Hesse was totally ignored. He watched quietly from the sidelines.

After the burned man was instrumented for vital signs and the activity in the med module decreased to normal again, Tom sighed and turned to find Von Hesse floating at his side, holding on to one of the oxygen pipes that crisscrossed the intensive-monitoring sector of the module.

Von Hesse didn't comment on what he had witnessed. He asked instead, "What happened out there?"

"Somehow, a fire started in the man's pressure-suit life-support backpack," Tom explained.

"How could that happen? Wasn't it tested to insure such a thing couldn't happen?"

"I imagine so," Tom admitted, "but things like that

do happen in spite of all the testing that's done on Earth prior to space use."

"Is the testing adequate?"

"Probably more than adequate. With safety bureaucrats such as yourself looking on, the tendency is to over-test—to the extent of putting safety devices on the safety devices until the safety devices themselves fail and cause disaster."

"I'm going to take that backpack with me," Von Hesse said abruptly. "We'll want to check it over to find out what went wrong."

"Can't let you, Doctor."

"What?"

"Herb Pratt will have his P-suit technicians check it out. They'll find out what went wrong. Whatever caused that fire—if indeed it was a fire—will be determined, and the backpack subcontractor will take whatever steps necessary to revise the design and to issue instructions for retrofitting all the packs that are currently up here."

"This backpack has now proved itself to be an industrial hazard!" Von Hesse snapped. "It has almost killed a man! There is a flaw in its design! I am going to use my authority to seize and hold that backpack for investigation and to enjoin the use of other backpacks of that design until the flaw is discovered and corrected!"

"Not likely, Doctor. There are probably a thousand of these backpacks in GEO Base alone, and they're used every day. Whatever happened, it wasn't a design flaw, or we'd have seen this sort of accident long ago. Herb Pratt and his P-suit technicians will probably discover that the fire was caused by some maintenance oversight."

"The use of that backpack design will be prohibited until the flaw is discovered and corrected."

"You do that, Dr. von Hesse," Tom said slowly, "and you'll shut down this entire program. There's only one backpack design in use."

"Then the program will just have to halt until the flaw is corrected," Von Hesse replied smugly. "We cannot permit the lives of the workers to be jeopardized by the faulty design of life-support equipment!"

Tom said nothing for a moment, then he turned to where Stan and Fred were drifting with the backpack and P-suit in their arms. "Fellas, take that equipment down to the P-suit maintenance facility. I'll tell Pratt it's coming."

"You can't do that!" Von Hesse exploded. "I'm confiscating that equipment for a government investigation!"

"I don't have the authority to turn it over to you, Von Hesse, because it's the property of Eden Corporation, not of Dr. T. K. Noels, P.C. You'll have to fight with the base engineer over it." Tom tried to control his temper. "And good luck, because you'll need it!"

Chapter Twelve

From the Galen Journal of Dr. T. K. Noels:

We lost Jed Hobart, the man with the fire in his backpack. The burn damage to his trachea and lungs was far too extensive, and he succumbed to lobar pneumonia caused by infection of the damaged alveolar tissues. I tried everything I knew, including penicillin G4B and direct IV injection of the spores of the coprinus *mushroom in normal saline—a bit of folk medicine I picked up in Recife, Brazil.*

When a man is dying and I have no other recourse, I'll use whatever medical knowledge I possess, regardless of where I obtained it, in an effort to save his life.

That didn't cut any ice with the great medical expert, Ernst Gustav von Hesse. What I did wasn't approved by the FDA or DHSS or XYZ or probably any of a dozen bureaucracies that try to tell American doctors how to practice their profession. When Von Hesse found out I was using a lot of remedies not officially approved by anybody, he stormed out in a huff—which isn't an acronym for some sort of spacecraft—and threatened to have my contract with Eden Corporation canceled and my license suspended.

Von Hesse was also upset over the fact that Herb Pratt is an even more difficult man to deal with than he is. Pratt refused to let Von Hesse touch that backpack, and got his life-support-systems experts on the track of the failure because, if it was indeed a design flaw, he wanted corrective actions taken now, not months from now, after we might lose others to the same malfunction.

It didn't take long to determine the source of the fire. Each backpack contains two high-pressure-oxygen storage bottles. A pressure switch valves a full bottle into the system when it senses the on-line bottle's pressure has dropped below a preset limit. The high-pressure oxygen then flows through a regulator that drops the pressure to about five psi absolute. The plastic O-ring that seals the upstream side of the regulator may have had a trace of contamination on it; the culprit seems to be aluminum shaved off the fitting when a maintenance tech overtightened it. When the pressure sensor switched tanks, a shock wave of high-pressure oxygen hit the upstream side of the regulator fitting and was heated by shock compression. This action ignited whatever was on the O-ring. The aluminum of the regulator body then began to burn in the hot, oxygen-rich atmosphere, and, in turn, sent an oxygen-rich flame right down the breathing pressure lines to the interior of Hobart's helmet.

A fifty-cent O-ring and an uncalibrated torque wrench killed a man. It could also call a halt to a multibillion-dollar project.

Pratt says it's a simple fix. He's got his maintenance techs replacing O-rings and installing a diffuser upstream of the regulator as each backpack comes in from vacuum for refurbishment at the end of each shift. This has kept his life-support mechanics busy, and he's had to move people from GEO Base life-support-systems maintenance over to backpack refurbishment, but Pratt's an organizer, albeit a slave driver.

Pratt also says it was a trillion-to-one happening. But that's little consolation to Jed Hobart.

The pilot SPS project's no different from any other huge construction program. Hundreds of safety engineers worry in advance about the big problems and the obvious hazards, but they can't possibly foresee all the little nickel-and-dime glitches that kill people. That's why I'm here with my med team.

As with all accidents resulting in death, I have to perform the autopsy and enter the results in the GALEN files. A waiver clause in everybody's employment agreement permits this because it could be the only way we'd ever learn how or why a person died here. Some people on Earth have objected, next of kin in particular, especially those whose religious beliefs prohibit autopsies. But if a person dies of an accident related to the space environment, and we don't probe to find out why and how and what happened, we won't learn enough to keep others from being killed the same way.

As if I didn't have enough problems with accidents and injuries in GEO Base, I've also got to worry now about Von Hesse and the bureaucrats breathing down my neck! They may not call it "socialized medicine," but the government sure as hell is creating just that by virtue of its mandatory standards and regulations, most of which don't have a thing to do with the way I have to practice medicine 22,400 miles from Earth. Sure, I'm the only game in town, but that's because ISHA and other government agencies demanded there be a medical facility here! Someday I won't be the only game in town, and people will have a choice. In the meantime, I must be conscientious and keep this setup from turning into a company-medical-center sham.

Lucky Hertzog stopped in, ostensibly to have me check her because she had a late and mild menses. On Earth, it wouldn't have mattered. But I've asked everybody who feels different or who has a change in normal body rhythms to let me know. Such changes in natural biological rhythms aren't uncommon in a place like GEO Base, where one's circadian rhythms can easily be screwed up. In additon, although we're still deeply immersed in the Earth's magnetic field, the natural flux through GEO Base isn't the same as on Earth. There's still the eight-hertz pulse in the field, along with daily and monthly variations caused by (we think) the interaction of the electrical and gravitational influences of both the Moon and the Sun. We've got a lot to learn about the effects of these kinds of factors on our physiology.

I mention Lucky's visit only because she apologized in a roundabout fashion for having lost her temper with me. So I took her to dinner. I find her interesting to be with. She's intelligent and has broad interests. She's stimulating from an intellectual and an empathetic point of view. Yes, she has sexual attraction, too. Most women here do, because, in spite of women's lib, the GEO Base population is only about twenty-five percent female, most of whom have that elusive pioneer attitude about them, but this doesn't make them any less female. In fact, I think it heightens the fact. They may be generally soft and feminine, but they possess a hardness and a resilience in their approach to life. Lucky shares those traits.

We haven't as much as kissed good-bye. Yet I'm growing very attached to this woman. I hope the feeling is reciprocal, but we haven't discussed it at all. Perhaps we're both taking it for granted.

Quite naturally, I'm comparing her with the other women in my life . . . and find there's no comparison whatsoever. At least, I don't think there is. Perhaps I'm overlooking something. Maybe we just have a few things in common, that's all. This could turn out to be nothing more than a friendship bred by the unique circumstances in which we both find ourselves.

"T.K., what the hell are you doing up there?" Owen Hocksmith's image on the screen showed a mixed expression of dismay and anger, but it was obvious he was holding both in check. "Did you deliberately bait that sonofabitch Von Hesse, or was it merely a coincidence he happened to be there when Hobart was killed by the backpack fire?"

Tom sighed. "I didn't bait him, Smitty. I dislike the pompous bastard, too, and I don't think he deserves his professional title because he probably hasn't practiced since his residency. What he saw was representative of what goes on every day. It's typical of the sort of thing you'll find on any construction job on Earth. The backpack's a minor thing; Pratt's people got that fixed a couple days later."

Hocksmith wasn't satisfied. "That's only part of it.

Von Hesse's report claims you're practicing black magic on your patients," he went on, looking through a hard-copy printout. "Have you seen his report on your facility and on you?"

"No."

"Get a printout. Memory code ISHA-45."

"I'll do that, Smitty, but can you briefly tell me what he says? Obviously, you're upset about it."

"Upset is putting it mildly, T.K. No, I'm not upset with you; you're doing your job. I'm upset with what these goddamn bureaucrats are trying to do to me because of Von Hesse." He sat back and sighed. "Tom, these bastards are trying to get a cease-and-desist order through the federal court in Phoenix to shut me down until we requalify every piece of hardware that's been involved in an accident resulting in personal injury or death."

"What?"

"You heard me. Look, I can't go into the politics behind this, but there're power groups and factions that want to shut down this project because of their own short-term vested interests. Now they have a handle to twist, and they're twisting it hard." Hocksmith swore under his breath. "Thus far, they haven't shaken my financial foundation, but they're chipping at it. They're playing Chicken Little—and the news media are falling for it."

"Chicken Little?"

"Poor simile. Never mind. The news media's yelling doesn't faze me—much. All it does is produce anti-space pickets at the rectenna site and the entrances to JSP, but damned few of those hairy freaks can last more than an hour or two out on the desert fifty miles from town. They're children of technology and television. They show up with the media crews in time to make the evening news, then crawl back to town in their smoking old wrecks." Hocksmith snorted in disgust. "Where it's really getting to me, T.K.," he admitted, "are the soft spots only my enemies know about. And to my friends who're a little chicken to begin with and are now afraid that I'm sending working people to a death trap in the sky."

"That's ridiculous, Smitty!" Tom objected. "Hills and Pratt counted on having fifty-five casualties by this time. I've been able to hold it to twenty-eight! That's better than a fifty-percent improvement."

"I know. But how many Americans realize that any large construction job *must* budget for casualties? And how many sob sisters would understand and not scream bloody murder about it? Never mind; you pushed my button! You're doing the sort of job I wanted you to do. But, T.K., why did you have to use South American witch medicine with Von Hesse looking over your shoulder?"

"Is that what he called it? Smitty, I was losing Hobart. I *had* to try everything I knew. I also realized that if it didn't work, I'd be a witch; on the other hand, if it had worked, I'd have been a hero . . . maybe."

"I doubt it. Von Hesse is a hatchet man who looks for anything that isn't certified true-blue and pure as the driven snow. Whether it works or not isn't important to him; the only thing that counts is whether it's been blessed by the bureaucracy. T.K., you'd better read the Von Hesse report. Bob Eddy and his partners can keep the wolves in the courts at bay long enough for us to finish assembling the pilot plant and put it on line. At that point, we're a success as far as both DOE and my backers are concerned—and then the rest of the screaming mob can just go fry ice!"

"I'll read Von Hesse's report, Smitty, but I probably won't have time to do so thoroughly."

"You'd better. They're after your hide, too. I'll run interference for you and figure out some way to protect you as a subcontractor, T.K., but you'd better be aware that the mob is baying for your head . . . and the women are knitting already."

"Smitty, level with me. You can handle the media and the lawyers, or you have people in Eden Corporation who can. Who's really giving you trouble?"

Hocksmith rose from his chair and stepped out of the

pickup field. Tom heard the sound of the bar fridge door opening and closing. Then Hocksmith returned to the chair and sat down with a can of beer in his hand. That told Tom that his friend was under real pressure. He had never seen Hocksmith take a drink of *anything* when he was on the videophone. Hocksmith didn't want to give an ounce of ammunition to anyone.

"T.K., I'm stretched tight on this one," Hocksmith began.

"We both are. So what else is new?"

Hocksmith took a healthy cut at the beer. Then he simply said, "Fran."

"What's she up to, Smitty?" From the moment Hocksmith first told Tom years ago that he was going to marry Frances Valencia, Tom knew it would be a marriage of political expediency, whereby his friend would be assured of the positions of majority leader in the State Senate and head of the State Democratic Party. It was the first step in Owen Hocksmith's rise to political power, which preceded his rise in financial and entrepreneurial power.

As an expedient marriage, it couldn't last, and it didn't. But it couldn't be dissolved. Neither Hocksmith nor his wife wanted a divorce, even if Fran's religion had permitted it. She needed the security of the Hocksmith name and fortune; he had to have the position and political clout that came from being married to the only child of a powerful political ally. In the impasse, Fran lived in splendor in Taos as both a patroness of the arts and a mediocre sculptress. As long as Bob Eddy kept her coffer filled with Hocksmith money, she hardly bothered to communicate with her husband.

"Making trouble," Hocksmith replied. "You probably don't appreciate the political ramifications of the problem, T.K."

"I was born in the state, Smitty. Try me."

"One of her young protégés convinced her to hit me for a million and a half bucks to build an art center in Taos so she could be the big wheel in state art circles and he could have a job that wasn't really very demanding," Hocksmith explained. "She's living with this long-haired, bearded, filthy fraud, who can't do anything except sponge off other people."

"Can you come up with the money yourself, Smitty? Would that get Fran off your back?"

"Yes, but I won't do it," Hocksmith stated firmly with a steady look in his eyes. "I won't mortgage Hocksmith land for an art museum. An *art museum,* for chrissake! So I've got to try to get the funds into the upcoming state budget. And I can't hack it, T.K. I collected all my political I-O-Us putting Eden Corporation together for the SPS program. In fact, I've got I-O-Us out now not only in Santa Fe but in Phoenix and Washington, too. Politically, I've got nothing to trade for her damned art center. Okay, this state supports a lot with tax money, but it all contributes to the educational and tourist situations. There's no way on God's little green Earth I can ram through the appropriations committee *or* the legislature any funds for an art center, not in the face of the Baca Amendment limiting the state's power to tax. Mostly, I can't swallow the project's being supported by tax money from farmers, ranchers, and small businessmen who couldn't care less about an art museum; they expect us to do something *useful* with tax money!" He sat back in his chair and exhaled sharply.

"Smitty, if you can't get the money, what can Fran do?"

"Are you kidding? The governor's her uncle, and Senator Otero's her first cousin. Do you know who backed me in Washington? And do you know what happens in Washington without that support in the face of the latest attack from ISHA, DHSS, and the Justice Department? Hell, Chaves and Otero and the rest don't have a penny of their money in this thing, although they hold some stock through untraceable trusts. If I go belly-up, they don't lose anything, not even political clout. If it looks like Eden Corporation and space solar power aren't politically viable things to support because we're killing people right and left up there, they'll finesse me, pull out in a manner that'll draw little attention to themselves, and leave me up the evil-smelling tributary with no visible means of locomotion and no knowledge of aquatics!"

"Smitty, I'm sorry what I've done has had such far-reaching effects on you."

"It's not your fault, T.K. You're doing your job," Hocksmith assured him. "They're trying to find a hook to hang me from. If it hadn't been you, they'd have looked until they discovered someone or something else.

Dorothy rapped on the coaming of the entrance to Tom's cabin. "Doctor, we have a patient you should see," she informed him quietly.

"Smitty, got to go. Patient waiting. Hang in there. We'll make it. I'll call you." Tom broke the connection.

It was Lucky Hertzog, but she had somebody in tow: Ross Jackson, the older astronaut who was now piloting Pot-Vees back and forth between LEO Base and GEO Base.

"Hi, Doc!" Lucky called brightly as Tom floated into the reception area. "Got a patient for you. Shall we discuss fee-splitting now, or do you want to settle for a flat commission?"

"I'll let you take it out in trade," Tom told her. "What's you doing up here, Lucky? I thought you were on your way down to LEO Base in the *Edison* with Ross."

"I was, except I didn't think Ross was in fit shape to drive," Lucky explained.

"What's wrong, Ross?"

The astronaut looked pained. "Had a dizzy spell during preboost checkout, and this redheaded broad, who's a big fan of yours, insisted I come and give you some business."

"Are you still dizzy?"

"A li'l bit." Ross' speech was thick and slurred.

"You didn't bust Rule Three, did you?"

"No, Doc—nothin' alcoholic in the last twenty-four hours. Just like the rule says. Why's everybody think

I'm drunk or somethin'? Dammit, gettin' so nobody around here trusts me anymore!"

There was no alcohol on Jackson's breath. "What'd you have at your last meal?"

"Nothin'. Not hungry. Hey, can I use your lav? I gotta take a leak bad." He pushed off in the direction Tom pointed to.

Lucky looked at Tom with concern. "Tom, I've never seen Ross this way before. It wasn't just the dizziness. We all get a little disoriented every once in a while. If it had been just that, I would've boosted with him. But not when he's in this condition."

"I agree with you, Lucky." Tom turned to Jackson as the astronaut floated back from the lavatory. "Ross, do you have an alternate to take your flight?"

"Sure!"

"Okay, I'm admitting you to sick bay here for a checkup."

"Hell, Doc, I'm all right! Just give me something for this dizziness and for my upset stomach, and I'll be good as new!"

"You're nauseated? Stomach hurts?"

"Yeah. Don't ground me, Doc! I've never failed my physical!"

"I'm not grounding you, Ross. I want to check you to find out if there's anything wrong with you. If there isn't, you'll get a clean bill from me. Okay?"

"Yeah, okay, but I'm getting damned tired of everybody pickin' on me! Jeez, I've got more time in space than any of you! I'm not gonna run off at the ears and do somethin' that'll kill me or anybody else!"

"I know you're not. Dorothy, let's get urine and blood samples from Ross. And give him ten milligrams of prochlorperazine IM to take care of his nausea and stomach cramps."

Lucky appeared concerned. "What do you think is wrong, Tom?" Her use of his first name wasn't lost on him.

He shrugged. "I'll tell you when I find out, Lucky. Thanks for bringing him here."

"No sweat. Hadn't you better tell Central to get his standby aboard? We've already missed the tick for this orbit."

"Thank you for reminding me." He pushed off for the comm panel, made his report to Central, and came back. "The *Edison* will be delayed three hours, Lucky. Nat Wallace just docked the *Steinmetz* and needs time to shift vehicles and run the checkout on the *Edison*."

"Can I stick around? Ross is kind of special to me."

"Sure. But special in what kind of way?"

"Tom, you've got a nasty, suspicious mind."

"No, *you* do, because of the way you always seem to misinterpret what I say."

"*Me?* Listen—"

"You listen. If you want to pick a fight, wait until we're somewhere else. Don't do it in my med module when I'm working with a patient, especially one who's a good friend of yours." Tom's voice was sharp.

Lucky *humphed*. "You are one of the most exasperating men I've ever known, Tom Noels!"

Tom left Jackson in Dorothy's watchful care and went to the GALEN terminal. He called up Ross Jackson's medical records.

The former NASA shuttle pilot was forty-seven years old. The record showed he had never varied from the medical norm during his entire flying career with the Air Force, NASA, or, now, SpaceLift, Inc. Tom went back through thirty-one years of medical records to Ross' initial FAA Third Class physical exam as a student pilot. There was nothing in the man's background that would lead Tom to suspect anything abnormal.

Was his problem something that resulted from thousands of hours spent in zero-g—the first symptoms of some syndrome that hit old-timers in space, something that would limit mankind's ability to live in space for long periods?

Tom gave that possibility a low priority. He knew many strange maladies affected human beings. He refused to jump to conclusions until Dave Cabot finished the urine and blood analyses and came up with some concrete data on which to base a diagnosis.

Suddenly he could feel Lucky looking over his shoulder. "This is confidential information, Lucky."

"So? It isn't telling me anything about Ross that I didn't already know. I won't run around to my girl friends, spreading rumors like a housewife. I know and respect the doctor-patient relationship. My father's a doctor, after all."

"I know. Just wanted to make sure you understood what you were reading. Technically, you shouldn't be in here when we're treating a patient, but I'll make an exception in your case this time."

"Why, thank *you, Doctor!*" she said with saccharine sweetness.

"Did I ever tell you of my overwhelming urge to wring your neck?" he replied with equal sarcasm.

"Tell me more about your overwhelming urges."

"Later. I've got a sick man here."

Dave was getting good at body-fluid lab work-ups. He was mastering the new tricks he had had to work out for handling liquids in weightlessness, using surface-tension effects and wetting characteristics to their fullest extent to control the liquids. It took him less than an hour to compile the complete data.

And it didn't make sense to Tom.

There was a slight electrolyte imbalance, but nothing beyond what he saw every day in the analysis of his staff's physiology.

The work-up showed a slight hypoglycemia, which might presage the onset of diabetes mellitus but which was not reflected in the urine sample. Tom had thought about this possibility. Ross was of the age when the disease could manifest itself. But the other symptoms weren't present. And the man said he hadn't eaten recently, which could also explain the low glucose level in the urine sample as well as the low blood-sugar level.

Ross couldn't be suffering from anorexia. By reputation the astronaut was something of a trencherman, and he did have difficulty keeping his body mass under control. Ross showed no tendency toward obesity; he just liked to eat well.

Serum calcium level was 12.1 milligrams per hundred milliliters—high, but not beyond what Tom saw occasionally, usually that was because of calcium resorption in the blood resulting from calcium loss in the bones.

Urine PH normal. Everything within normal range except for the usual suppression of steroids and increases in primary hormone levels associated with orbital living.

"Damn!" he swore under his breath.

But Lucky heard him, anyway. "Stumped, huh?"

"You've got it."

"I thought you were a smart doctor."

"Sometimes I wonder."

"It's a relief to hear a modern doctor admit that. My dad never ceases to admit he doesn't know everything."

"You must admire your father."

"I do. He's a fine doctor. Know what he'd do in a situation like this?"

"Yes. Excuse himself, and in the absence of the patient, take down a medical book and look it up."

"Right."

"And that's just what I'm going to do," Tom decided and pushed off for the GALEN terminal, "except this place isn't conducive to privacy."

"I don't think Ross is paying any attention to you," Lucky remarked, indicating where Dorothy had secured the astronaut to a treatment table. He was nodding because the prochlorperazine was relaxing him.

Tom keyed the terminal and fed in the blood and urine data. He then typed in the observed symptoms and called for a probable diagnosis.

As usual, GALEN was fast. Almost as quickly as he had hit the *RUN* key, it flashed its answer across the screen:

FIRM DIAGNOSIS NOT POSSIBLE WITH DATA PROVIDED. DIAGNOSIS ONE OF THREE POSSIBILITIES: 1. ADDISON'S DISEASE, BUT DATA INDICATING INCREASED PIGMENTATION OF THE DERMIS AND DISCOLORATION OF ORAL AND

NASAL MUCOUS MEMBRANES NOT PROVIDED. 2. HYPER-
CALCEMIA, BUT DIAGNOSIS REQUIRES CONFIRMATION
THAT Q-T INTERVAL OF ECG IS SHORTENED. 3. DIABE-
TES MELLITUS, EXCEPT URINALYSIS DOES NOT TOTALLY
SUPPORT THIS AND THEREFORE POSSIBILITY MUST BE
CONSIDERED REMOTE. PLEASE PROVIDE ADDITIONAL
DATA FOLLOWING POSSIBILITY NUMBER GIVEN ABOVE.
STANDING BY.

"Dorothy, warm up the ECG," Tom called.

Ross revived at this and understood what Tom was
talking about. "Oh, no, Doc! Not my heart! I haven't
got chest pains! I've got gut pains."

"Don't worry, it's not your heart, but I have to check
your ECG to confirm a diagnosis," Tom tried to reas-
sure him.

In less than five minutes, Tom had the answer.

"There it is: shortened Q-T interval on the electro-
cardiogram." He showed the printout to Ross.

"What's that mean, Doc?" The anxiety in the astronaut's voice penetrated the lethargy that the relaxant
drug had caused.

"Hypercalcemia. I'd call it the Ancient Astronaut
Syndrome. You've been in weightlessness more than
anyone else in GEO Base, Ross. All of us are suffering
from some decalcification of our bone mass because
our skeletons aren't supporting the weight of our bodies. The calcium is resorbed into the cellular fluid and
then into the blood serum. You're reacting in a text-
book manner to the fact your body's having trouble getting rid of the excess calcium being poured into your
system from your bones."

"Will it ground me?" Ross asked

"I won't ground you, Ross, because I can treat this
syndrome," Tom told him. "It's no more incapacitating
than any endocrine imbalance, and it can be treated
and controlled. People are flying airplanes all over the
world with hyperthyroidism, hypothyroidism, hyperuri-
cemia, and a whole list of other endocrine and metabolic disorders. Chemotherapy solves their problems
and permits them to function normally. I'm going to do

the same for you and put you on fifty milligrams of prednisone every day; you'll just have to take a pill every time you have breakfast. You're the first case of hypercalcemia I've seen in space. Frankly, you're going to be a guinea pig for the rest of us. For right now, I want to keep you here under observation for twenty-four hours—just to make sure I'm right. Then I'll clear you to flight status, but only for a single mission to LEO Base and back. You've got to report back here for a quick test every time you hit GEO Base. Understood?"

"Roger your last, Doc! Hey, thanks. I know doctors who'd ground me for less than this." Relief was evident in his voice. "Doc, you can use me as a guinea pig any time you want," Ross said.

"Okay, now get some rest," Tom instructed. "Nat's taking your flight down to LEO Base. Don't sweat it."

Tom turned to where Lucky had been watching. "He'll be all right, Lucky. Better get moving if you're going to catch the *Edison*."

Lucky was staring at him with a strange look on her face. It was almost an expression of sudden recognition—or, Tom thought, of admiration that was no longer grudgingly given. He thought he knew why, and he anticipated that Lucky would react to cover it by putting up her defenses again.

She did. "There's over an hour left. Don't try to get rid of me!"

"If you act like a child, I will. I prefer adult women."

His rejoinder was a bit too sharp for her, although he had said it jocularly and had a smile on his face. "Well, that hasn't been obvious from your immediate past! Dorothy, try to keep him from cradle-robbing before I get back to make sure he's behaving himself!" And with that she was gone.

Tom had to admit it would be a real challenge to try to blunt Lucky's temper and bring some security into her life again. He wasn't sure he could do it, but he was finding himself increasingly anxious to give it a try.

Chapter Thirteen

From the Galen Journal of Dr. T. K. Noels:

Ross Jackson recovered from the attack of acute hypercalcemia within twenty-four hours, just as I'd anticipated.

I feel stupid that I didn't spot the problem immediately from the symptoms, because I should have been looking for the consequences of calcium resorption at a greater rate than usual, and therefore having a greater effect on an individual's physiology. I'd been lulled into thinking of it as a nonproblem because everyone else appeared to be coping with calcium resorption.

This should reinforce what I was taught: People can and usually do react differently from individual to individual. Homo sapiens Mark One Model One is a generalization. There's something known as a Gaussian distribution, the bell-shaped curve. It gives us headaches occasionally, but better the bell curve than total equality that narrows the curve to a single point on the graph. We don't need to worry. Not even our mass-produced machines can avoid the statistical reality of the Gaussian distribution. Why should we try to shoehorn humanity into a single point on the graph when the universe is constructed differently? There's no such thing as "equality" in the universe, or in—

Sorry that this journal was suddenly interrupted, but we just went through a major crisis in GEO Base.

It was caused when Pratt pulled his life-support techs off GEO Base maintenance and had them modifying P-

suit backpacks to prevent any possibility of another backpack fire.

Within eighteen hours, a patient showed up with a 101.2 fever, mild nausea, and influenzalike symptoms. I was in sleep phase at the time, so Dorothy hospitalized the rigger and tried to make him comfortable. When I awoke, she had the work-ups ready, but there was nothing to indicate the nature of the complaint. Even GALEN couldn't come up with anything, which was unusual. So Dave and I ran every test we could think of. It was only when Dave suggested we try zero-g electrophoresis separation of a liver biopsy sample that we found acute viral hepatitis type A3, for which there's no serologic marker; that's why it didn't show in the blood work-up.

Hepatitis A3's a nasty one, with a very short incubation period. There's been some speculation it got out of a Soviet bio-warfare lab. I wasn't worried about where it came from on Earth; I was primarily concerned with (a) finding out where it came from in GEO Base, and (b) how to protect the people here against contracting it, if possible.

Dave found the virus in the drinking water. We traced it back to the recycling system, where it had penetrated through a break in an osmotic filter. The malfunction of the filter hadn't been caught in routine maintenance because the life-support techs were working on backpack mods. The break was immediately repaired, but the barn door had been opened and the stuff was loose in GEO Base.

We didn't have enough whole blood in GEO Base to permit Dave to fractionate sufficient gamma globulin for eight hundred people. And we had no facilities to synthesize neogamma globulin-F. We needed it fast, but almost a day would be required to get it up from JSP because the Pot-Vees and Cot-Vees were located between LEO Base and GEO Base.

Colonel Owen Hocksmith provided the answer. We tend to forget about the military presence in space because it's highly secretive and because we don't interface with DOD on this job. But it's there, and it sure *saved our necks on this one. Smitty got on the horn to the Pentagon. I'm not exactly sure whose arms he twisted or how he managed to get hold of them to twist in the first place, but he got results. The Air Force replaced the warhead of a ground-launched satellite interceptor missile with enough neogamma globulin-F to immunize a thousand people and shot it at GEO Base. The direct boost from the surface was much faster than staging the payload through a transfer at LEO Base, and the boost could be faster because the missile was unmanned and remotely controlled from something the Air Force has over at the L-5 lunar libration point. We're not supposed to know about that. Fred and Stan had the Pumpkin rendezvous with the missile as it crawled past GEO Base, pulled the serum out of the warhead compartment, and the ranch was saved—so to speak. The Air Force didn't want us to say a lot about it, although they had acted in a humanitarian role much in keeping with American military history. The Air Force destructed the bird after we removed the payload.*

Most important, we didn't lose anybody to the hepatitis epidemic, and the eight people who came down with it bad enough to require hospitalization were back on the job shortly.

We earned our salary on that one. Even Herb Pratt has come around to accepting us fully, and now there's nothing but friendly cooperation from him. We might have lost some people; then again, we might not have.

Even at that, the Grim Reaper Count now stands at thirty-one. We can't protect the world from idiots, and any idiot out here can't look forward to living very long. Here, you live and learn—or you don't live, period.

We're learning.

"Med Center, this is GEO Base Central."

"Central, Med. Go ahead," Dorothy replied on the intercom.

"Med, emergency in progress. Please stand by for possible rescue attempt."

Tom had been updating the GALEN file with Jackson's latest data, but he powered-down and activated the intercom switch. "Central, this is Dr. Noels. Let me speak to Herb Pratt, please."

"The base boss is pretty busy."

"Put him on when he has a moment—unless you can give us some more details on this emergency," Tom told Central.

"Better stand by with Pumpkin," was the reply. "Array Subassembly Module Two Zero Two's on its way up from LEO Base. They've had an accident. The survivors are in the personnel module, with the life-support system out and only a UHF emergency locator transmitter with limited voice capability."

"How many casualties?" Tom asked.

"The brief report said three dead—one on EVA, the other two in the control module when it dumped to vacuum. The remaining four are apparently alive and uninjured in the personnel module, but they have life-support air for only an estimated seven hours."

Tom turned to Fred Fitzsimmons. "Stumpy, power-up the Pumpkin and be ready to go. I don't know where the subassembly is or whether we can reach it with the Pumpkin. I'm going to Central. Dorothy, get things ready here for hypoxia therapy and possible abaryia resuscitation."

Tom located Herb Pratt surrounded by a bank of readouts and panels at Central's main overview consoles. The base boss was on a four-way conference hook-up with Charlie Day at LEO Base, Dan Hills in Albuquerque, and Owen Hocksmith, who happened to be in his offices in Santa Fe that day, there being a legislative session in progress.

Tom floated up and arrested his motion by grasping a handhold and swinging around to where all the screens were visible.

"We've got Doc Noels here now," Pratt addressed the other three images on the screens. "Doc, are your people standing by to handle whatever medical problems might arise from this?"

"We're always ready for whatever crisis arises," Tom replied curtly. "Can you tell me what's going on, please?"

"Good idea, Doctor." Owen Hocksmith was being formal with his friend. This was no private videophone chat. "Herb, run through it again. Maybe one of us will come up with an idea how to save these people."

"You've got a problem? Where are the *Edison* and the *Steinmetz*? Can't those Pot-Vees rendezvous?"

"Doc, if you'll listen, you'll discover what our problems are," Pratt told him with uncharacteristic tact, either because he had really come to respect the GEO Base doctor or because the Hawk was on the conference net.

"Array Subassembly Module Two Zero Two left LEO Base on schedule," Pratt forged ahead. "According to its trajectory, the electric thrusters would boost it to GEO Base in seventeen-point-two hours. The normal crew of seven was aboard—two guidance-and-control technicians, two electric-thruster mechanics, two power-bus controllers, and the array commander. At fourteen-twenty-one, Zulu time, one of the electric-thruster mechanics, Bob Henson, got into his P-suit, cycled through the transfer lock, and powered-up the Eff-Mu to go out and check Thrusters Five and Eleven on the far dorsal surface of the array. Both thrusters were acting intermittently. There was no telemetry on the Eff-Mu, so we don't know what happened when Henson started to move out along the array. Maybe a thruster valve stuck—we'll never know. But he put the Eff-Mu right through the side of the pressurized control module.

"The pressure in the control module dumped immediately," Pratt continued soberly, "killing Lem Udevitz, the subassembly commander, and Sally Renquist, a control tech. As a matter of fact, they were blown out through the hole in the module wall. The presence of that much gas in the vicinity of the array, plus the pres-

ence of the Eff-Mu, which may also have dumped to
vacuum and added to the outgassing, caused the main
array bus-bar junctions near the control module to arc.
You don't short out a nineteen-megawatt array subassembly without fun and games. All the protective circuits activated. The bus bars acted like massive fuse
links and vaporized. We don't know what happened to
Henson and the Eff-Mu, but our radar signature says
the Eff-Mu isn't anywhere around the subassembly
now. It may have been vaporized in the arc-over, or it
may be tumbling out of control with all circuits dead
somewhere between here and LEO Base."

Pratt checked two computer display readouts. "They
lost most of the pressure in the living module before
somebody slapped something over the holes and sealed
them. Three of the survivors suffered the bends from
the rapid decompression. Fortunately, one of the
power-bus controllers was in her P-suit and was able to
act quickly enough to save most of the life-support con-
sumable gases for the module.

"At this point, four of them are still alive in P-suits
in the living module with emergency battery power for
illumination. They've got their P-suits plugged into the
emergency life-support fittings, and they're trying to
scavenge as much of the life-support consumables as
possible. The power-bus controller found the emergency locator transmitter, got it on the air, and transmitted the basic elements of this report. Then she shut
down the voice-transmission capability to conserve battery power. We're still picking up the locator signal."

Pratt looked around at the three screens and con-
cluded, "Here's the problem: They've got . . . uh
. . . seven-point-eight hours of life-support consumables left, according to calculations based on information
received in the brief ELT report. The *Edison* is one-
point-three hours from docking at LEO Base; no way
for Nat Wallace to turn it around and head for the accident scene. He's running heavy. He'll have to be re-
fueled, and that will take at least two hours after he

docks. There's no way he can make it to Two Zero Two before they run out of air.

"The *Steinmetz* is two-point-nine hours from docking at GEO Base, and Ross Jackson's running loaded with enough delta-v plus standard reserves to make GEO Base rendezvous, period. There's no way he can re-shape orbit to get to Two Zero Two in time, and when he got there he couldn't do anything because he has only enough life-support for his passenger manifest, plus normal reserves. He wouldn't have the delta-v cap-ability to get to either LEO Base or GEO Base after-ward. We'd just have a Pot-Vee and fifty more people stranded along with the subassembly."

Pratt looked around again. "That's it in a nutshell, confirmed as best we can by radar track and signature analysis from here. We're rechecking as many permuta-tions and combinations as possible with computer runs, looking for some trajectory that would let us rendez-vous a Pot-Vee with Two Zero Two, but we haven't found it yet."

"Who're the survivors?" It was Owen Hocksmith.

"One guidance-and-control tech, Pat Mulligan. One electric-thruster mechanic, Jim Service," Charlie Day announced from LEO Base as he checked his departure manifests. "And two power-bus controllers, Ed Swen-son and Lucky Hertzog—Lucky was the one in the P-suit when the accident happened, and she was the one who sent the report."

Lucky? In that accident? With less than eight hours of life-support left? And no way to get to them with the Pot-Vees? Tom swallowed and tried to think straight. Given the situation, what could be done? What could *he* do?

Finally, Owen Hocksmith broke the brief silence. "Four people and damned little time. Anybody got any ideas? To hell with the schedule, and to hell with the rules! Somehow, we've got to make an effort to get to them. No, we've *got* to get to them and bring them out of this alive!"

There was silence from everyone on the conference net.

"Dammit!" Hocksmith exploded. "We move thousands of tons of cargo and hundreds of people around in orbit every day! Surely there's some way we can get to four people in a transfer orbit within seven hours and with enough life-support to keep them alive, even if it's for just long enough to get a Pot-Vee turned around and on its way."

Dan Hills spoke up earnestly. "Let's think about that one. We don't have to get them and get back. We just have to get *to* them within seven hours with enough oxygen to sustain them until we *can* get a Pot-Vee there. Charlie, Herb, what do you have up there that one man can boost and control, carry about fifty man-hours of Oh-two, no guidance system, vectors being fed to the pilot verbally from analysis of the radar track?"

"I haven't got an Eff-Mu big enough," Charlie Day replied. "How about it, Herb? You've got Eff-Mus that are bigger. Do any of them have the delta-v to reach Two Zero Two in time with a pilot and fifty man-hours of Oh-two?"

"Hold on, let me get a readout on the delta-v required for a seven-hour rendezvous." Prat turned and began to dance his fingers over the keypad of the computer. "Dan, I haven't got the computer power here to figure it. Get your big general-purpose unit on line so I can work with it."

"Why don't you feed me the data, Herb, and I'll input the computer here. It would take fifteen-twenty minutes to set up the link," Hills told him.

"Okay, this is radar data I'm reading off our plots here, reference is GEO Base, and time is . . . Mark! Now!" Pratt began to call strings of numbers to Dan Hills in Albuquerque.

Tom moved to another keypad and display. He had an idea. He didn't know if it would work or not. He couldn't do the math, and he couldn't program the computer. But he had access to a very large general-purpose computer net: GALEN. He didn't know if

GALEN could handle celestial mechanics, but he could certainly ask.

It could, using its links through EuroMed to computers in Brussels and London, plus a link into a DOD computer net through Bethesda Naval Hospital. He asked GALEN and its peripheral systems to solve the problem for him. GALEN already had all the parameters on the Pumpkin. All Tom had to do was feed it numbers on the location and trajectory of Two Zero Two and the location and orbit of GEO Base. He asked for graphic visual displays of the results as well as hard copy.

When he was through, he had the answer.

Dan Hills and Herb Pratt didn't. "Mr. Hocksmith, the mission's beyond the delta-v capabilities of any of our Eff-Mu vehicles," Dan Hills announced. "They were designed as short-range craft for getting around the SPS during construction. They don't have very much delta-v as a result."

"You're the most negative problem solvers I've ever seen!" Hocksmith snapped back. "Four people out there, and we can't come up with a way to get to them in time? Do you know what this could mean, gentlemen? It could mean that we get shut down for killing too many people. The hue and cry of the press could trigger the politicians and bureaucrats to do something, anything, to stop what they consider to be slaughter. We're already in that position, as you damned well know. We're supposed to be the world's brightest people when it comes to space transportation. We've built and operated the biggest space transportation system in history. And we can damned well figure out some way to make it work to save four people! *Think!*"

Tom tapped Pratt on the shoulder and motioned for him to move over so he could get in the pickup's field. The action came as such a surprise to Pratt that he moved immediately without a word. Tom didn't bother strapping himself into the GEO Base engineer's seat, he curled his legs underneath and held himself effortlessly in position as if he had been doing it for years. "Smitty, I've got an answer," he told his old friend.

Pratt looked at him with a start. Nobody used a nickname when talking to the Hawk!

"What is it, T.K.?"

"The *Pumpkin,* the GEO Base ambulance you designed for us, Smitty," Tom explained. "It's got more delta-v than any Eff-Mu because we need to move around *fast* here, which means high-g and gobs of thrust—in comparison, that is. It's normally rated for a thousand pounds of payload. I've just been working with the GALEN computer, and I asked it whether or not I could get there as a single pilot in a P-suit with a cargo of five fifty-cubic-foot Oh-two backpack bottles. That's about a hundred fifty pounds, plus me in a P-suit at two hundred pounds. Just to be on the safe side, I figured five hundred pounds; I may need some medical gear because three of those people are in severe pain with the bends. I can get there with the Pumpkin and enough Oh-two to save them. But I can't get back. You'll have to come rescue me with the *Edison* or the *Steinmetz.* That'll give you ten hours after I make rendezvous. *I* can do it! Can *you* get to me in seventeen hours?"

"I won't let you go," was the comment from Hocksmith.

"I won't let Stan or Fred go. I'm a doctor, and those people may need a doctor, not a paramedic," Tom explained.

"We can get to you," Pratt put in, looking at the display screen linked to GEO Base computer. "It'll be close, but we'll get there. Better take a couple of spare bottles, Doc, just in case."

"Can't. I'll be rendezvousing with electric thrusters as it is. Barely enough propellant to get me started and almost stopped. When it's that critical, I want about five-percent reserve. Just get there within ten hours after I do, Herb."

Charlie Day broke in. "We'll start from this end with the *Edison,* too. We'll come after you from LEO *and*

GEO. This operation's got to have some redundancy built in somewhere!"

"Okay, I'll be depending on both of you after I get to Two Zero Two," Tom said. "I'll fly by vectors from GEO Base radars and lidars. Herb, have your gang track me and give me those vectors. You'll have my position, my trajectory, and your computer power—in short, all the data you'll need. All I need is communication with you. No other way to do it."

"You're right," Herb remarked.

"Tom, forget it! You're not going!" Hocksmith yelled.

"Smitty, *you* forget it! And shut up! You're sitting on your ass down there with gravity and an atmosphere around you. Don't try to run this operation by long distance. Herb, Charlie, and Dan work for you as employees—they've *got* to follow your orders. But I'm one of your contractors, and the *Pumpkin* was bailed to me by Eden Corporation. So you can't tell me what to do at all! Or do you want four people to die?"

Hocksmith threw up his hands. "Goddamnit, go get 'em, T.K.! But please be careful!"

"A martyr I'm not," Tom replied flatly. "Let's go, Herb. Time's a-wasting!"

Tom didn't mention that one of the four castaways was a woman he didn't want to see die. He had already had too many women in his life die. As far as he was concerned, this was the turning point; he wasn't going to let Lucky Hertzog die. And that was all there was to it.

Tom was a little under his mass estimate. He did take a few extra backpack bottles and the equivalent of a spare fan belt. "I want a hand-portable communicator or a booster amplifier on my backpack radio, Herb. I will have to go EVA to get aboard Two Zero Two, and I want to be able to talk to you if necessary. I also want the unit as an ELT if something happens."

"We'll give you a little extra delta-v, Tom," Pratt told him. "I'll have three of our Eff-Mus couple to you during GEO Base departure boost and supplement your own thruster on the *Pumpkin*. They'll undock after they've boosted you. Sort of a two-stage vehicle. Computer says that'll give you a ten-percent reserve—slim, but a hundred-percent improvement on the five-percent reserve you thought you'd need."

"Still going to be close, but thanks for the additional help," Tom said as Fred buddy-checked the P-suit connections.

"Doc, I'll go aboard with you and check your connections into the Pumpkin's life-support system. No use using up your suit bottles until absolutely necessary," Fred pointed out.

Tom slapped Herb on the shoulder, an unexpected movement that almost sent the base boss spinning off across the docking module. "Herb, I'll be talking with you!"

"Fly low and slow," Pratt said in the pilot's classic farewell. "I've got my best people on this one, Tom."

"As long as you're in charge, I'm not going to worry," Tom said over his shoulder. Then he passed through the hatch into the Pumpkin.

Fred fretted over him as he strapped in, and began checking hoses and fittings.

"Dammit, Fred, you're like a mother hen!"

"Just don't want this mission to lay an egg, Doc. Okay, you're wired up as if you were in intensive care! Don't try to be a hero and end up dead, huh? I know what's between you and Lucky."

"Oh? Get out of here Fred! See you when I get back!"

The undocking was very gentle. Tom was reluctant to use any delta-v he didn't have to. As he backed away from the med module's docking port, he saw on his displays that three Eff-Mus had drawn alongside. Into his helmet speaker came the voice of one of the Eff-Mu drivers. "Pumpkin, Eff-Mu Fourteen. We're ready to move in and couple. Don't try to hold position; let us move on you."

"Roger, Eff-Mu. GEO Base, Pumpkin, radio check."

"Loud and clear, Pumpkin. How me?"

"Five by. While the Eff-Mus are coupling up, let's check the data links."

"Go ahead, Pumpkin."

Tom exercised his small on-board computer, testing its megabyte memory and squirting the test data on the up-link to GEO Base, where the GEO computer examined it, determined it was all there, and echoed it back to the Pumpkin accompanied by its own test data. Within three seconds, the two computers were happy with each other and in communication.

"Pumpkin, GEO Base," Pratt's voice called. "The Eff-Mus will maneuver you into boost attitude. We're working this mission with Earth-oriented references, equatorial category."

Tom informed his computer and control systems. "Okay, Geo Base. Pumpkin's ready for attitude positioning."

The three Eff-Mus gently lined up the Pumpkin.

"Close enough," Herb told Tom. "Your down-link data matches. Computer's grinding out the final trajectory elements. Stand by for real-time updates on the up-link."

When the Pumpkin boosted from GEO Base on its errand of mercy, the computer estimated that Two Zero Two had six-point-nine hours of life-support available. The estimated trajectory time was six-point-eight hours.

"I don't like those numbers, Herb. Too many chances for error, and I know this is only a quarter-percent data."

"No, we've got very accurate info on Two Zero Two. Air Force is feeding us their SpaceTrak data, too, and it cross-checks."

"Okay, Eff-Mus have separated," Tom reported, "and I'm getting a solid up-link data signal. I'm on manual control."

"Roger."

When Tom had taken flight training from Dick Callins at the Roswell airport years before, he never thought he would find that detestable simulated-instrument hood training useful in flying a spacecraft.

But that was exactly what he was doing. Instrument flight training had taught him to ignore the inputs from his otoliths and his kinesthetic senses, to give up flying by the seat of his pants. Then, as now, he was forced to rely only on the data that was presented to him by instruments. And it required the same degree of control precision—only the data presentation was slightly different.

He still had a gyro attitude indicator and a gyro vector indicator. Otherwise, the instruments were fully electronic.

It was a simple task for computers. Radar and lidar from LEO Base, GEO Base, and the Earth's surface tracked the Great Pumpkin's beacon, providing the computers with direction, range, and Doppler relative velocity. The computers were also receiving tracking data from the ELT beacon in Two Zero Two; they knew where it was and where it was going to be. The instructions for right-left, up-down, and fast-slow were transmitted to the Pumpkin on the data up-link, where the ship's computer converted the data for display, telling Tom how and how much to change direction or thrust. The Pumpkin's simple autopilot couldn't be used on this long flight because neither it nor the Pumpkin's inertial guidance system had the accuracy required. They didn't have to be accurate for operating around GEO Base and the SPS assembly; they just had to keep general track of where the Pumpkin was. Thus, Tom had to fly the Pumpkin by hand, keeping dots of light centered on displays and making sure that the indicators on graphic displays stayed right on the lines.

It wasn't difficult, because nothing happened very fast as long as Tom kept on top of things constantly.

"Going right down the tunnel, Pumpkin," Pratt told him.

"Any further messages from Two Zero Two, Herb?"

"Nothing but the beacon signal," the base boss reported. "Its code hasn't changed and indicates the situation's the same."

"Any way to get word to them that we're coming?"

"They have no receiver, and they're sealed in that living module, so there's no way to send even a laser signal to them."

"That's got to be grim," Tom observed.

The Pumpkin was coming up on final trajectory velocity. Tom concentrated on the displays, his hand on the main throttle with the vernier throttles just below. He was also receiving a verbal countdown from Pratt. Five feet per second short of final velocity, he chopped the main engine and used the verniers to bring the Pumpkin to precisely the required velocity.

"Looks good, Pumpkin. Right down the pike. Take five, because we won't do a mid-course correction for two hours yet. I want to let the trajectory errors build until we've got a reliable track that we can correct with greater precision. No sense burning up vernier delta-v by correcting every little glitch in the radar track."

Tom couldn't help but think of Lucky Hertzog, trapped in that can, knowing how much oxygen was remaining but not knowing whether anybody was on the way, and not being able to find out. He agonized because he knew it must be hell. On the other hand, he didn't think Lucky would come apart under the circumstances. She was made of stout stuff. He knew there would be no hysteria, only tight-jawed discipline right to the very end if necessary.

He didn't realize that he was fantasizing long-cherished ideals of his mental image of a perfect woman, one he could admire as well as love. Real or not, he was building his psychological perception of Lucky Hertzog perhaps far beyond her true characteristics. But he didn't think so, and he wouldn't have cared if he had known. At that point, he was only obsessed with reaching her in time.

He hadn't been able to get to Julie Lea in time.

He was determined not to repeat history with Lucky.

"Pumpkin, GEO Base. Here's your latest ETA at Two Zero Two." Herb's voice returned him to reality. "It's tight, Tom. The estimate's converged with the flight time. We show a rendezvous only five minutes before life-support exhaustion. I think it's too close to call. Let's hope Two Zero Two has instituted drastic conservation measures. If they have, you'll make it."

"I refuse to trust any computer when it comes to that close a call on the chances of living or dying," Tom snapped back. "I'll make it, Herb, because we're dealing with people, not with computers."

He hoped he was right.

Chapter Fourteen

Tom saw it on the forward screen through a ghostly haze of electric-thruster plasma. The huge solar array gleamed in the sunlight and bright specular reflections overloaded the video pickup, causing streaks of overexcited display phosphor to paint wiggly lines on the tube face. He fired the vernier thrusters carefully to rendezvous as precisely as possible with the personnel module that appeared only as a tiny polygon on the near end

According to the digital readout, he didn't have a foot-second of delta-v to spare.

The computer also told him he was running out of time.

He'd have to move in on the personnel module with one single continuous application of the thruster in order to save time. Then he'd have to do a fast EVA.

He had prepared for that. During the hours of coast-in, he'd pumped the Pumpkin's cabin atmosphere back into the ship's life-support system and carefully blown-down the cabin to vacuum; in fact, he had used the blow-down to provide some fractional delta-v, which gave him a trifle more reserve. He'd even opened the hatch to vacuum. When he got to Two Zero Two, he was ready to move—*fast*.

Suddenly his instruments began reporting relative velocity between the Pumpkin and Two Zero Two. The computer was presenting projections and forecasts of future velocities, positions, and closing rates. He knew he would have to be exceptionally precise and that he had only one chance. He realized that this was the same degree of precision he had to exercise as a surgeon, and, as in surgery, he had only one opportunity to succeed.

"Gently! Positive pitch! Too much, back it off! Bang yaw right a couple of times. Coming right on in." Tom talked to himself as he often did during an operation or during instrument approaches in his Maule. "GEO Base, Pumpkin! Closing nicely. I'm videotaping the monitors, but I'll give you a verbal . . . There's a big hole in the side of the command module and a series of smaller holes in the personnel module. The ones in the personnel module look as if they've been sealed from the inside. There're no lights showing. I'm receiving only the modulated r-f signal from the ELT. Okay, closing slowly . . . Ten feet and dead in space. I'm holding it there. I don't want to bump the personnel module because I don't know what internal damage it's suffered, and it could collapse if I whanged it. How's my timing?"

"Tom, it's too close to call," Pratt admitted.

"Okay, I'm uncoupling, going to backpack. My transmission may get garbled because I'm switching to the booster transmitter strapped to the backpack. Now I'm free. Moving to the hatch, hauling the backpack bottles with me. Out of the hatch. What a mess! Everything seems to be covered with a grayish deposit. Probably vapor deposition caused by the arc-over. The survivors are lucky. The reflectance of that coating is probably just enough to maintain a comfortable interior temperature in the personnel module."

Tom pushed off the five feet across the void to the damaged module, not even taking the time to latch a safety line. He hit with both feet and bounced back in spite of the fact that he had used his knees to absorb his momentum. He would have bounded right back to the Pumpkin's hatch except for the two-hundred-pound bag of backpack oxygen bottles in his left hand. Its momentum forced him around as it kept going and thudded into the module. He planted his feet on the module again, looked for handholds, found them, and pulled himself to the hatch.

He banged on the closed hatch and could feel the vibrations through the soles of his P-suit boots.

There was no response.

"Dammit, I'm too late!"

He tried to twist the latch, but couldn't do it. He had to hold on to the bag of oxygen bottles with his left hand and, therefore, could work only with his right. His body twisted instead. So he banged again, hoping he might somehow dislodge the hatch-closure dogs or that someone might detect his banging and open from inside.

"Open up! For God's sake, open up!" He found himself screaming in his helmet that was pressed against the hatch. Maybe his voice would penetrate by direct contact.

He almost fell into the module when the hatch suddenly swung open.

And he found himself faceplate to faceplate with Lucky. She touched helmets, and he heard her say, "Well, you took long enough to get here, but did you have to make such a racket?" She reached out, put her arms around the neck of his P-suit, and hauled him into the module.

And she continued to hold him tight.

It's not easy to do a good job of hugging somebody when both parties are in P-suits. But Lucky did her best, and Tom found himself reciprocating. They held their helmets tightly together, and Tom reached up to turn off his booster radio transmitter. What he wanted to say was for Lucky alone, not for the universe, and the range of the P-suit radio wouldn't carry back to GEO Base.

If it hadn't been for the helmets, Tom would have kissed her, but kissing in a P-suit isn't exacty the most exciting way to do it. There hadn't been tears in Lucky's eyes when she opened the hatch, but she was crying now, and that wasn't a good idea in a P-suit, either. Her lips were slightly blue instead of their normal red, and she was acting punchy.

Disentangling himself, he reached for the bag, grabbed a bottle, and snapped the hose fitting into the auxiliary fitting on her suit. As he was doing so, she switched on her suit radio. "Oh, I'm glad to see you!" her voice came to him. "I'm *so* glad to see you, honey! I knew you'd come! I knew where all the Pot-Vees were, and I knew you were the only one who could get to us because of the Pumpkin!"

"The Pot-Vees are on the way. Lucky, how did you stay alive? The pressure gauge on your backpack reads only one psi—and it may be stuck."

"You weren't born at ten thousand feet," Lucky told him. "I can get by on very little oxygen when I have to. And I know a little yoga."

"If I'd had communications with you, I would have told you about some techniques I picked up in India. But, God, I'm glad you didn't need them!"

"No, I don't need them, but I think I do need you, dear. Come on, my partners are in worse shape." She was breathing hard, her lungs taking up oxygen she had been denying them, but she was ready and willing to go to work on her three companions.

They *were* in worse shape than Lucky. In the first place, they had suffered from decompression, which had resulted in the bends. Their lips were blue. All three were either unconscious or semiconscious, but they soon had oxygen flowing into their P-suits.

"How are you?" Tom asked her once he had made sure that Pat Mulligan, Jim Service, and Ed Swenson had an adequate oxygen supply. "Are you okay? Anything broken? Anything bruised? Do you feel all right?"

"One hundred percent better than I did a few minutes ago, dear."

"What's with this 'dear' stuff?" Tom asked.

"If we weren't wearing P-suits, you'd find out! And when we can take them off, you'll find out for sure," she promised.

"You're obviously suffering from hypoxia," Tom

said, but he really didn't mean it. "And claustrophobia as well. You've been in this can too long."

"You bet I have! Long enough to do a lot of thinking when I wasn't providing entertainment for my compatriots," Lucky admitted.

"Entertainment?"

"Longest poker game I was ever in."

"Did you win?"

"Of course!" She bent over to read what was scribbled on a pad of paper on the eating table. "Only six thousand bucks, which is kinda lousy for all the time it took! The last pot was five hundred and fifty bucks before Ed finally became so uncoordinated he dropped out, leaving me no one to play with."

"Listen, my lucky girl, do you mean to tell me you spent all those hours since the accident playing poker in here?"

"Oh, no! We had to work out our survival plan first. Once we did that, there was nothing else we could do but wait," Lucky explained. "I wasn't going to sit around, stare at the walls, and go stir-crazy. So we had a friendly little game. Kept me from going bonkers. Same with the others. They were more worried about how much they were losing than about whether or not somebody would come to save our necks in time."

Tom grinned. "You are something else!"

Even through the transparent plastic of her helmet's faceplate, Lucky's eyes twinkled. "My dear, you are going to find out even more than that the instant I can manage to get you trapped alone somewhere."

"You're still running a tad shy on oxygen. I'd better check you for brain damage when we get back to GEO Base."

"When we get back to GEO Base, you can check me for anything you want. Tom, my dear, I had a lot of time to think."

"Pumpkin, GEO Base! Pumpkin, GEO Base! How do you read?" Pratt's amplified voice boomed into his helmet.

"Hang in there, Lucky. Hyperventilate if you want.

Get all that carbon dioxide flushed out of your system. I've gotta talk to Pratt." Tom switched on his transmitter booster. "GEO Base, Pumpkin here. Sorry; I got shielded from you. Read you loud and clear. I got them, Herb! I got to them in time! They're all right!"

"Hot damn!" It was the first time Tom had ever heard joy in the GEO Base Engineer's voice. "Damned good work, Tom! Right on the button all the way! Jackson just boosted out of here with the *Steinmetz* to pick everybody up, and Nat's on the way up from LEO Base with a repair crew. Ross also has a load of propellant so you can bring the Pumpkin back."

"How long do we have to wait, Herb? We've only got ten hours' oxygen."

"Jackson's scheduled to rendezvous in five hours and ten minutes. Think you can keep yourself occupied until then?"

Tom looked at Lucky and saw her smile. "We might, Herb," he reported. "We haven't got much on-board power here, just enough for one or two lights, but we can move to the Pumpkin if we have to. Just don't dawdle; these suit collection bags are designed for only an eight-hour shift."

"Fill up the boots if need be. I think we can give you clean P-suits when the Pot-Vees get there." Herb's voice was greatly relieved now, and his sometime sense of humor crept in, which was highly unusual. "How about shooting me a status report every hour just so we know you're still there?"

"Can do. But we'll be okay. Where do you think we can go without propellant? Right now, I've got work to do. I'll be back with you, so stand by this freq." He switched off his booster transmitter.

The other three were groggy but coming out of their hypoxia. Most had headaches, and all complained of aches in their joints. Tom managed to get analgesic capsules through their helmet pass valves. It was easy enough to put Pat Mulligan to sleep and make Ed Swenson and Jim Service groggy.

But he couldn't keep Lucky down. "Lucky, dear,

you've been through a rough stretch. Your system's loaded up with cee-oh-two and you're probably acidotic. Come on, now. Take this sedative and rest. Everything's okay."

She put her helmet against his. "*No!* Tom, I've *got* to talk to you. Not later. Not at GEO Base. *Now!*"

"Okay, talk," Tom said. He stowed his medical kit and returned to where Lucky floated in the wan light of the single bulb that illuminated the module. He touched his helmet to hers. "My transmitter's off. Ain't nobody here but just us chickens as long as we use helmet contact for communications."

"Tom, dearest, I didn't play poker the entire time we were waiting for you to come," she admitted.

"I know that. You said so." He paused, then continued. "And there were long hours during coast-in when I'd done everything I could except wait. I wasn't even sure I was going to get here in time. The computers said it was too close to call. I wouldn't have made it if all of you hadn't gone to a reduced metabolic mode."

"Oh, stop using medical terminology!" Lucky remonstrated. "We all knew we'd last longer if we cut our Oh-two consumption. Tom, do you know what I was thinking about while I was waiting?"

"Do you know what I was thinking about while *I* was waiting?"

"I don't have to guess. Do you?"

"Not really, Lucky." He wished the P-suits weren't between them. It made the conversation decidedly nonphysical. "Lucky, let's stop taking each other for granted, shall we?"

"Tom, you remind me of my dad. That's what attracted me to the med module every time I was in GEO Base."

"I spotted it, too, Lucky. But I'm not your father, and I could never measure up to that man."

"What do you know about him?"

"A great deal. As much as I know about you. I looked up your med records, then I asked GALEN for a bio on your dad."

"You dirty dog! No, I shouldn't say that . . . because I had Dad look you up, too. I know a lot about you, Tom."

"I think," Tom observed, "that's going to save us both a lot of time."

"Yes, because I don't want to wait to get to know you, not a day more than is necessary. But I *do* want to get to know you better—much better." She was quiet for a moment, as if debating with herself whether or not to say what she wanted to, then went ahead anyway. "Do I remind you of Julie Lea, Tom? Am I going to be able to replace her in your life?"

"Julie Lea's dead," Tom said suddenly, and then realized it was the first time he had admitted it aloud. "Nobody can ever replace her in my life, but that doesn't mean there's no place for you. There's a lot of room—a whole lifetime. I don't have the slightest notion why I slowly fell in love with you, and I don't know when it really happened. I only know that I thought a lot about us when I was piloting the Pumpkin here, and I honestly didn't know how I'd handle things if I were too late."

"You didn't?"

"No."

"I thought you had that good old professional detachment toward people."

"You know better. That's a fiction dreamed up by writers. If it looks as if a doctor's being professionally objective, it's because he's fighting hard to control the extreme empathy he feels for *everybody*, sick or well."

"You're an exasperating, hyperlogical, overly sensitive doctor who tries to cover up with that good old professional detachment. But I love you for it anyway! I'm going to demolish that professional attitude of yours and turn you into a simpering, lovesick swain. Let's sneak back into the Pumpkin and pressurize the cabin!"

"Not enough air to do it." He disentangled his left P-suit arm and looked at the digital timer strapped to it.

"We'll be at GEO Base in about ten hours. Think you can control yourself until then?"

"Won't people talk, or were you figuring on admitting me to the med module for observation?"

"I'm going to observe you plenty. Does Herb Pratt have the authority to perform marriages as the civil as well as the technical boss of GEO Base?"

"Why, Doctor, I never thought you'd ask! If that's a proposal, it's the strangest one I've ever received."

"How many have you received?"

"Just that one, which makes it automatically the strangest," Lucky admitted. "I accept. But Ross Jackson's a minister in a church that was formed by some of the old NASA astronauts. He can perform the ceremony in the Pot-Vee heading back to GEO Base. We'd save a couple hours that way."

"No," Tom said, "let's wait until we get to GEO Base. I think you should be properly dressed for the wedding . . ."

From the Galen Journal of Dr. T. K. Noels:

This is the last entry I'm going to make in my journal. I will continue the professional log, but I no longer need this personal catharsis. Yesterday, Ellen Adele Hertzog and I were married by the Reverend Ross Jackson.

Smitty was madder than hell. He had to play best man by videophone and he didn't get to kiss the bride. Herb Pratt comported himself in a manner he can be proud of and managed to handle the assignment that Smitty delegated to him for the occasion. Smitty discovered some things can't be delegated.

It was a good party, I'm told. Even a day later, I don't remember too much about it except Lucky, and she occupied my full attention.

One of the secrets of good medical procedure is to know when to stop using a crutch or depending on a prescription. Julie Lea, I still love you, wherever you are. But I also love Lucky. And there's enough love in me to share it with both of you.

* * *

"Smitty, why did you demand I come back now?" Tom complained. He preferred to remain sitting; the persistent tug of terrestrial gravity seemed strange to him. "Jim Bradley's been with me only two weeks, and I'm not sure he can handle everything yet, in spite of Dorothy."

"Tom, you went up there eight months ago and you didn't know a thing about how to practice medicine in orbit," Hocksmith pointed out. "I knew you'd manage to cut it. Now you've got to have the same sort of confidence in the doctor *you've* hired."

"It isn't just that, Smitty."

"Why didn't you bring Lucky with you, then? I want to meet her," Hocksmith told his friend as he leaned back in his working chair.

"You'll have to come to GEO Base, Smitty. She's three months pregnant."

"So? Bring her down here, and she'll get the finest possible care. I'll see to that."

Tom shook his head, a most unnatural action for him now. It didn't bother him. He felt better than when he had landed at JSP the day before. His strength and old habit patterns were returning. "We don't want to. More particularly, Lucky doesn't want to. And she's getting good care in GEO Base, Smitty: my care."

"But why take the chance? Nobody's given birth in weightlessness before."

"That's one reason she's staying up there. Somebody has to be first," Tom said firmly. "Smitty, I'll need more gynecology capability than I have now, and I'll have to expand my obstetrics capability and facilities sooner than *you* think. People are people. They come in two sexes and have a tendency to fall in love and make babies. They're no different in GEO Base." He paused, then added, "It may be safer for Lucky up there. She has a small pelvis and a rare blood type."

"Aren't you afraid you'll lose her in that different environment?'

"No. Not Lucky. Not in GEO Base. Not even if we

' have one hell of a flare storm. In spite of sixty-seven deaths putting the pilot satellite on line, Smitty, GEO Base is a healthier place to live. In the twenty-four hours since I've been back, I've caught a head cold, and I've got to kick it before I leave."

"Well, don't worry about it, because you're not going back up for long," Hocksmith suddenly announced.

Tom started to rise from the easy chair, then decided against it. "What?" he exploded.

"I don't want you to go back permanently for a number of reasons, T.K. First of all, you've got a going thing up there now, and you've got to train more people to handle the medical services of LEO Base and two more GEO Bases coming up. You knew your rescue of Two Zero Two put us over the top, didn't you?"

"You didn't mention it to me."

"Well, we haven't talked by videophone as often as we did before you and Lucky were hitched. If you watched TV, you know that you, Lucky, and Ross Jackson were big heroes. Your marriage to Lucky was splashed all over the news, and the media were madder than hell they couldn't get interviews with you."

"I told them to go climb a rope; they were trying to invade our privacy," Tom explained. "Besides, I was busy. We had a lot of people in GEO Base making all those final assemblies and adjustments on SPS-One."

"Sure. Anyway, acts of personal heroism and bravery have always been of interest to most people down here because they lead such boring, ordinary lives. I didn't realize that, because you and I have always wondered what would happen every day when we got up, even on the Hill. The Two Zero Two rescue was the most positive thing to come out of the pilot plant project. Looking back on it, maybe we should have hired a PR firm and planned some cliffhangers.

"Happily, your good Dr. von Hesse ended up looking like a damned fool for reporting you were a witch doctor and weren't following accepted procedures. ISHA didn't fare much better, not when Bob Eddy, Pete Otero, and Jerry Cleator got finished with them.

Then Governor Chaves and Governor Winslow jumped on the bandwagon. Politicians will bust their butts to be associated with a hero and the things he stands for."

"Speak for yourself, Smitty."

"I am. Hell, you ought know you can't insult me after all these years, T.K."

"I can try. Okay, it must have helped, because you're looking pretty good—a lot better than you did a few months ago. How long since you've had a checkup?"

"About two years."

"Better let me look you over while I'm here. I'm anticipating your visit to GEO Base, and then I'll give you a complete physical."

"T.K., I want you to come back to Albuquerque and open a training clinic there for the doctors, nurses, paramedics, and med technicians we've got to have for the expansion."

"What expansion? Did you get your financial dealings squared away?"

"Thanks to you, yes. The media coverage of your rescue didn't hurt a bit, because until then nobody really understood what we were doing up there. Because of the rescue, the media couldn't ignore us anymore. To get your story out in a meaningful way, they had to tell the *whole* story." Hocksmith stood up and went to the bar. "Bourbon and branch, the usual?"

"Nothing, thanks."

"When'd you quit drinking?"

"After four men in GEO Base almost killed themselves with moonshine, I don't have much of a taste for liquor anymore. Actually, I couldn't afford to drink in GEO Base. I was on call all the time and didn't dare drink anything that might screw up my reaction time or dexterity."

"Anyway," Hocksmith continued as he dropped his big form back into his work chair and put his booted feet up on the coffee table, "things smoothed out after you rescued the crew of Two Zero Two. And when Governors Chaves and Winslow threw the switch to put the Hassayampa rectenna on the grid and then went over and shut down the Palo Verde nuclear plant, there was no stopping us. Most of New Mexico, Arizona, and southern California are now run by SPS-One. DOE agreed to license two ten-gigawatt SPS units per year because of long lead-time elements involved. Oh, sure, they can still waffle if the pilot plant reveals problems—but it won't. Dan Hills is a competent engineer and a damned good manager."

Tom looked around the rustic study of the H-Bar-S ranch house. Strangely, it no longer seemed so much like home; the reason was that he had found a new one. "I notice you've still got the ranch. How'd you solve the problem with Fran?"

Hocksmith grinned and drained his glass. "I didn't. She rode on your publicity, too, and some foundation showed up at her doorstep one morning, drooling at the prospect of being tied in with the Hocksmith name, and asked how much she needed. Seems the foundation gets its money from art buffs, so the art lovers are springing for the art museum, which is as it should be as far as I'm concerned—I guess I'll have to go up to Taos for the dedication next spring. You ought to be pretty well established in Albuquerque by that time, so I'd like you and Lucky to come to the opening with me, more to keep me company than for anything else. I can't stand those nutty artists!"

"Smitty, listen to me for a change," Tom interrupted. "Maybe we'll come down from GEO Base for this affair, if we aren't in the middle of something. But you must understand one thing: I am not coming back to Earth to stay."

"T.K., don't buck me, you lousy plebe. I need you down here teaching people what you've learned."

"Let me repeat: *I am not coming back to Earth to stay*. Did you hear that, Colonel Hocksmith?"

"Goddamn it, I'll cancel your contract!"

Tom shook his head, again with an unnatural feeling. "Read what your own man Bob Eddy wrote up. That contract can be broken unilaterally by Eden Corporation only in the event of unsatisfactory performance on my part. Cutting your planned death schedule by more than fifty percent at GEO Base alone certainly gives you very shaky ground for claiming unsatisfactory performance. And nothing in that contract says I have to come back!"

Hocksmith leaned forward, put his hands on his knees, and glared at the doctor. "What the hell's got into you?"

Tom shrugged. "Simple. As your boyhood hero Duke Wayne once said, 'A man's gotta do what a man's gotta do.' You're very much like the image he projected, Smitty. I'm surprised you don't understand what I'm trying to tell you."

"I *don't* understand you, T.K. I'm offering you what you wanted—again: that Albuquerque clinic, but this time dealing with *real* frontier medicine!"

"Smitty, that dream's as dead as Julie Lea. As dead as any frontier on Earth." Tom stood up. It took a lot of effort. He knew he'd have to work out in the GEO Base gym more strenuously from now on. Decalcification wouldn't prevent him from coming back to Earth, and muscle atrophy didn't seem to be a problem. But he found he had to use different muscles to get around on the surface.

"I can't train people in orbital medicine here on Earth. Everybody here has a distorted notion of the universe." He picked up an ashtray of bright Arizona copper that had been crafted by some skilled Navaho. "What happens if I release this, Smitty?"

"You'll ding a fifty-buck copper ashtray, T.K."

"In most of the universe, it'll just stay put if I release it. We're now in a warped part of the universe, Smitty. Things don't behave naturally. Look." He released the copper work of art; it clanged to the wood floor. "Smitty, I *can't* train people in orbital medicine in Albuquerque—only in GEO Base. I've got to train them in the environment. I learned the hard way how to cope with living and work conditions so different that my Homesick Angel couldn't adapt at all. Some of the medical procedures I use up there *can't* be used down here; some of them wouldn't be permitted here."

Tom had to lean on the back of the chair for support. "How can I explain it to you, Smitty? It's nothing you've ever experienced. There's no grand sweep of the horizon; the horizon's the module wall no more than fifty feet away. There's no blue sky, no crimson sunset, no smell of ponderosas, no crunch of pine needles under your shoes. You don't see the stars except when GEO Base happens to slip into the Earth's shadow, and even then you see them only through a six-inch port or the faceplate of your P-suit helmet. Beauty? In its own way. The Moon's a dirty beach ball. The Earth's a blue and white glob that's always there with its changing cloud patterns. The real beauty's elsewhere, Smitty. It's in the *people*, not in the *surroundings*." He gestured toward the video window displaying the real-time image of the Gallinas Mountains and the blue sky beyond. "How could you possibly explain *that* to your New York financial colleagues who've never been west of the Hudson River? You can't. And I can't explain the experience of space to you; you'll have to come yourself. You'll be a better space entrepreneur if you do."

Owen Hocksmith sat there looking strangely at his old friend. He said nothing for a long minute, then remarked, "Welcome back, Tom."

"Huh?"

"You're the Tom Noels I knew in Roswell. You're the Tom Noels I knew fresh out of med school and just married to his childhood sweetheart, But you're even more now. I'm damned glad I've got you training people up there in GEO Base." He grinned and rose to his feet. "Can I be the godfather?"

"Only if you're willing to come up to GEO Base and see the boy."

"Boy? You know already?"

"Medical technology doesn't stand still, any more than other technology does. I knew I was going to have a son before Lucky and I created him. With electrophoresis and other new biological techniques in weightlessness, we can do things that can't be done down here—like determining the sex of an offspring." Tom walked over and took his friend by the elbow. "Come on, Smitty. Dinner isn't for an hour yet, if Mrs. Cameron's sticking to her usual schedule."

"She is. But where are we going?"

"For a little exercise. I may not want to come back here to stay, but that doesn't mean I don't want to watch the clouds move and listen to the wind through the pines while I'm here. Do you good to stop and smell the flowers occasionally, too. It'll be a while before we have such things in GEO Base."

The two old friends walked out in the late-afternoon sunlight. Both rammed their hands in their pockets and crunched through the forest. Hocksmith finally said to Tom, "You sounded as if I'd be moving up to GEO Base."

Tom nodded. "I think you probably will once you see it. After all, you can run your empire just as well from GEO Base as you can from the H-Bar-S Ranch. Better, in fact. Much better. All you really need is communication, the same thing you've got here. And, Smitty, someday soon somebody's going to have to set up some sort of government. There'll be too many people up in GEO Base to run it like a company town. And, quite frankly, we're going to need the best politicians we can get, because nobody will put up with the sort of political situation he left behind down here. How's that for a challenge?"

Hocksmith was quiet for only a moment. "Well, I never thought about the possibility of being the George Washington of space."

"You'd never qualify."

"Why?"

"No false teeth and no slaves."

"I could remedy that."

"Be yourself. That's good enough to save the world."

"With a little help from one of my friends who's doing the same thing."

"It's not a one-shot job, Smitty. We've got to keep at it constantly, even after we think we've saved it."

"Tell me, T.K., do you think it's worth it now?"

"Yes, but not for the reasons I once thought, Smitty. It's only because my children will have to live with it."

Epilogue

"Tom, sweetheart, they're coming every four minutes now. How am I doing?"

"Fine, Lucky, love. No problems. The cervix has dilated to about ten centimeters."

"Oh, I wish I could see what's happening!"

"Dorothy, bring in the ultrasound unit. Do you want me to rig a mirror, Lucky?"

"Yes. I don't want to miss a thing—uh, sorry, contraction coming on."

"BP normal. Pulse rate normal. Respiration returning to normal."

"Thanks, Fred. Keep an eye on it. Stan, we don't need it yet, but how are we doing on the AB-negative donors?"

"We've got plenty, Doc."

"Good. I'm trying to cover all bases. Ask Dr. Bradley to scrub just in case I have to do a Caesarean."

"Does it look like you'll have to, dear?"

"Not thus far, Lucky, love. I thought I might because the baby's head is larger than your pelvis would accommodate in passage. But this is one time where zero-g decalcification of the bones has turned out to be a blessing. Here, look at the ultrasound image. Your pelvis appears to be more cartilaginous, or softer. It's got a lot more give in the pubic symphysis than normal. I think you'll be able to do this quite naturally."

"Oh, good! Well, here we go again—oh! Rough one this time."

"Do you want anesthetic?"

"Huh? Whu . . . ?"

"Do you want me to give you some anesthetic? Acupuncture?"

"Uh . . . uh . . . no, no, I told you this was going to be natural if I could do it. Oh, look at that on the screen! He's in the birth canal!"

"Dave, get me that bottle labeled Sumatra Midwife and a cotton swab, please."

"Doctor, what *will* the AMA say? Witch doctoring again, sir?"

"It'll help dilate the tissues. If it works on Sumatra, it'll work in GEO Base—and it's approved by the OMA."

"Hi, Lucky, Tom," Jim Bradley greeted them as he floated in. "Well, looks perfectly normal to me. Still want me scrubbed and ready?"

"You bet, Jim. I'm not taking any chances. I'd appreciate having another doctor standing by in case I blow my cool."

"You won't, but I'll stand by anyway to give you moral support, if nothing else. That's what an assistant surgeon's for. Ah, there's the *hoquet,* the O-K!"

"Okay, Lucky, the cervix is dilated. I can see the little guy's head, sweetheart! He's a redhead! At least on the top of his head, anyway!"

"Oh, good . . . good. I'm so happy that everything's working right! It's glorious . . . uh . . ."

"Dorothy, sponges! I've got to keep these liquids under control."

"Right here, Doctor. Let me get that sweat out of your eyes."

"Perfectly normal, Tom," Bradley commented, "Everything looks good. Frankly, I never thought it would be this easy in weightlessness."

"That's why I'm bringing people up here to train them. Now you know."

"You're right. Orbital medicine's a whole new field!"

"Okay, sweetheart, *push!* Good girl! Keep it up—you haven't got gravity to help you. No, Jim, I refuse to use forceps! He's coming out fine! *Who said the hu-*

man race needed gravity to do anything? One more, sweetie, *push.* That's the way! I've got his head! Once more, *push!* That's it, Lucky! That's it, lover! And here he is!"

"Oh, Tom, he's beautiful!"

The human race was in space to stay.

The first birth cry of a newborn human being sounded through the weightless halls of space.

The first but not the last as Dr. Thomas K. Noels cut the umbilical cord, and Lucky Hertzog-Noels held Owen Noels close to her. The frontier and its future lay cradled in her arms.

ABOUT THE AUTHOR

Better known under his real name, G. Harry Stine, Lee Correy is a rocket pioneer, a futurist, an expert in space industrialization and high-technology marketing, and the author of or contributor to more than twenty books on science and technology. He uses his pen name "Lee Correy" for fiction to separate it from his nonfiction.

He has been the director of an industrial research laboratory and marketing manager for a small industrial company. He is an instrument-rated private pilot with over a thousand hours, owns a Cherokee (N95439), and is an aerospace historian and a consultant to the National Air and Space Museum.

He lives in Phoenix, Arizona, with his wife, a cat with twenty-four toes, and three golden retrievers.

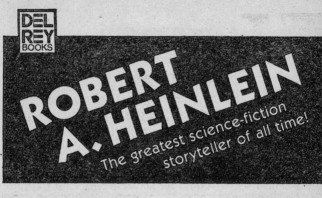